CRAVING THE CEO

IONA ROSE

Some Books

Author's Note

Hey there!

Thank you for choosing my book. I sure hope that you love it. I'd hate to part ways once you're done though. So how about we stay in touch?

My newsletter is a great way to discover more about me and my books. Where you'll find frequent exclusive giveaways, sneak previews of new releases and be first to see new cover reveals.

And as a HUGE thank you for joining, you'll receive a FREE book on me!

With love,

Iona

Get Your FREE Book Here:
https://dl.bookfunnel.com/v9yit8b3f7

Craving the CEO

Publisher: Some Books
978-1-913990-12-1

CHAPTER ONE

Grady

"Where's your secretary?" Allen, my Chief Financial Officer and best friend for as long as I can remember, asks from my door.

I lift my head from the training development report I'm reviewing and look at him as he nonchalantly takes his seat at my table and with furrowed brows I move my gaze to the door. "Has she not arrived yet?"

"Nope."

Irritation begins to simmer in the pit of my stomach.

"Wow," he says. "You look murderous. Have you ever given her this look before?"

I release a heavy sigh. My annoyance at my secretary's absence is beginning to boil over into anger. I put the report aside. My concentration is already shot to hell. "I need a new secretary."

"We'll get to that, but what I need you to do right now is to express your excitement at the Inc 500 ranking. We're at number twenty-three. Twenty fucking three! Can you believe it? Just a few years ago we were at zero and pitching our business to anyone who would listen."

"The list's not officially out yet," I say. "How did you find out?"

"Got a call from Scott, Inc's Editor in Chief." He seems mighty pleased with himself. "He told me he was going to give you a call too."

My gaze darkens once again as it returns to the door to my office. "He probably tried to, but *she* wasn't at her desk."

"Yikes," Allen replies. "You really do need a new secretary, but you can't fire her. She was my dad's secretary."

"If that's the only fucking reason she's still here, I'm screwed."

"All right, fire her then," he says. "There must be lots more qualified candidates in the company. My dad will understand. We've just received our billion dollar evaluation. It's almost laughable that one of your problems is finding a proper secretary."

"She's not completely incompetent," I reply, thinking of the stern man who had been my greatest mentor. It felt wrong to criticize any of his decisions.

He flashes a blinding grin at me and holds his arms apart. "You'll actually be doing her a favor."

I frown. "How so?"

"The only thing that'll make her happy is finally getting a good acting role somewhere. She's dying to do it, but she doesn't have the guts. Pushing her off the ledge would be a blessing."

"Hmmm..."

Just then, there's a knock at the door. It is pushed open without the courtesy of waiting for my permission to come in, and that clearly indicates who it is.

Mariam Stean walks in, my actress in waiting secretary.

I have to do a double take at her appearance. On her cheeks are patches of red with bold whiskers painted over them.

"I apologize, Sir," she says with a smile. "My acting class had a production last night, and the paint has refused to come off. Most of it will be gone by the end of the day. Also, I apologize for coming in late. That IT security lady just dropped this off for you. She says you are expecting it?"

"You're having wild nights, Mariam," Allen teases.

She flashes a coy smile at him.

I, on the other hand, have no words for her. Thank God, I have no business meetings or clients coming in today. I accept the folder she hands to me and immediately pull it open and start looking down the row of sales figures. "Have you scheduled the meeting with the Bloom executives for tomorrow?" I ask.

"I'll get right on it, Sir," she replies.

My head shoots upwards.

Before I can chastise her once again for dragging her feet on such an incredibly important task, she turns around and hurries away.

"She sure knows how to escape, I'll give her that." Allen says.

I rub the back of my neck. "How's it going with the baby?"

"Don't ask," he laments. "My entire last week was spent literally hands deep in shit, changing Alexa's diapers, and trying my best to survive with the stack of disgusting almond flour waffles my wife left for us before she went on her trip."

I smile as I resume my perusal of the training development report.

"I mean I'm not complaining," he continues quickly. "I love my wife and daughter very much, but good Lord that kid can shit for England—"

"What does England have to do with it?" I ask, amused.

"Well, her maternal grandmother is English."

"You need to get out more, man."

He looks dreamily out of the window. "Yeah, somewhere there's alcohol."

"Do you want to come along to the meeting with Bloom?"

"Nah," he says mournfully. "Alexa's still recovering from her illness stunt last week so I'm on toddler duty while Meredith goes to Tampa for another business trip over the weekend."

"You can't call her illness a stunt."

"That was exactly what it was. She threw tantrums no less than a dozen times, and during one of those she fell to the floor in tears. I just left her there. I got a beer, and turned the volume up on the TV to catch up on my game."

My mouth falls open. "You're joking.'

"I swear it. I'm not bringing up an entitled snowflake."

I grin. "Yeah, right. How long did your nonchalance last?"

"Three minutes. Meredith called to find out how we were doing and I couldn't let her hear Alexa wailing over the phone. Plus, my conscience was beginning to eat at me. So I calmed her down and called her back. After lying to her that we were doing great, she asked for another kid."

I drop the report and burst out laughing. "So more dirty diapers then?"

He laughs heartily too and ends our little detour with his domestic tales.

"Will you go on your own to the meeting?" he asks.

"Yup."

"I see why my dad was never worried about the company for even a second. We're already this big and you're still in the trenches. You love that grind, don't you? As the CEO you're meant to manage and leave all the grunt work to the lower guys, but here you are, still recruiting clients on your own."

"The chase is thrilling."

With a tap on my desk, he rises to his feet. "Maybe, but I can tell you of a much more thrilling pursuit."

I don't even bother asking. I return my attention to my report.

Of course, he speaks anyway, "A woman. That's the greatest pursuit that man has been called to."

"You're an ass," I say, just as my phone begins to ring.

"I mean it," he says.

"Hello," I put the phone to my ear.

A few seconds go by as I listen to the man complain to me.

"I'll call you back," I say and end the call.

Allen is still watching me, especially at the deep frown on my face. "Mariam still hasn't set it up, has she?"

"She really knows how to piss me off," I hiss, and storm over to the door. I jerk the door open and walk out to reception to find her on the phone.

She is cackling out loud with her feet on the table, and her forefinger twirling the curls in her hair. She immediately sits up when she sees us walk out. "Brenda, I'll call you back," she says, and clears her throat at my approach.

"You haven't set the meeting up?" I ask quietly.

Her expression turns sheepish for a moment. "I'll do it now. Sorry, I had to take a call."

I lose my temper. "You're fired. Pack your things and leave. Right now."

The shock strikes her face like a hand slap. "W-what?"

Without answering her I turn around to leave.

"You can't fire me," she blurts out.

I stop for a moment to process her response, and then turn back to her. "Excuse me?"

"Mr. Canter owns a part of the company. He guaranteed that I'd always have a place here."

I cock my head at her. "Which Mr. Canter are you referring to? The one behind me right now, or the one who passed away some time ago?"

Her lips parts dramatically in distress. She really is a much better actress than she is a secretary.

"Mariam you can't say that to him," Allen states. "My father only passed fifteen percent on to me. He owns the rest."

Her eyes fill with tears. "B-but, he promised I'd always have a place here."

I walk back to her, the heat of my anger scorching the pit of my stomach. "Is that the reason why you've taken the liberty to be absolutely useless around here? We have a thousand employees to manage and you think this is a joke?"

"I gave this company ten years of my life. All I'm trying to do now is to—"

"Leave," I growl. "Right now. Out of respect for Robert, I've given you more than enough chances and you've screwed up over and over again. I'm not going to take it anymore."

Tears flow down her cheeks.

I turn away to return to my office.

After a few puffs of grief, she calls after me, "Fine, I'll leave! I don't need you. I don't need this company. I have an audition tomorrow and I'll make sure to ace it and everything else that comes my way. I'm going to be big, do you hear me? I'm going to be really big!"

"Good. Go do what you love and stop wasting your time here." I slam the door to my office shut, and return to my desk.

A few seconds later, it reopens, and Allen stands at the entrance. "I guess now, you really need a new secretary, but don't worry I'll handle it personally," he says. "Do you have anything in particular you need?"

"An ability to work hard. This is the last time I'll ever keep a useless employee out of sentiment."

"Roger that." He grins evilly. "I think I have the perfect candidate for you." With that, he turns around, and takes his leave.

For a second I wonder about that grin, then I lose myself in the report.

CHAPTER TWO

Blair

"When are you going to find out?" I ask. "If the baby's a boy or a girl?"

"In about two weeks," Layne replies. "We have a visit scheduled for the 28th."

"We? Matthew's going to be around?"

"He will. He'll be back from the oil field by then."

"Nice," I say and once again press my ear to her protruding belly. Suddenly, there is a slight movement against her skin and I scream.

"'Blair!" Layne looks startled.

"'They just moved. I mean he—or she."

"Yeah," my sister laughs. "They, or he or she moves from time to time.

"Oh, my God," I squeal again.

She shakes her head and moves my hands away from her stomach. “I’m not having twins,” she says.

“I know.” I laugh. “I just lost it for a moment there. Oh, my God. I can’t wait to be an aunt.” My heart is racing in my chest.

“Well, I’m scared out of my mind,” she says as she heads over to the refrigerator to retrieve a carton of milk.

“Don’t be.” My voice softens at the worry in her tone. “You’re going to be fine. Everything is going to be fine.”

She sighs as she opens the carton, her face away from me. “Yeah, but I’m scared of handling it alone.”

I return to my seat on one of the stools in the corner. “What do you mean alone? You have Matthew and you have me.”

“I have Matthew but Matthew’s not always here. And neither are you. You’re just in to visit for the weekend.”

My lips part to speak but I have nothing to say, so I give it all some thought. “Well, I could move. It’s not like I have anything holding me back in Texas. I just graduated, so all I’m doing now is looking for a job. And to be honest, I’d rather search for one here where I can be close to you than somewhere else random.”

She turns to me, her eyes sparkling at my words even though she tries not to show it. “Are you serious? Would you have any prospects here in Denver?”

“Layne, I have a degree in computer science. I think I’ll have a pretty good chance wherever I go.”

She thinks on the idea for a moment and then turns away. She pours herself some milk, and then downs it all at once. “No,” she says as she wipes the corners of her mouth.

I'm not surprised at her response. I know exactly why she's refusing my idea, and it warms my heart.

"This is the best time of your life," she says. "I'm not going to let you squander it on me. Go out into the world and apply to wherever you want. You've always said that you wanted to try New York or somewhere in Europe? Do that."

I sigh. "Layne, I'm not squandering anything on you. There are great opportunities here in Denver and rather than reside in some strange place where I won't know anyone or have anyone, I'd rather be here with you. I'd be happier. That's what you want, isn't it? For me to be happy?"

She spins around to face me. "Of course it is."

"Exactly. So, I'm going to increase my focus in applying to positions here in Denver. An exciting offer can come from anywhere but I'll prioritize here."

"No, prioritize your interest. I'll be fine."

My phone begins to ring so I roll my eyes at her and head over to where my purse was abandoned on her sofa. "We'll be fine Layne, and I'll be here for you. Stop overthinking everything." I glance down at my phone, and am slightly taken aback that there is no caller ID.

I consider ignoring it, but then it occurs to me that it might be regarding one of the countless positions I have applied to. So I lift the phone to my ear. "Hello?"

"Hello," a man's voice comes through the receiver, smooth and strong. "'Is this Blair Tatum?"

"Yes, this is Blair. Who am I speaking to?"

"Allen Canter. We met a couple of weeks ago at the job fair at the University of Texas,"

My heart fell into my stomach. "Allen Canter? The CFO of FireEye?"

"Yes, that's me. How are you doing?"

My airway constricts. "Um, I'm doing great... sir." I'm not sure but I think I can feel his smile through the phone. When I met him a few weeks ago at the event, he had been open and friendly, so it is probably the same countenance that I'm projecting onto him now.

"I'm calling regarding a position that might be a fit for you. I remember the last time we met you spoke about your interest in cyber security and your experience during your internship at Zimperium."

"Yes, sir," I reply, and turn around to glance at Layne.

She has her attention on me, surprised at my sudden formal tone.

Even I'm rattled, not exactly sure if this is some sort of courtesy call, or if I am now in an interview for a potential position. It's 7 PM on a Friday night, and if the latter is the case, I'm not at all prepared for this.

"I have an opening that I think you might be able to fill considerably well," he continues. "Would you like to come in, so we can talk about it further?"

I become too nervous to remain still, so I begin to pace the living room, one hand underneath my elbow to support the weakened hand holding my phone. "Most definitely, sir."

"Alright," he says. "How soon can you make it to Denver?"

I clear my throat. "I'm already here, sir. I'm visiting family."

"That's fantastic," he replies. "How about we set up a meeting for Monday then? Sound good?

"Sounds great... sir."

"Alright. You'll be able to find your way to FireEye right? It's downtown."

"Most definitely, sir."

"Okay. I'll slot you in for an appointment at 9 AM. Have a great weekend."

"Sure. Thank you... sir," I respond. The call comes to an end and I pull the phone away from my ear as though in a trance.

"Who was that?" Layne asks.

I turn to her. "I just got an interview. Here in Denver."

"Oh, my God!" Her hand covers her mouth. "We were just talking about this. Where? I mean what company."

"FireEye."

"FireEye? I've never heard of it, what do they do?"

"It's a cyber security awareness company. It's massive."

"Wow, that's great. You applied for it? What position are they interviewing you for?"

I head back to the stool to take my seat. "That's the thing. I didn't apply. I just met the CFO about two weeks ago at a job fair at school. I was still interning at Zimperium then, so I gave him my card."

"And he kept it? You must have made quite the impression."

"Absolutely not," I replied. "I was a babbling idiot. I kept asking stupid questions and making the most awkward jokes, which now that I think about it, he did actually find quite funny. What is going on?"

Her smile is angelic. "The stars are aligning in our favor." She rubs her stomach.

I couldn't hold back my delight either. "Oh, my God, if I get a position there I'm going to collapse. That's a freaking unicorn company!"

"A what? Unicorn? I thought you said they're in cybersecurity."

I laughed at her naivety. "I don't mean an actual unicorn. I mean they're really successful, fairly new and privately owned and valued at a billion dollars. Companies like that are called unicorns because it's so rare to be that successful within a short frame of time."

Her eyes nearly bulge out of her sockets. "A billion dollars? Wow, that does sound massive."

"Exactly. Wow... I'm shaking. It would be such a privilege to work there."

"It does sound like a great opportunity," she agrees. "What position is he calling you in for?"

"He didn't say. All he did was set up a meeting for Monday. And oh, my God, he's the CFO... and he called me himself. His father founded the company along with the current CEO, and he called me himself. Not through personnel but directly."

"Okay, calm down." Layne laughs. "You're hyperventilating."

"I know but this is unreal," I say, close to jumping out of my skin. Overwhelmed with emotion, I do realize I need to calm myself down, so I take deep breaths, and focus on reducing my excitement and subsequent nervousness.

"Okay we need to celebrate," Layne says. "Tomorrow night. I've had a tiring day and this momma to be needs to crash."

I laugh. "What do you mean? There's nothing to celebrate. This was just to set up the interview."

"Well, we're going to celebrate you even getting the call. Then we're going to toast to your acing the interview and getting some fantastic position there."

"Well, I'm not going to say no to that, but are you going to be able to come out?" My eyes lower to her bulging belly.

"Honey, this night out is more for me than it is for you. I need to get out of this house." She does a little swirl with her hips. "I can't wait."

I laugh again. "Neither can I," I reply. "Neither can I."

"Ask Jodie if she wants to come along with us. The more the merrier."

I lift my phone to pull up my best friend's number. "I doubt it. I think she has to work at the restaurant tomorrow."

"On a Saturday night? I doubt Jodie would ever give up her Saturdays to work. I think you have the day mixed with Friday or Sunday even."

I dialed her number and lifted the phone to my ear.

CHAPTER THREE

Grady

Both men, the Senior Vice President Mark Cuomo and the recluse, Jack Clay share a look with each other before placing their documents on the table.

The marble surface is filled with two bottles of aged malt whiskey and platters of stingray fins and squid tempura. Allen's secretary had secured the private room for us at the downtown club with the perfect ambience for the conversation I intend to have with them.

It is set against the backdrop of a dim and rowdy dance floor below, lit with colorful lights, and the deafening music hitting the panels of our glass encased lounge. It is just enough to remind us of where we are, but yet allow us the detachment that I paid heavily for.

"Grady," Mark begins. "What you're proposing we can do internally."

Both men share a look with each other once again, so I pick up my tumbler of whiskey and take a swig of it.

I pull out two more folders and hand them over. Both men receive their copy and quickly start reading through it, as I continue to sip calmly from my glass.

I watch their eyes widen in shock.

"Where did you get this?" Mark asks, his voice now cold.

"Through our analysis. Even your team hasn't picked up on this security issue. So you see, even your waiting room feature is flawed and if I can discover this, someone else out there will sooner or later. I'm disclosing this vulnerability to you as a courtesy. Fix it and give me a call. Now let's push all this aside and get back to the second reason we're here."

Mark leans back into the sofa with a laugh. "Oh. I thought this was the end of the road."

"What do you mean?" I ask innocently.

"Thus far, you've hosted us in a lounge and then brought us here. We've been waiting for this shoe to drop. Now that it has and you've hassled us into doing business with you, I expected that you'd call it a night and be on your way."

"I don't hassle, Mark," I correct. "That's for people that don't know what they're doing. What I've done is given you a chance to save your house before it's engulfed in flames, and it's up to you to take or reject it. But it wasn't my sole intention in bringing you here either, otherwise we could have handled this discussion in either of our offices."

"So what is this second reason then?"

I rise to my feet. "To dance, of course."

Mark laughs again. "I can do that."

"You're joking," Jack says, his face frigid with horror. "I don't dance."

Their reaction amuses me. "That's alright, Jack. I'm joking. Neither do I. I'm sure we'll come up with better ways to have a good time. In the meantime, have a look at these." I hand them my proposals.

Then I excuse myself from the room and head to the restroom. After handling my business, I'm about to return to them when I decide against it. It is better to give them some more time alone to look over the data that I have presented. So instead I head towards the bar.

It has been quite a few months since I've come to a club like this. My insane schedule and unending responsibilities have kept me away from most social pastimes like this unless it is business related, but since my goal for the evening is somewhat complete, I allow myself to bask in the simple pleasure of herd excitement for a few minutes. I weave through the throngs of gyrating bodies in the humidity, and soon arrive at the bar.

I want a cocktail, something I haven't had the liberty of enjoying of late. So the moment the bartender comes up to me I make my order. "Sidecar."

He nods in understanding. "Coming up."

Soon he delivers it and I flick away the orange peel attached to the glass.

To my surprise however, a slender set of fingers catch it before it can roll off the counter to the floor. I follow the fair limbs all the way up her glistening alabaster skin, to the dark red strap across her delicate shoulders.

The face on those shoulders is even more exquisite, and as my gaze connects with the deep green eyes of the shiny blonde woman before me, I feel my breathing hitch.

For a few seconds, I don't say a word or rather nothing comes to mind, so I look away to try to recollect my thoughts. It occurs to me then, what just happened. The sight of her—literally fried my brain. The hand holding my glass freezes midway to my mouth. I glance at her once again.

She has turned her face away from me and makes her order, "Cranberry with ice,"

I listen to her velvety voice. She is speaking louder than usual as we all are so that we can be heard over the racket, but I can still make out the creamy flow to her tone. "You don't drink alcohol?" I find myself asking.

She hears me and turns with a smile on her face.

I empty my drink without realizing it and set the empty tumbler down on the counter.

"I do," she replies. "This is for my sister... she's pregnant."

I hear every word of what she says mainly because my gaze is so focused on her lips, and the forms that they are shaping into so she can communicate with me. Her lips are covered in lipstick the same exact red shade of her dress. They are plump and curved in a way to seemingly solely entice me. I want to kiss her badly... to sink my teeth gently into that warm and tender flesh... feel her heat and scent swirl around me.

I take a step closer to her, almost needing to inhale her scent more than I need my next breath and it makes me wonder what is so severely attracting me to her. Is it the way the color compliments her skin, or is it her almost doe eyed gaze? I can't remember the last time I'd ever been this immediately drawn to a woman. "Let me pay for the drink," I say.

Her smile widens. "No need, I can handle it."

I am even more intrigued. "Why?" I ask.

She blinks. "Why what?"

"Why are you refusing me?"

"I'm not refusing you." She laughs. "I just... want to pay for my own drink. "

"Fair enough. So what would you have me do for you then?"

This time around, she boldly holds my gaze, and tells me exactly what she wants, but I can't possibly have heard it right. How could I have when I heard her say...

Fuck me. Brutally, until I lose my mind. Against a surface, in the air... everywhere.

CHAPTER FOUR

Blair

Fuck me. Brutally, until I lose my mind. Against a surface, in the air... everywhere.

These are the only things I want to say to him, but thankfully the glasses of cosmopolitan I have consumed thus far haven't tampered with my head yet. I turn my gaze away from his to recollect myself.

I wonder if he can tell that my breathing has become labored and that it has absolutely nothing to do with the rowdy space we are in.

Yes, we are surrounded by a multitude of people but from the moment I laid eyes on him, it has seemed as though only the two of us exist. I spotted him a few minutes earlier.

Actually, Layne was the one who spotted him, and then she drew my attention. "Isn't that the hottest fucking man you've ever seen?"

I had turned to take a look and my jaw had dropped.

He was dressed in a simple black T-shirt, tucked into equally dark, checkered tailored pants and I couldn't look away. It wasn't the outfit, but the man, and like a possessed zombie, I had risen to my feet to chase after him.

At first, it had been a joke and I'd almost changed my mind, but Layne had spurred me on. Therefore, I had gone after the stud with broad sculpted shoulders, coiffed dark hair and tastefully bulging olive toned biceps.

Catching the flicked peel had been reflexive, and thankfully, it had given me the opening I'd hoped for. What I can't believe now is that he is the one leading the conversation. My expectation was that he would barely give me a second look, but I can see in his sparkling eyes that I have caught his attention.

His scent is of tobacco and lavender and it's messing with my head. And then there's his striking blue eyes, so light that they can pass as grey.

My panties are already soaked with arousal, and that brings my excitement to an intense level. My drink is delivered then, and since I can't think of anything to say, I turn around to leave.

He however, places a hand on my arm. "What's your name?" he asks.

I'm stopped in my tracks and I spill my sister's drink. "Blair," I reply. "What's yours?"

"Grady." His tone of voice is hoarse, but quiet and grating on my insides. "You're really not going to give me a chance, Blair?"

Unconsciously, I bite down on my bottom lip, and to my surprise, he swears.

"*Fuck*!" He hisses as his eyes rove down my body.

I'm taken aback. Then I immediately applaud myself for the decision to go with this red dress. It is provocative and plastered to my frame and I can see that his eyes are brimming with appreciation. With one long drink, I empty the glass of cranberry juice and return to the counter. "You'll have to replace my sister's drink?" I say to him.

With a smile, he calls the bartender over. "No problem. What do you want?"

"Whatever you'll have. I want to share." I cannot believe the words coming out of my mouth, and at his narrowed gaze I realize that my eyes are probably also emitting smoke.

He places the order... another cranberry for my sister and a refill of what he had been drinking earlier.

I slide onto the stool.

He leans against the bar and faces me.

"So," I begin. "Mr. Grady. What brings you here?"

"Business," he answers, his eyes boring into mine. "I have some people up there that I want to show a good time."

My eyes dart over to the VIP section above and I'm not surprised. That is exactly where the likes of him belong, especially since it's impossible to miss the creamy, gold watch wrapped around his wrist. He exudes extreme wealth and style, but yet it is all presented with a simplicity that draws me to him like a fly to honey.

"What about you?" he asks.

I turn to glance at Layne's direction. "We're celebrating. My first official job after college." I feel a twinge of guilt at the half lie since technically I've not been employed, but I don't want to feel inferior to him right now, so that little white lie is eventually approved by my conscience.

Our drinks are delivered but there's no way I'm leaving now.

"Sidecar," he says as he offers his to me.

I take it from him. I take a sip of the golden liquid and it slides down my throat with a slight burn.

When I hand it over, his lips cover the same spot that mine has just perched on.

I feel the tease like a kick to my gut. "That's an indirect kiss," I blurt out and for a moment I stop. I'm being too bold. He is a complete stranger and I am flirting like I'm out of control. Perhaps the alcohol has kicked in and I don't realize it.

With a low laugh, he responds, "I am aware. I'll take what I can get."

It was a clear nudge for me to offer more and I did not intend to hold back. I needed to be in his arms even if it was for a few seconds otherwise I might just implode. So with a smile, I place my hand on the side of his arm and lean in. My palm burns at the warmth of his skin and I'm ready to lose myself in him. "Kiss me," I breathe. "It's an offer."

His gaze darkens and in a step he is so close to me that I can see the specs of grey in his eyes. His hand settles on my waist and it zaps a burst of pleasure through me. He is incredibly tall, so I have to raise my head to his. With a smile, he slants his head and my eyes flutter shut.

He takes my top lip in his mouth and my bones begin to melt. He then moves to the bottom and the plump flesh is expertly sucked into his mouth... at just the right tempo and with just the right amount of pressure. My heart is beating so wildly in my chest that I can barely breathe and before I know it, my arms are wrapped around his shoulders.

I'm floored by how delicious he tastes... how warm and clean and how intoxicating his scent is. His very existence seems like an extreme aphrodisiac and it completely scrambles my brain. All I can feel is his heat and the tension quickly building in the pit of my stomach at the avalanche of sexual excitement.

A groan follows and we are so melded into one that I cannot even tell who it is from. It doesn't matter either way, because in the next movement, his tongue slips into my mouth and the heightened intimacy completely possesses me.

We ravage each other with languid strokes and it is as though my entire being has been transformed into some sort of ethereal instrument, plucked by the expertise of his kiss.

I can no longer remain seated. I need my body as close to his as possible so I stumble down from the stool, my grip on him tightening for dear life. I'm on four inch strappy heels but they are not enough, so I lift myself further on the tips of my toes and push my body hard against his.

His is bulging, and at the undeniable proof of my effect on him, my alcoholism infused promiscuity is driven up a notch.

My hands move away from his shoulders to slide down his rock hard chest and the ridges of sculpted muscle I detect turns me on even further.

"Fuck," he breaks the kiss to exclaim.

I'm in equal and parallel concurrence with the sentiment. I register his arms curving around my ass to lift me up and once again, I'm deposited back on the stool. It registers that my dress has slid dangerously up my thighs to the point of certainty that I am somewhat exposed but none of that matters because he presses his groin hard into my sex before I can protest.

My back arcs at the ground breaking contact and this time around, a clear shuddering moan escapes my lips.

He traces deep, scalding kisses down my neck as he grinds his crotch into mine, and then his mouth closes around my nipple.

With a jerk, of staggering ecstasy and shock, I am brought back to the present.

This is a complete stranger and we are surrounded by a multitude of people, yet I'm seconds away from being fucked in the midst of it all. And my sister... she is probably watching all of this with the shock of the century. I pull away from him and if not for his hold on my waist, I would have fallen off the stool.

He immediately respects my retreat and steps back, but keeps his hold on me to ensure that I don't fall.

My hand is on his chest to hold him at bay, but I can't look him in the eyes just yet. That was much more intense than I had anticipated and it had freaking rocked my world.

With a quick smile, I turn away to get myself together and soon recover my senses. Now all I can think about is his mouth on other places of my body or perhaps in every part of my body. "Thanks for the kiss," I say, unable to further hold any semblance of a conversation with him.

He leans in, his lips to my ears and I cannot push him away. "Let's go somewhere," he says.

I'm of a mind to do exactly that. But then I am not drunk enough to not realize this has gone much farther than I had intended. "I have to get my back to my party," I breathe my response as I come off the stool. My feet are a bit wobbly.

He catches me by the arm, and only releases me when I assure him that I am fine. "Your sister's drink." He says as he lifts the glass.

I accept the glass from him. I don't know if I'll ever see him again, so I curve my hand boldly around the side of his face, stare into his eyes for a brief moment and then plant a kiss just on the underside of his jaw.

I can see that he is quite taken aback by the endearing touch, but I don't linger. A second longer and I would be sold on doing absolutely whatever he wants.

With the glass in hand, I head back across the floor in search of my sister and best friend.

CHAPTER FIVE

Grady

I watch her leave and almost have to physically restrain myself from going after her.

Perhaps it's because it's been too long since I've had a woman. I've been so occupied with the company that I have given no time whatsoever to sexual relations, and I can now see that it's messing with my head.

After releasing a deep breath, I return back to my meeting on the second floor and we continue with our discussion. However, I have gone considerably quieter and can't help but stare down the glass view, hoping to catch a glimpse of a blood red dress amidst the sea of people. I know it's fruitless but still I try, because I can't get that kiss out of my head. My cock throbs with a delicious ache as it relays to me its desire to be sheathed inside of her... to be milked free of its excitement and frustrations.

"I'm going to call it a night," the recluse finally announces, and both men rise to their feet.

"Me too ," Mark says. "I've gotta get back to the wife and kids."

I, too, am ready to bring this meeting to a close, so I rise with them and head out. They go on their way when we reach the ground floor while I slip my hands into my pockets. My eyes scan across the sea of writhing bodies and I realize now, I should have at least gotten her phone number.

After paying the tab, I make my way out of the club and call for my car. The night is still quite young at 2 AM but then I figure it's time to get a good night's sleep. I toy with the idea of going home with someone else but I can't work up any motivation for it. Especially after *that* girl. Blair. I can even still remember her name.

"*Fuck,*" I curse, wishing once again, that I had gotten her number. The oversight makes me want to smoke a cigarette and it's been quite a while since I'd indulged in the habit. My Mercedes soon pulls up at the curb.

The young, curly haired valet brings the key over, his eyes wide with excitement. "Sick ride, man."

I give him a smile as I round the vehicle and get in. In no time, the ignition is started but as I'm about to pull away, there is a tap on the passenger window.

I turn to it, wondering who it could be and meet the view of ample cleavage, and full lips.

I roll the glass down and a pair of green twinkling eyes meets my gaze. That red dress telling me who this is. My heart freezes inside my chest.

"I need a ride," she says. "My party abandoned me."

Without a second thought, I unlock the door and watch, mesmerized, as slim fair legs slide into the car.

She shuts the door with a smile and turns to me. "Nice car," she says.

The compliment barely registers with me. "Where do you want me to take you?"

"Anywhere," Blair replies, her gaze darkening.

With a half-cocked grin at the double meaning, I turn away, put the car in gear and pull out into the traffic.

I don't take her to my house. The Brown Palace is a pretty luxurious option, so I get a room for us, and in no time we're alone.

"What do you want to drink?" I ask.

She settles down on the end of the bed. "Red wine is good," she says.

Now, I take a second to look at her and realize there is a slight problem. Under clear, bright lighting, I can see that she is much more beautiful than I had thought but her beauty right now is more innocent, than sultry.

She is still wildly appealing, but now rather than the sophisticated lady I had painted in my mind, I am now considering how to go softly on her, or if it's even legal for her to be in the same room as I am. I think for a moment on how to phrase my question lightly, but when nothing comes to mind, I just revert to normal and say just what I want to, "How old are you?" I ask.

Just as expected, her response is a slight frown. She uncrosses her legs and glares at me. "Excuse me?"

I'm not moved by her reaction. "You look way younger than I thought."

"I'm of age," she answers coldly.

"Let me see your ID."

She rises to her feet then, indignation across her face. "Are you fucking kidding me?" She grabs her purse and turns.

For a moment I watch her storm away, but then I can't let her leave. So I go after her and just as she jerks the door open, I reach out above her and slam it back shut.

"Hey!" She spins around to protest, but finds herself trapped between my frame and the door. "Move!" She orders, her eyes glowing with annoyance.

I note that she is doing all she can to avoid touching me. My voice lowers, "Don't get me wrong," I say. "I want to fuck you, in a hundred different ways but I need to know that I'm not going to be put in jail after that."

Her eyes maliciously bore into mine, but her offense has come down a notch. Her hands begin to move and without taking her eyes from mine, she produces her driver's license. She holds it so close to my face that I can barely see it. "I'm twenty-one," she says. "Is this enough proof for you?"

I confirm the numbers that I want to, and she puts it away. "You've asked your question," she says. "Now, it's my turn."

I laugh at the challenge in her tone. She is indeed feisty and I feel my cock swelling in the exhilaration with each passing moment. "Go ahead," I say.

A mischievous smirk lifts a corner of her mouth. "I want you on your knees," she says. "Eat me out. Let's start there."

I laugh out loud, the sound hearty and rumbling and it's a surprise to the both of us. It has been a while since I have been so out rightly challenged and disrespected like this, and it is thrilling. Perhaps she had expected that I would be offended. However, I am anything but. I lower my frame, and grab the back of her thighs to pull her towards me.

I hear the little gasp that escapes her lips, and look up to see her slightly widened eyes. My hands reach up to grab her ass, and my grip is so hard that she falters, almost falling into me. I can hear her breathing becoming harsher as her hands move to my head to steady herself.

My fingers hook into the strap of lace on her waist, and with a sharp tug, I begin to pull the thong down her thighs. But then halfway through, I change my mind. I rip the flimsy lace apart and fling it away from her.

"Hey! That's expensive..." She begins to say when the words suddenly die on her tongue. Her dress is now bunched around her waist, completely exposing her and it seems it has made her quite shy.

With a smile, I run my hand down her pretty crotch then I slide my middle finger through the slick folds.

Her hips begin to writhe, almost as though she wants to escape but that is no longer a possibility.

"Hold onto me," I order and lift one of her legs. I hang it across my shoulder, tilt my head, and seal my mouth over her pulsing clit.

Her gasp resounds across the room, and its sharpness spurs me on. She tastes sweet, warm, and sinful and it messes with my head.

"*Grady...*" The breathy call of my name registers to me from a distance, but I pay it no mind. I suck greedily on the swollen bud of her arousal in a hard rapid rhythm, and in no time, her body is squirming and contorting uncontrollably above me. With a hand across her stomach to pin her to the wall, I dip my head even lower and give her entire cleft a thorough lick from the top through the completely drenched slit.

Then my tongue spears into her opening.

Little Blair buckles with an even louder grasp. "S-stop," she tries to say.

I can only laugh darkly in my mind. I haven't even begun.

CHAPTER SIX

Blair

I am losing my mind

This is not the first time a man is ravishing me with his mouth but it's definitely the first time that my soul is on the verge of slipping away from my body. I cannot stay still or silent as his heated tongue expertly thrusts and weaves in and out of me. My entire body is burning up to a dangerous degree as wave after wave of disconcerting ecstasy crashes through my body.

Nothing registers, but then at the same time everything does so when he thrusts a finger inside of me and then another, all of the strength seeps out of my leg, I collapse.

Luckily, his reflexes are fast and with a quiet laugh, he rises to his feet to catch me before I can land on the floor. His fingers however remain inside of me. With his body, he holds me to the door trying to meet my gaze.

I am no longer coherent. "S-stop," I shudder, grabbing weakly onto his wrist. "I-I need some tim—?" Once again, the words are stolen from my lips as he begins to thrust those infinitely long fingers in and out of my sex.

It wrenches a tortured whimper out of me, but then to my shock his speed becomes viciously rapid. I hold on to his bulging biceps so I won't break, and when my eyes manage to flutter open, I meet the grim look in his eyes. He knows what he is doing... just how severely he is unraveling me, and it makes me feel victimized.

I had thought that we'd be on the same level, but I can't even take this brutal fucking from his fingers. He pauses only for the moment that it takes to slide a third finger into me, and then resumes drilling me like a machine.

The sounds that are coming out of me now are near animalistic, as I struggle to pull myself away but my frame is solidly pinned to the door.

All the muscles in my lower stomach begin to tense in preparation for my release and from the distance, I can hear my body's rhythmic slam against the door.

He doesn't stop until I explode and as I do, it is with an intense cry into his shoulder. "*Holy fuck! Oh God.*" I bite down hard on his skin in a bid to ease the mortifying intensity of the release, but nothing softens the high.

He proceeds to massage my sensitive clit with the pad of his finger; coupled with my slickness all over his hand, and the soothing motions through my cleft, his touch is nothing short of magical.

My feet suddenly leave the floor and before I can register what is going on, I am thrown onto the bed. I immediately try to get away from him, my eyes barely able to even stay open and once again, that dark chuckle of his comes to mind.

He allows me to run until I'm pressed against the headboard and by then some of my coherence has returned. I look up at his handsome face to see the smile across it, at just how whipped I look. It spurs the return of my temper.

He is on his knees and unbuckling his belt.

I lick my lips and gear myself up to return the favor. His cock is jutting out of his briefs and I don't even allow myself the time to appreciate it. I pull him to me and close my mouth around the thick, damp head. For some reason, it tastes so delicious to me and I realize then that I'm not in a normal state.

With my grip on the rock hard shaft, I pump him in fluid strokes as my lips suck feverishly on the head.

This earns me a long groan of appreciation from him and it gives my heart wings. My eyes raise upward to see his head thrown back and his Adam's apple bobbing enticingly. I want to kiss it and him... to leave my mark on every inch of his virile body. In much clearer lighting, I realize that I had caught an even bigger fish than I had initially thought.

On my return to my sister, I had indeed met her in shock at the behavior I had exhibited at the bar with a complete stranger. My immediate excuse had been that I'd never done that before, and it had earned me a painful slap across my arm. Not long after however, we both decided he was worth the bit of promiscuity, and lamented at how things had ended where they had. She'd then become too tired to continue on and I'd escorted her out to get a taxi.

Jodie was deeply occupied with grinding with some guy on the dance floor, so my intention had been to return to the club when I had spotted Grady on his way out. I'd watched, too nervous to speak until I'd heard that engine start up. It was either now or never I'd realized. So, I hurried over to pound on his window.

And now here I am, with his dick down my throat and I can scarcely believe it.

I've never been this promiscuous but his kind of hotness is possessing. He seems aloof and withdrawn, but at the same time warm and inviting and its complexity excites me. His gorgeous structured face and dreamy eyes are a bonus, and that taut ass, toned torso and those broad shoulders have done me in.

Tilting my head, I lick up and down his cock, smearing saliva and cum all over the soft pale flesh. Then I move on to his balls and his response is a slam of his hand against the headboard.

I grab onto his taut ass when I return to the head, and almost jump in excitement when his hand curves around the back of my head. With the most animalistic male grunt I've ever heard, he holds my head in place as he drives himself into my mouth. Briefly handing the reins over to me, my teeth scrape lightly along his length while my cheeks are hollowed to fully accommodate him. When he eventually climaxes, he pulls out to spill his seed away from me and I'm a bit disappointed. Pouty, I watch his release and the intensely erotic sight more than makes up for my annoyance.

Damn, he is a beautiful man.

I watch as he brutally pumps himself, his release seemingly endless as it spills onto the mattress. His head is thrown back and his ass clenched with the tension of his release. I want to see more of him so I head over, going behind him to slide my hands underneath his shirt. I move them up his heated smooth skin, feeling the ridges of muscles as I go along and my mouth waters with hunger.

His breathing is still harsh and labored but now he has brought himself under control, so he turns around to glance at me with a smile across his beautiful face. In one swift, fluid motion, he pulls the T-shirt over his head and at the hypnotic move of muscle in response, I almost orgasm again right there.

I press a kiss to his shoulder and it immediately graduates into a flurry of starved worship as I taste every part of his skin. I'm just moving down to his ass when I feel his hand grab by arm. So I move quickly and am able to take a nip of that delicious ass before he swings me around like a doll and throws me on the bed.

Our combined laughter rings out into the air at my naughtiness but it soon changes into something else. He leans down to hover just above me and for a few moments, all he does is stare into my eyes. Then his gaze roves all over my face and down my body.

I find myself unable to breathe.

"You're a wonderful surprise, Blair," he says in his buttery smooth voice.

I feel my heart make several somersaults within my chest. I can only dare to breathe when his attention moves to my dress and in no time, he has the hem of my dress, pulling it up and over my body.

"I love this dress," he says. "But it has to step aside for a little while. He leans down to press a kiss to my lips and then places another right on the skin above the pulse on my knee. "I also love the color red on you. Coupled with your beautiful eyes, it makes it seem like you just jumped out of a painting."

He is succeeding in bed and advancing dangerously in the romance department.

I don't think I'm emotionally detached enough to handle this, so I need him to shut up before I'm in trouble. Leaning forward, I seal my lips over his and thrust my tongue into his mouth. This produces the desired effect as it completely captures his attention. He lowers onto me and I am over taken with the burn of his skin against mine. I writhe, moan, and gasp underneath him as he begins to trace the kisses down my skin and soon he arrives at my breasts. Firstly, he pulls some of the alluring, plump flesh into his mouth and it produces a slight sting that I know is going to leave a mark. I don't mind it at all and look forward to the memories that this night will forever plant in my memory.

His mouth soon moves on to my nipple. When his lips close over it through the sheer material of my bra, I begin to leak incessantly from between my thighs. I can't remember being so turned on in my life and I cannot believe just how stimulated and on fire I am.

His touch and his scent and even his very presence has entrapped and entranced me in a cocoon of mind blowing pleasure and I never want it to come to an end. His hands proceed to cup my breasts and even the tender, sensitive mounds flush in excitement. I am obsessed with just how wild it feels to be possessed by him in this way, and by the low grunts from the base of his throat, I know he feels the exact same way.

His hands remain on my breasts but then his face moves even lower and my entire body squirms with maddened anticipation. He dips his tongue into my navel and that draws a giggle out of me to his amusement. Soon, he is back at my crotch and my legs automatically slam shut, all too aware of the assault that they have just endured from him.

He isn't having it however. With a stern look at me, he straightens and with his impeccable strength jerks my legs apart. "You're hiding?" He rasps.

My throat constricts at the barrage of emotions coursing through my body.

He roughly pulls me over to him and then grips his cock in his hand. He strokes the head up and down the middle of my drenched sex.

My hands shoot out to my sides to grip the bed sheets. I am burning all over and yearning, and it is all too much but yet not enough at the same time. Brimming with anticipation, I await his entrance but then when it is not immediate, I look down to see he is slipping on a condom.

He meets my gaze from beneath his lashes.

I almost feel shame. I am so out of it that I practically forgot the most important thing. My safety. Covering my face, I try to control my breathing and the frantic racing of my heart until once again, I feel his cock at my entrance. My eyes shoot open to gaze into his electric blues and I can't look away. He gradually slides into me and I lick my lips at the most welcome intrusion.

He watches me, one hand underneath my back to support his weight, while the other is guiding his cock into me.

In moments, I am filled and stretched to bursting while guttural moans reverberate through my body. For a few seconds I stop him, my hands gripping his biceps to halt his movement. He is too big and too tight and I don't know if I can take any more of him.

Then his warm breath fans over my face, his nose softly stroking mine before he moves his lips to my ear. "How are you doing?" he asks.

My emotions are struck at his concern. I nod after a few more moments. "I'm good."

He kisses my neck. "I'll go slow."

I wrap my arms around his shoulders but my embrace is too hard and it weakens the elbow that is supporting most of his weight. He collapses on to me with a laugh but I am unable to share the sentiment as his hefty cock plunges further into me. A deafening gasp sounds from my throat.

Suddenly, his hand cradles my face. "Oh shit, are you all right?"

That final plunge is indeed a surprise but I can't exactly blame him can I? I can't help the smile that bubbles up to my face and it widens even further when he leans down to kiss me. He rolls his hips so I can get somewhat acquainted with his length but instead it hits a dangerous spot inside of me that almost triggers my climax right then. My fingers dig into his ass.

He withdraws, his cock glides out of me and although I love the feeling of being so connected with him, I can't help but wish that rubber barrier wasn't there between us. I want to feel his flesh grating directly on my walls. I reach up to nibble on his chin and with a low laugh he slides back into me. I begin to completely relax, and a couple of thrusts later his rhythm is quickening. I love the harshness of his breathing on my skin as he pounds ferociously into me.

I cling onto him for dear life, and it makes my entire body shudder in response. My heart is racing in my chest, my bones melting at the stream of ecstasy washing all over me until my eyes begin to water.

"Oh God," I croak out as I tighten my hold around him. My hands then slip down towards his ass to grab onto the tense cheeks. I'm soon displaced however because his thrusts soon become even more severe. His following lunges are so hard and wild that they tear intense gasps out of me and slam the headboard constantly against the wall.

"*Fuck, fuck, fuck*," he groans.

I completely lose control of myself. My hips are driving forward to meet his thrusts but I soon lose even the ability to contribute. He fucks me so hard that I collapse back onto the bed with my eyes rolling into my sockets.

With one last brutal thrust, he plunges into me and it hits just the right spot.

My orgasm explodes from within and I cry out at the earth shattering release. I am shuddering and trembling underneath him and he seals his mouth over mine to muffle my sobs. Then from a distance, I also feel him receive his own climax and his animalistic groans in my ear reverberates through my body. It triples my pleasure and excitement that I have been able to give as much as I have received, and I bask in the euphoric aftermath of us.

Afterwards, and as we both slowly return back to earth, I am unsure and a tad bit worried about the correct etiquette to follow. I know this indicates that I want to spend more time with him, but at the same time do not for a second want to hurt my pride. So I watch for what he will do and I am taken aback when he kisses me over and over again before falling to his side.

With an arm around me, he pulls me into his frame and rests his head in the crook of my neck. "That was fucking amazing, Blair," he says and soon falls right to sleep.

My own lids are heavy too, so I allow myself the guilty pleasure of falling asleep with him this one time.

I shut my eyes, and melt into his embrace.

CHAPTER SEVEN

Grady

"How did the meeting go?"

Once again, I am jolted by the sudden entrance into my office. I look up from the stack of reports on my desk.

Allen is brimming with cheer as usual, as he takes his seat in front of my desk.

For once, I want to ask him just what the cause of his seemingly ceaseless breezy persona is, but I decide against it. It will no doubt lead to a lengthy conversation that I currently don't have the time for. "It was all right," I respond.

"Did they officially come on board?"

"Well, I haven't gotten the call yet."

"It's only a matter of time," he says. "I know you and I'm sure you drove the message home that they would be extremely stupid if they don't bite on this."

I nod in response as my mind returns to that night, but instead of the two executives he is referring to, my memories conjure up a different person and a different venue.

The person I had woken up to and almost refused to get up from.

Again, I wonder what that was about. In my experiences from the past with one night stands, the routine afterwards is standard. No matter how exhausted I am, I've never been able to stand being that filthy from and with a stranger for too long a period of time. So I've always gotten up to clean myself, and with that behavior, the message is usually sent that when I returned, I didn't want them to still be there.

With her however, I had fallen right to sleep and I'd been aware of it.

And I hadn't minded. Even with the sex. I had let loose in a way that I usually didn't and the results had been staggering.

Somewhat alarmed, I'd gotten up to take a shower to clear my head and by the time I had gotten out of the bathroom, she had disappeared. The only thing I know is her name, and I am not going to use it to search for her, although for a short while after her disappearance I had entertained the idea. The previous weekend is in the past and I am done with it.

Suddenly, there's a knock on the door and I look up once again, upset that there isn't a secretary to screen these impromptu visits.

Allen, able to read my face is inherently amused. "You can't believe it can you? You're the owner of a company worth a billion dollars and you don't even have a secretary."

I give him a hard look, and answer the knock on the door.

Monica, my head of Human Resources comes in with a smile on her face. "Good morning, Grady," she greets, and her smile widens even further, when she notes that Allen is also present.

"Monica," he greets, with an equally wide smile and a wave.

"I just came from your office but your secretary didn't know where you went."

"He was on a bathroom break when I stepped out," he replies.

"Alright," she says before turning to me. As usual, she seems just a bit wary.

Allen's admonition comes to mind that most of the employees would not mind it if I cracked a smile or two once in a while so they would find it a little bit easier to relate to me.

There is currently nothing to smile about, so I just wait to hear what she has to say.

"I'm here about Mariam," she says. "How do you want me to go about her replacement?"

"He's handed that over to me, Monica," Allen says. "Sorry I didn't inform you, it slipped my mind." He then lifts his wrist to gaze at his watch. "I have a meeting with her replacement in about eight minutes."

"Oh," she says. "That's what I wanted to talk to you about. Since I didn't get any directive from Grady, I presumed that perhaps he told you to take care of it."

"He did." Allen smiles.

Alarm creeps up my spine as I note the glint in his eyes.

"I'll send her straight to you as soon as I'm done with her interview."

I lean back into the chair, my arms folded across my chest, and my brows raised. "She?"

"Yes, *she*," he affirms. "I had a great time speaking to her at the job fair I attended at the University of Texas a few weeks ago. She made a great impression. "

"She's a recent graduate?" I ask dryly.

"Yes, she is."

"I don't want her. Monica, please handle this and pick someone who can keep up with me for once."

"Hey!" he exclaims at me, and then turns to Monica. "No! I've got this, Monica. Don't do anything." He then returns his gaze to me. "Why can't you trust me?"

Monica is amused by him. However, I am not. I am incredibly alarmed. "Monica, please get me a temp in the meantime. There's too much going on around here for that desk to be unmanned."

"Sure," she says and exits the room.

My glare never leaves Allen's, even though his response is an audacious grin. "What is it about this candidate? This is not some sort of prank is it?"

He pushes away from the desk and rises to his feet. "It seems that I have to remind you, sir, that I am the CFO of this company, and that I got to this position by merit, not because of my father, like most of you have concluded.

I shake my head at his insincere tug for sympathy. "Get out."

He laughs in response. "Just relax. I'm sure you'll be pleased with her and if not, then we can get someone else."

I don't bother responding anymore. Suddenly, there is an incoming call on my cell phone and I can immediately see who it is. "It's the recluse," I tell Allen, and rise to my feet.

He gives me a thumbs up as I turn away from him to head towards the floor length windows covering the north wall of the office.

"Jack," I greet and we begin our conversation.

CHAPTER EIGHT

Blair

I'm in one of the seats in their massive, glass encased conference room and I can't stop shaking. Their damn headquarters is much, *much* bigger than I thought. Eighteen fully utilized floors encased in glass and steel and furnished with polished oak and marble.

I feel absolutely under-qualified to even be in the building, especially with the constant stroll of busy looking employees up and down the corridor beyond. I'm still not even aware of the position that I will be interviewing for.

My instinct is to pick my purse up and scram before the CFO gets here, but even my body seems to have stopped responding to me. I don't understand why I am this nervous as I have been to quite a number of interviews. However, none have terrified me as much as this. Maybe it's because the stakes are incredibly high? In fact, they're the highest they have ever been.

An invitation to work for an industry renowned company, and I didn't even have to send in an application?

I need to get this position even if an arm or a leg is sacrificed in the process. Opportunities like this I imagine don't come along very often.

Suddenly, the door to the conference room springs open and I immediately rise to my feet. I'm dressed in Layne's satin, olive green pant suit, wearing rosy pink makeup on my lips, cheeks, and eyelids. My hair is held back in a simple chignon, and on my feet is a pair of black, suede, medium heeled pumps.

The comment that Grady at the bar from the weekend had made about me looking too young comes to mind, and it makes me even more nervous. Perhaps the CFO calling me is a mix up with one of the other candidates from the job fair? Perhaps he still doesn't realize that apart from my internship, I don't have any concrete experience in my chosen field of cyber security.

The polished, tall man in a tan suit and a buzz haircut walks in and offers his hand to me with a big smile on his face.

I am immediately drawn to that smile and his kind eyes, and for the first time since arriving here, I take my first real breath.

Soon, we are both seated opposite each other, and the interview begins. It however does not go the way that I expect.

"So," he says. "Have you tried our green chili smothered burrito yet?"

I blink... *hard.*

My expectation was that he would first of all ask for my resume, so my hand is poised on the folder inside the briefcase on my lap, ready to immediately retrieve it.

When I see this is not the path he intends to follow, I take my hand out of the briefcase, and straighten my back. A smile is tugging at the corners of my lips but I'm not certain yet if it is all right to relax. "No, sir. I can't say I have."

"Call me Allen." He waves his hand. "Well, why haven't you? You haven't been in Denver long enough?"

"Uh, I just came in for the week to see my sister. She lives here with her husband."

"Ah, I think you did mention that you had a relative here when we spoke at the job fair."

I can't believe him. How and why does he remember all of this? There were at least a hundred people at the event, and I am certain that more than half of them came up to speak to him. A quick glance at his hand shows the simple gold wedding band on his finger so it cannot be that he is interested in me, right?

"Again, I'm glad that you were able to come in especially at such short notice. A position opened up that made me think of you and it just so happens that you are in town. It does seem like fate doesn't it?"

"It sure does." I smile, beginning to relax. "Thank you sir, for the call. I've admired your company for a very long time."

"You said as much during our first chat. You also said that you would get me the Tex-Mex and that I would be blown away. That was how our debate on the state with the best smothered burrito in the country was concluded. I never did get that burrito though."

My laugh is nervous but at the same time my heart feels like it's doing somersaults. I recall it all and don't even know how to respond to his recollection of a conversation that had at the time seemed to solely be a momentarily thrill between two people absurdly connecting amongst a sea of other more anxious and severe individuals. “Well, I did hand my card over so that you could contact me. I even offered to get it delivered to you before you left Texas if you couldn't find the time to get one yourself.”

He chuckles. “Yes, you did make that offer. Well it's not too late, and seeing as we might be working together, I am certain that we will have many opportunities to taste both burritos and make the final judgement.”

My heart lurches in excitement. “That is my hope too, sir.”

“Allen,” he corrects yet again.

This time around, I take special note of it.

He then claps his hand together as he straightens from his slouch against the chair. “Alright then, let’s get down to business. Where do you see yourself professionally in five years?”

CHAPTER NINE

Grady

There's a knock on my door, brief and assured.

I don't need to respond to know it's Allen. Therefore, when he knocks again and again and then calls out to me for a response, I am a bit perplexed.

"Come in," I reply.

A few seconds later, he walks in to meet the confused look on my face.

I notice the massive smile on his face and wonder what he's up to now, especially since it hasn't been but forty minutes since he left my office. I'm about to ask him what's his problem when I notice that someone else has come into the office with him. I recall then that he left to conduct the interview for my supposed new assistant.

"Blair, I want you to meet our CEO, and the co-founder of FireEye, Grady Abbott."

I turn towards the woman behind him... and my heart stops in my chest.

Allen continues speaking but I swear that I cannot hear a single word of what he is saying and I am sure that she is in the exact same state.

Her eyes are wide, her lips slightly parted and her complexion deathly pale.

"Grady... Grady?"

It is a few seconds more before it registers that he is calling out to me. I drag my gaze away from hers and rest it on Allen.

"This is Blair Tatum," he says. "We've just had a great interview and I'm sure that she'll be the perfect replacement as your assistant."

I set my pen down and take a deep breath. "Blair, would you excuse us?" I ask without even turning to her.

"Um, sure," she nods and turns around to hurry away. She however moves too quickly and as a result her leg tangles with the other. This causes her to fall to the ground.

Seeing this, my heart lurches in concern.

"Oh God," Allen says as her knees connect with the floor. He hurries over to help her.

I'm automatically out of my seat to do the same when I see that I am not needed. I settle back into my chair and try to remove the concern away from my face as he gently helps her back up.

"I'm alright," she says. "Thank you. I'm so sorry."

"Don't be," Allen says and soon she's back on her feet. She walks out of the office, this time a bit more slowly but her knees are still very visibly wobbly.

I don't blame her. I myself feel a bit jarred after seeing her, but luckily for me my current seated position does well to keep my appearance calm.

The moment she leaves the office Allen turns to me. "Would it have killed you to be a bit warmer to her?"

I don't even try refining my response, "Yes, it would have."

That stops him for a moment, but he soon recovers. He moves towards me and begins to make a case for her. "I'm not going to let you reject her," he says. "I've already offered her the sun and the moon and I'll be damned if you make me look like a fool by refusing her."

"I'm not going to accept her," I say. "Give her a check and apologize for wasting her time. You can go as high as five thousand. Tell her that the position has already been filled."

The usual care free air about him immediately disappears. His gaze hardens and his brows crease in annoyance.

It's rare for him to be this offended and I am not particularly pleased that I'm the cause of his annoyance, but this is a more complicated situation than he will ever know.

"Why?" he asks. "You haven't even asked for her resume." He flings the folder to my table.

Even after it lands, I don't even spare it a single look. "I don't want to work with a woman," I reply calmly. "Especially one as attractive as she is. It'll be too distracting."

He considers my response for a moment.

I wait for him to accept it.

His smirk returns to his face.

I begin to breathe easy, but then the next words that come out of his mouth are not what I expect at all.

"That's exactly one of the reasons why I'm hiring her. As your best friend, I have been concerned about your abject state of solitude and your unhealthy obsession with work. Therefore, I am taking it upon myself to—?"

"Allen, I'm not joking with you." I've run out of patience. "Send her away and that's final." I return my gaze to my desktop's screen and get back to work. Or at least I try my best to. It is definitely impossible to concentrate especially when I feel his glare on me, but I ignore it all.

This entire situation has shocked me and I need quite a while alone to process what has just transpired. I don't much believe in fate or coincidence but this is most definitely one sick twist that I want nothing to do with it.

CHAPTER TEN

Blair

I'm panicking.

I try to listen to what they might be saying outside the door but I can't hear a single word. It's as though in the space of a single minute I've been taken to Heaven and then cruelly kicked back down to the ground. I don't understand this fucking joke.

He is the CEO of FireEye?

Him? The man that had fucked me senseless, barely two nights prior? I've been so focused on the CFO Allen, that I didn't even bother doing any research on the CEO. I had expected an entry level position in one of their departments, but instead Allen has offered me what I am certain is one of the most prized positions across the company.

To become the personal assistant of Grady Abbott, a man whom I have heard mentioned over and over again amongst other industry professionals for his sheer genius and business acumen, is not a casual opportunity. He has however kept such a low profile that very few are aware of what he looks like. I should have done my research before this damn interview and I would have been able to find some information about him despite the fact that the majority of FireEye's publicity is handled by their PR officer along with the CFO, Allen.

Grady Abbott was rumored to be more focused and concerned with the development of the company's products.

His name should have struck some sort of chord with me at the bar, but I had been out of my mind with lust at the time and now here I am about to lose a position that I would probably never have obtained ordinarily. My hands are trembling and my heart is racing, so I fish my phone out of my purse to call Layne.

Tears sting my eyes, and by the time she picks up my voice is now shaky, "Layne," I say.

She immediately knows that something is wrong. After a quick, scattered explanation of the situation, she goes silent for a little while. "Did you know who he was before you slept with him?" she asks.

"Of course not," I almost squeal out in my defense.

"Hmm," she says. "I'm just trying to see if this is some sort of orchestration by them."

"I don't think so," I reply. "It's just my cursed, twisted fate."

"You weren't cursing your fate on Saturday when you picked him up from the bar."

"*He* picked me up," I retort, "and why the fuck do I have to suffer for what I did outside of work?"

"Exactly," she says. "*Exactly*. You deserve this job and you've earned it. So don't you dare allow him to take it from you."

"That's the thing," I mutter. "I don't know if I've earned it or if I'm even qualified. This is a job anyone with more working experience than me would kill to get."

"If you're not qualified for it then why were you hired?"

"The CFO and I clicked over burritos at the job fair, and I think I mentioned my experience with creating the development kit that my internship company packaged and sold as a defense solution against app attacks. I even forgot about that because he so casually slipped the inquiry into our conversation, but apparently my answer impressed him and made quite the impression."

I moved to grab my hair in frustration when I recall that it's in a very delicate chignon, so I restrain myself just in time. The last thing I need right now is to go back into the office again looking crazy. "Layne, what the hell am I going to do?"

"Blair, listen to me very carefully," she says. "You might not believe that you're qualified for this job and nothing I say is going to help you change that perception. But what I need to know is whether you're certain of this opportunity. Is it as special as you claim it is?"

"Of course it is!" I exclaim. "This is the fucking position of the century- to learn directly from Abbott. I'm prepared to work my fucking ass off. Having him anywhere on my resume automatically puts me above seventy percent of the entire industry."

"Okay," she says. "Now go in there and tell him that and demand your job. The CFO has already offered you the position right?"

"Yes he did but—"

"Did you accept it?" She cut me off.

"Of course but—"

"Then it's binding. A contract has been established between you two even if it's a verbal one, so he is obligated to offer you the job. Tell Abbey or whatever his name is that you will sue him for wrongful termination if he fires you or refuses to give you the position solely based on your personal affairs beyond the workplace."

For the first few seconds after her statement, I'm speechless. Thereafter, I have only one word as a response: " What?"

"Suits. Season two, the sucker punch episode. I watched it last week and this moronic CEO put up his company as collateral during a poker game in Atlantic City."

I am even more confused. "What the hell are you talking about?"

"The TV show- Suits. The one about the lawyers, Harvey and Mike."

"Ah," I say. "Why the hell are you bringing that up?"

"You're not listening to me! An offer was made and you accepted it. You're already under a contract of employment even though at this point, it is verbal and no one can break it without reason. If he does, you can sue him."

I finally understand what she is talking about. "Are you telling me to threaten to sue him if he doesn't hire me?"

"Exactly," she says.

I pull the phone away from my ear and stare at it. I don't know what to feel or think but before I can decide how to respond, the door is pulled open. My heart slams against my chest as I spin around.

Thankfully, it's not Grady but Allen that has come out.

I don't like the look of disappointment on his face but at this point, anything is better than seeing Grady.

"Blair," he begins. "I apologize for... that. Your boss can be a bit... difficult to relate with sometimes. He's just informed me of his preference for someone a bit more experienced so I'm going to have to reassign you to a different position in the company."

Immediately I feel relief, but then Layne's words come to mind. I'm however, too shaken right now by everything to muster up such courage. "Okay."

"Alright, let me escort you out," he says. "I kind of had only this position in mind for you, so I'm going to need some time to speak to human resources to get you set up with something else. I'll give you a call the moment we're ready for you."

I realize then that I am going to walk out of here today without the job that I actually want, only to be reassigned to something mediocre later on.

I turn to leave in dejection, but then once again Layne's advice comes to mind. Why should I be judged for something that happened in my personal life, and at the time had no connection whatsoever to my professional activities?

I stop in my tracks and so does Allen. "Can you give me a few minutes?" I ask. "I want to speak to him."

Surprise fleets across his face. "Uh, I don't think that is a good idea."

"Neither do I," I say nervously, and turn around before my brain can talk me into reason. I knock on his door but I am too nervous to wait for a response so I just walk in and make sure to shut it behind me. The last thing I want is for Allen to hear anything that I'm going to say.

Mr. CEO lifts his head at my entrance and fuck, he is intimidating. His hooded gaze watches me but his face is completely expressionless so I have no idea what is going through his mind. I take a step forward and then another knowing that my mouth will not work the way it is supposed to unless I am directly in front of him.

He straightens to watch my approach.

I pray for my knees not to give out.

"I didn't give you permission to come in," he says.

I stop in my tracks. "I know," I reply. "I just wanted to say something to you."

"Go ahead."

I refuse to think. "I'm going to sue you," I say.

Now, there's finally an expression on his face.

It is confusion, and I am quite certain that the exact same one is on mine. This is definitely not the way I wanted to start but it is quite apparent now that I just really want to get to the point before he throws me out. With that threat, I'm pretty sure any chance of working here is lost, so I just throw caution to the wind and say exactly what I want to.

"Excuse me?"

"If you fire me, I'm going to sue you for wrongful termination."

He leans back into his chair, and his hands slowly fold across his chest. "What contract?" he asks.

It almost seems like he is enjoying this and it terrifies me even further. I can't even look him in the eye. "I-it w-was verbal," I reply. "Allen - the CFO offered me the position as your assistant and I accepted it. So the agreement has been created."

"Really?" he says. "Well, I'm not aware of that. As far as I know what you were called in for today was an interview. For a contract of employment to be established and binding, we have to extend a formal written agreement to you, which you then have to accept and sign. So tell me Miss Tatum, on what grounds exactly is your accusation of wrongful termination going to be based on?"

In that moment, I curse Layne. I've never watched the episode of that show, so I don't have a clue as to what I am talking about, and she didn't give me enough details that would help me to formulate some sort of comeback. The best I can do now is to finish strong even though every word out of my mouth is borderline moronic. So I square my shoulders and lift my chin for my grand finale, "That's all I have to say. A verbal offer was made and accepted and the cameras in the conference room can prove this. By the time those records are subpoenaed and shown, then I'll be able to establish all the grounds that I need."

"The camera in our conference room doesn't work," he says.

My gaze meets his in shock. I am a bit surprised though to see that his eyes are sparkling, and a ghost of a smile is tugging at the corners of his lips.

"That can't be right," I say.

Now, his smile breaks free. "Really? How so? Because if I say the camera in the conference room is broken then it is, and if I say that it is not, then that will be the case. This, Blair, is my turf and I call the shots here."

This, I think as I watch his face brighten up. *This right here is the sinfully haughty and massively appealing demeanor of his that made me offer myself to him on a silver platter during the weekend.* Suddenly, recollections of him pounding his hips into me flashed before my mind, and the sexual pangs that ensue feels like several severe kicks in the gut.

I don't know how to respond to him anymore so I turn around to take my leave. I *have finally lost.* This whole situation is a bust and I am ready to save myself from the shame before it kills me.

"Can you really work with me?" he asks. "After last weekend?"

He hits a nerve and I turn back around. "Last weekend has absolutely nothing to do with today! That was personal and I didn't know who you were. This is my professional life."

He remains calm despite my explosion. "That's why I'm asking you. Can you separate the two?"

"Of course I can," I reply.

Silence.

"Then you're hired. Relay my decision to Allen and tell him to instruct you on all you need to know. Please shut the door on your way out." He returns his attention to the documents on his desk.

My knees wobble from the shock. Before I can fall again, I force the strength back to my frame and immediately turn around. I want to express some form of gratitude but I can't muster up a single word or thought for that matter, so I just walk out of the office and shut the door behind me.

Allen is outside the office and speaking to a woman in a corduroy pant suit. The moment they see that I have emerged, they both come over to me.

"Blair, this is Monica Herring, our head of HR. She is going to be assisting me in reassigning you. Monica, this is Blair Tatum."

"It's a pleasure to meet you," she says.

I reply in kind, before turning to Allen. "He says I'm hired," I tell him. "So I don't think there will be a need to reassign me."

Both of them go silent at my statement.

"What?" Allen asks while looking stunned. "He changed his mind?"

I nod and hope to God, he doesn't find out the backstory behind all of this.

Allen inhales deeply and then releases a deep, and heavy breath. "Monica, please orientate Miss Tatum. I'll speak to Grady." With that, he returns to Abbott's office.

While trying to control my nervousness, I go along with Monica.

CHAPTER ELEVEN

Blair

There is a sudden commotion in the cafeteria. I look up from my simple but tasty meal of grilled rockfish and pecan dumplings to search for the source and my gaze meets a man with a small toddler strapped to his torso. The baby is giggling with excitement, it's stubby arms and legs outstretched to receive all the attention that is coming her way from the myriad of employees, most of which are female, that are gathered to welcome them.

Her father is none other than the affable CFO, Allen, whom I've become quite fond of, and who is very clearly enjoying the attention even more than the toddler is. I want to go over and give my greetings, but I am still somewhat of a strange presence amongst the sea of employees. So I glue my butt to my seat, continue with my meal and remain content with just watching from afar.

A message arrives on my phone, so I turn my attention to the screen to see that it is from Jodie.

It's about her escapades at the diner she works in, and at the picture of the stranger's Ferrari that she went home with the previous night, my heart nearly jumps out of my chest.

You got in a freaking stranger's car and went home with him? I texted

You're one to talk, she texts back.

I'm immediately reminded of the dilemma I'm in with my new boss who by the way, hasn't spoken a word to me in the week that I have been working here. *Touché*, I reply with a sullen face just as a deep but breezy voice sounds behind me. I turn to see the highly esteemed CFO Allen, arrive at my table with his toddler and I immediately rise to my feet. He has two packed lunches in hand, and to my surprise pulls out the chair in front of me to take a seat.

I immediately feel self-conscious, knowing that a lot of eyes from the cafeteria will now be on us.

"How's it going, burrito debtor?" he asks.

I can't help but laugh. It makes me immediately relax enough to enjoy his company. "Quite well, so far," I reply, and don't bother to add the *'could be better'* part of the sentence. It turns out however that I don't have to.

"Establish any sort of rapport with your boss yet?" he asks.

I'm about to brush the concern off but then I see the glint of true concern in his gaze. "Can I be honest?" I ask.

"Of course."

"It won't come back to bite..." I quickly catch myself "I mean, it won't be used against me in the future, right?"

He laughs, and the boisterous burst startles the toddler strapped to his torso. "No, it won't come back to bite you in the ass. And no need to censor yourself either on account of this one, we say ass around her all the time. She's still unimpressionable."

I laugh again as I gaze at the blue eyed toddler.

Her head is covered in dark tufts of curly hair and her limbs outstretched as she fights to be free of her father.

"She's so beautiful. What's her name?"

"Alexa," he replies, "but back to your frigid boss."

"Alright," I respond but quickly drop a disclaimer. "And I didn't call him that, you did."

"Of course." He smiles and sends me a wink.

My gaze moves to his bowls of salad. "Don't you need to eat though? I don't want to keep you."

"These are for my wife," he says. "She's visiting me today and loves our Greek salad, so she's going to take them back to work with her. Now will you stop changing the subject and talk to me about your boss?"

I sigh. "He's not bad... it's just that, I wish he would be more... that he would communicate a bit more. He hasn't said a word to me since I've been here." I do suspect it has to do with the fact that we've slept together, so he is ensuring to keep his distance from me. Since he made the decision to hire me it is a bit difficult to accept that his complete animosity towards me will be the nature of our working relationship.

I do not however want to alarm Allen enough to go poking around because of my complaint, since this will almost certainly reveal this backstory, so I immediately try to brush it all away.

"It's all alright," I say. "I mean he's been really busy and I've been able to tackle the schedule left by his previous secretary. Although he doesn't seem to use it most of the time. I take the calls that come in and schedule appointments, then I leave them on his desk. I do think he works with it, but I just expected that there would be more input from him on how he wants me to manage his office and time. Look at me rambling on." I catch myself at his endearing gaze. "I guess I just want to be as useful as possible and maybe with time that will be the case. "

He smiles as he glances down at his restless tot. "Can I have that?" he asks referring to my half emptied bottle of water.

I quickly hand it over.

He puts it in Alexa's hands and immediately, the toddler is occupied with wrinkling the plastic. "I understand you," he says. "And I'm surprised at all. Grady takes quite a while to warm up to people and can even sometimes, just remain completely closed off. This is one of the reasons why I hired you. Because of your youth and easy going personality, I am hoping that perhaps you'll be able to lighten up the air around there."

Well, you're not the one getting slowly killed by frostbite, I think to myself.

"The second reason why I hired you is to bring some fresh perspective into his projects. From what you know so far of his schedule, is there any part of it that you would like to improve upon? If there is, then perhaps you could bring this up with him, and if he appreciates your suggestion, then that will most definitely break the ice between you too. The way to Grady's heart is work and solely work."

I consider his suggestion. "Well, he has an event in Breckenridge on Friday; the annual security conference. He has to give a short presentation about cyberattacks, via package delivery, and I was thinking that perhaps he could incorporate a short demonstration during his speech to increase its impact? There are going to be a lot of companies and potential massive clients at the conference."

He nods in agreement. "That's pretty good," he says. "So bring this to his attention."

I hesitate, a small breath sifting through my teeth.

He studies me. "You have to bring it up to him," he stresses. "This is the surefire way to melt the ice between you two."

"What if he doesn't respond positively?"

"Then you try again, and again until he eventually does. He's your boss so although, I am rooting for you, the heights that you climb here will depend on your resilience and proactivity."

I nod promptly, reminded that the CFO isn't my personal therapist.

His baby throws the bottle across the table and that becomes his cue to leave. "Gotta get back to the wife," he says and rises to his feet. "And on a final note, I'm certain you've done well thus far because despite how withdrawn he can be, he's incredibly vocal about bad performance. He hasn't said a word of complaint to me about you, so I'm sure you're handling your tasks properly. However, you need to build a rapport so that you can truly be a great assistant to him, and through that, find opportunities to grow."

"Yes, sir," I reply.

"Also, make some friends," he says. "It's not good to be too alone over here as there are many tedious and long hours coming your way. You've just been CFO certified so say hi to some people and they'll be very happy to welcome you to a conversation."

I give a quick glance around the room. "I will, sir," I respond with a smile.

He takes his leave.

I wave to Alexa, and soon they are gone. Then I take the time to think hard about what he has just advised me on.

On my way back home from work later that evening, I stop by Jodie's diner for a quick meal, and to catch up with her. I also share Allen's suggestion on how to tackle my boss with her.

She then gives me her advice on how to 'truly break the ice'. It's a pair of bright blue lacy lingerie she had picked up a few days earlier. "This is all you need," she says. "Wear this into his office, and you'll have all the attention you need from him."

I snatch the package to inspect it, but roll my eyes at her devilish suggestion. "Fix the problem that sex created with more sex. You're a genius aren't you?"

She fights to take the gift back at my sarcasm, but I eventually succeed in leaving the diner with it. The next day, I wear it to work beneath my cobalt blue suit, and there is just something about its decadence that makes me feel just a little bit more empowered and sexy.

He arrives right on time at 8 AM, and once again walks past me without a word. I rise to sound my usual greeting and his response is a quiet nod.

I don't sit back down, but of course, he doesn't notice. He shuts the door to his office as usual and I'm left to wallow in the silence of the massive reception. I pace the front of the door for a good twenty minutes before I finally find the courage to go in. Inhaling a shaky breath, I knock on the door and do not give him the chance to pretend that he doesn't hear it.

I walk in and of course, he only spares a brief glance to check who has come in uninvited.

When he sees that it's me, he continues right on with whatever he's doing with his desktop.

"I haven't yet had the chance to ask how you like your coffee in the morning," I say as I approach his desk, my gaze on the paper cup that he usually brings in himself.

"Don't worry about it," he says.

I try my very best to calm my annoyance at his snobbery. I place the folder on his desk and open it up. "Here's the schedule for the conference at Breckenridge tomorrow and the lineup of speakers. I've also included the companies that will be present and the best potential prospects as major clients. The names of the CEOs that will be in attendance are also here."

He doesn't respond which is my cue to leave, but I'm not going to back down this easily. So I begin to circle his desk.

At my approach, he lifts his head.

I don't dare meet his eyes as I come over to his side, slightly bending over to point out what I want his attention on from the schedule. "Here's my recommendation for—"

"Step away," he says.

The words are like the slash of a blade through my chest. *Perhaps I have gone too far?* I can't help the burn of tears in my eyes, but in the following moment, I clear my throat and force myself to take the rejection in stride. "I have something to show you, sir."

"You can do it from across the table. Please maintain your distance."

"Why?" I ask, hating how he's making me feel. In this moment, I have ceased to care whether I keep this job or not. "You've seen me naked and been inside me, and you didn't seem to hate it at the time, so why are you treating me now as though I'm a leper?"

His eyebrows arch. "We're at work Miss Tatum," he says through gritted teeth.

"Good," I reply. "Since we're at work then award me the professional courtesy of at least looking me in the eyes while I'm addressing you. It's alright if you say that you do not have the time, but don't treat me like a fly on the wall."

He leans back into his chair, and folds his arms across his chest.

Now, against my better judgement, my lower body is struck numb with arousal. It doesn't help that he looks extra damn fine today in a dark green suit jacket, and a white dress shirt.

His skin is glistening like satin, his hair swept smoothly away from his face, and the dark rimmed glasses that sit on his nose doing more damage to my heart than I can bear.

Why does he have to be so fucking attractive?

Once again, flashbacks come from that night, my clit in his mouth comes to mind and I quickly look away. I almost desperately want him to take me once again. I can see the problem now. How could I think that we could so easily work together?

"Are you done?" he asks.

I don't respond and to my surprise, he keeps waiting.

My gaze falters from his. "Yes, sir."

"Okay. First of all, I'm not treating you like a fly on the wall, I'm treating you like your boss. Which means that I can choose to just listen to you rather than stop what I'm doing to give you the attention that you for some reason, feel you deserve. Secondly, before I hired you, you assured me that you could keep things professional between us. Therefore, this is my first and last warning to you, to not to breach my personal space again. If I call you over to point something out to me, then you do so, but if I don't please don't cross the line."

I am speechless, and can no longer remain under his scathing gaze. My tone of voice dips till it's almost inaudible. "Yes, sir. Um, I included some suggestions on how to improve your presentation. I went through a couple of your old clips and I think that this will help us further engage your audience. The revised contract sent over by Bloom is also included in the folder so please go through it when you get the chance so that I can send it back to legal. I want to do more here than warm a seat, so I sincerely hope that you'll give me the chance."

With that, I turn around on somewhat wobbly legs, and it is nothing short of a miracle that I make it out of his office before crumbling. I shut the door behind me, and immediately sink to the exquisite mosaic flooring.

CHAPTER TWELVE

Grady

I watch her leave and don't miss the tightened fists by her sides.

I don't blame her. I know I've been less than welcoming to her since she officially accepted her position at the beginning of the week. But snubbing her isn't wholly intentional either. I'm just not certain of how to properly process her presence and I haven't taken the time either to reflect on it. So, I've just altogether pushed her out of my mind.

Except for the times when I arrive at the office. It's too difficult then not to notice her. She's usually either busy on her computer or going through documents, and each time it hits me just how unreal it is that I've had mind blowing sex with the woman. She is fucking stunning and in the tranquility of these mornings, it is almost impossible to get the notion out of my head that perhaps I will someday, be able to have her again.

Right now, I'm as hard as steel, making it very clear that I get some sick kick out of watching her fume. The last time was in the hotel room when I had challenged her age and the defiance in those deep green eyes had doubled my arousal. Now, and at the recollection of the fists by her side, all I can think of is binding her hands behind her and pounding my cock into her. Over and over again. Stretching and filling her till she is pulsing and panting from the passionate barrage. Her ass would repeatedly slap against my groin, flesh passionately hitting flesh, filling the room with the wild, maddening cadence of our grunts and moans.

My heart is now thumping against my chest, my breathing hard and heavy. Am I some sort of sick sadist? How can I intentionally ignore her and then relish the thrill of the aggravation it produces?

With a push, I move away from the desk and rise to my feet.

There is no way in hell that I'm going to be able to keep working without some sort of release, so I head to the bathroom.

Soon, my cock is in my hand and I'm pumping it ruthlessly, my other hand against the tiled wall to support my frame as I chase the release I so desperately need. I will otherwise be unable to keep functioning.

I have never done this beyond the confines of my home before, as nothing and no woman has ever pushed me to such a frivolous brink. Therefore, this goes to show more than anything, just how much trouble she is, and how susceptible I am for hiring her, regardless of my knowledge of this fact.

A long groan flows from my throat at the intense release, my knees almost buckling from the violent burst of pleasure. It takes all of what is left of my self-control not to sound out the fucking mesmeric orgasm, my hand barely able to keep from slamming against the wall.

I smear some of the discharge down the delicate skin of my cock and to some extent, it vividly brings to mind the feeling of being inside her. My body shudders as I bask in the delicious aftermath, and when things eventually subside, I lower my gaze to take in my current state.

I'm still somewhat hard, but anymore and I just might rip the skin off my dick. What and whom I really need is just a wall away but there is no way that fantasy can ever occur here. I try my hardest to ignore the wisps of shame that surrounds me as I pull my pants up and head over to the sink to wash up.

After putting myself in order, I glance back at the reflection of my blue eyes in the mirror and cannot deny that I look as haunted as I feel.

I acknowledge now that this can't go on for much longer. It's either I fuck her, or fire her, but which one of the two however will help me keep my sanity, I have absolutely no clue.

CHAPTER THIRTEEN

Blair

The hard, painful punch of my fist into the couch startles me back to my senses.

“Fuck,” I wince.

“Blair!”

Layne’s alarmed tone sifts over to me. I turn to see the worried look on her face.

“What the hell is going on? You’ve been so out of it since you got home.”

“Nothing," I quickly reply, but I’m all too aware of what she is referring to.

Ever since I walked out of Grady’s office, I’ve been on edge. After his scolding, I’d quickly returned to my seat and tried to wipe the daze off my face.

I didn’t see or hear from him again until the time came for me to leave for the day. Usually, I waited until he left, which was sometimes almost midnight and it had brought more than enough scoldings from Layne that the company was working me too hard. I didn't have the heart to tell her the truth, that I was the one who chose to wait on my boss, who still didn't bother to acknowledge my existence, so that I didn't make the mistake of leaving in case he perhaps still needed me. Today however, I returned early, my altercation with him completely shattering my mood and self-esteem.

"Everything is fine," I try to assure her.

Of course, she's not buying it. "Really? What about him?"

The mere mention of him causes my chest to constrict.

"He still hasn't warmed up towards you?"

I don't want her to be worried but at the same time, I also want to speak to someone before I lose my mind. However, one look at her bulging stomach and I change my mind. "Everything is fine, Mom," I groan softly and rise to my feet. "I'm going to get more iced tea, do you want some?"

She shakes her head, so I simply bring my now empty mug with me and the glass bowl that had been filled with potato chips an hour earlier.

I spend a longer time in the kitchen than is needed to get my refill, but I need the time and space away to give the rampant thoughts in my head the chance to run wild, especially without Layne's watchful gaze mere inches from mine. I start on the dishes in the sink, but then my phone begins to ring. It is however all the way in the living area so I tell Layne to get it.

"Who is it?" I ask.

She stares at the phone. "The person's not on your contact list. Do you want me to bring it over?"

I give it a thought. "Nah, take a message for me."

She proceeds to answer the call while I return to my mindless chore. It's a few seconds later before I realize that she has gone a bit too quiet. Beyond her initial salutation, all she is doing now is listening intently.

"Yes, sir," she eventually speaks, but before I can go over the call comes to an end.

"Who was that?" I ask.

"Your boss," she replies.

The ceramic I'm holding onto slips from my hands. Luckily it only clatters into the sink and is saved. "What?"

"Yeah. He introduced himself as Grady Abbott."

I'm stunned, speechless, unable to even ask for any further information. She starts relaying his message to me: "He says that you should ensure to get to the office on time at 8 AM tomorrow so that you both can commute together to the conference in Breckenridge."

My heart lurches into my throat. "What? Are you serious? I-Is that what he said?"

"Yeah," she answers, a bit startled by my reaction. "Why, is it strange? Isn't this a part of your job?"

I can't answer any of her questions, even if I wanted to at this moment. My heart is beating too fast with excitement.

She immediately notices this switch in my mood. "What's this about? Is there something special happening in Breckenridge?"

I glance at her to respond but when a smile attacks my face, I slap my hand over my mouth to try to control it.

She can't help but share in my excitement albeit her confusion. "What's happening? Fucking talk!"

After I'm able to bring my smile under control, I move my hand away from my mouth. "My boss just spoke to me as his employee for the first time since I started working there."

All the blood drains away from her face. "What?"

"Long story," I reply.

She sits up straighter on the arm chair she has been lounging in. "You better start fucking talking."

I'm well aware of the rant and aggravation that is going to follow my narration but it doesn't matter much to me. I can take it. In that moment in fact, it seems that I can take anything because finally, I have a goddamn fucking chance with that godforsaken boss.

CHAPTER FOURTEEN

Blair

The next morning, I arrive with just a few minutes left before the stipulated arrival time of 8 AM.

When I see that neither my boss nor his driver Andrew is outside the building, I head on up to the office. I'm still very much on edge, though the source of my agitation has now switched from the concern that he wasn't giving me any attention whatsoever as an employee, to the even larger concern that he now is. Somehow, it all feels like some sort of trap. Perhaps the goal is to give me an opportunity to mess up so he can find a real reason to fire me?

Or perhaps my tantrum the previous day truly got to him and has earned me a real chance? None of it really matters either way because regardless of the motive behind this move, I'm going to take it and run with it.

I stayed awake late into the night, reviewing the materials for the event and examining the previous ones so that I can be of thorough assistance with whatever he will possibly need.

The elevator finally reaches his floor, so I wait until the doors slide open to step out.

It does not however register that there is someone in front of it until it is too late.

My heart jumps into my throat as I all but crash into the person in my haste. "Oh, my God!"

Our bodies stagger dangerously backwards and it seems like forever before a hand clamps down hard on one of my arms. We are both brought to an abrupt stop and as I notice the magnitude of the damage that I have caused, the apologies burst from my mouth. "I'm so sorry," I gasp, but I become so stunned by the brown stains that have soaked into his shirt that my heart just fails me altogether.

My boss glares down at me.

I can't keep from relating the rage in his eyes to that of a bull preparing to charge me.

He remains silent but his grave annoyance at the accident is painted all over his face.

I have on a beige chiffon blouse underneath my dark suit and it is now pitifully soiled, but that is not my concern. The stained light blue dress shirt he has on is thoroughly ruined.

The higher concern however is that I have burned him. I'm too in shock to feel my own burns if there is any, so I focus solely on him. After putting the half emptied cups down, I pull my jacket off my body and begin to tap it against his chest. "I'm so sorry." Tears sting my eyes.

He stops me with an impatient, startling tone. "You need that." He pulls the jacket away from his chest and then turns around to return to his office.

I'm left with a soiled floor, empty cups and trembling knees.

I don't know what to do.

I consider just turning around and walking away from the building. There's no way I'm going to have a job after this, and the *event*! He is going to be late if he doesn't recover on time. I decide then to at least try to be of some sort of help before I leave.

So I head to his office and find his door open. I hear the sound of a tap running, but hesitate to go inside, so I just wait by the door and gaze nervously at my watch. I hear him begin to approach and hurry behind my desk to hide. I can't even meet his eyes when he comes out.

I'm sorry, I prepare myself to say, but then when I look up, I see that he has changed.

He still has on the same dark suit jacket but he is now in a white dress shirt. He looks surprised to see me just standing there. "We're running late," he says. "Aren't you going to change?"

I'm shocked. "Um, I d-don't—?"

"Go into my bathroom. There's a small closet there so pick one of the shirts and hurry downstairs." He places my jacket on the table and walks away.

For the first few seconds, I can't move but then a quick glimpse at the wall clock reminds me of how urgent things are. So, I rush into his office and head for the closet. There is indeed a small provision of extra suits and dress shirts and I immediately go for a white one.

Of course, my petite frame is drowning inside it but, I quickly make it work. I tuck it into my pencil skirt, leave the collars and a few holes unbuttoned, before gently folding the long sleeves up my arms. Coupled with the delicate gold jewelry around my neck, I conclude that things don't seem too bad.

I grab my jacket and hurry out of the building. His car is waiting out front so I knock nervously on the front door, unwilling to sit beside him.

The driver rolls down the pane. "I'll take my car and drive behind you—"

"Get in." Grady's crisp, cold voice comes from behind me.

Reluctantly, I pull the latch of the door open but it doesn't budge.

"Come around," he says.

I hurry around the vehicle in my dark pumps and try my best to slide in as gracefully as possible despite my flustered state.

The driver immediately moves, so I busy myself with staying as still as possible. I'm even almost afraid to breathe.

A few minutes pass by before he speaks to me, and the first words out of his mouth are, "You're late."

I swallow, hard. "I'm so sorry. I would have been at the office a few minutes earlier but I stopped by to get us the cups of—"

"If I tell you to be somewhere at 8 AM and you arrive by then, you're late. If you arrive earlier, you're on time and if you arrive later than that, then don't even bother showing up. Keep that in mind for next time."

Next time? My heart skips several beats. "Yes, sir."

CHAPTER FIFTEEN

Grady

I know that she feels incredibly remorseful.

But she seems so damn shaken and afraid that I'm the one who is becoming even more contrite. There is no doubt that this is the effect of my one week of ignoring her in the office and it makes me feel like a monster. And that rant about her being late. Otherwise, a small incidental coffee spill shouldn't seem like a death sentence to her. I want to speak to her, to calm her down especially at the hands that she can't stop wringing on her lap.

Her gaze is outside the window and she's as still and pale as a corpse.

I take a deep breath and part my lips to speak, "Which demonstration are you recommending that we perform today?" I ask.

She looks away from the window but still can't fully meet my gaze. "Um," she clears her throat. "I suggest the Remcos backdoor. We can get some of them to install that by downloading the deceptive email attachment and through that extract their data. I think that it'll leave the biggest impression."

"Alright," I agree, my gaze on her. I know it is somewhat uncomfortable but I'm hoping I can cajole her to look at me, so she can see in my eyes that everything is okay.

It doesn't.

"Do you know how to infiltrate with spyware?"

"I do," she replies with a brief nod.

"Which?"

"I'm familiar with Bsymem Trojan."

"Then would you like to headline the demonstration event today?"

Her head snaps towards mine, and in this moment she looks so much like the doe eyed girl I had suspected her to be in that hotel room. Her face loses even more color.

But I can't tell if it is out of excitement or dread at my request.

She then looks away, her gaze returning to the window but not before she briefly assesses her attire.

I figure then that she might be a bit self-conscious about the change with her appearance. "This looks fine on you," I say quickly, not wanting to reveal how I currently feel about seeing her in one of my shirts. When she still doesn't say a word, I add. "If you don't feel comfortable we could stop quickly to get you something to change into?"

"No need, sir," she says. "The shirt is okay and... regarding the event, I think that it will definitely have more of an impact if you lead it yourself. If you still think otherwise, then I'll certainly handle the demonstration as per your request."

"Alright," is my response as I unlock my tablet and return to work.

CHAPTER SIXTEEN

Blair

The way the day is unfolding is so outstanding that I don't know how to feel.

One moment, it seems as though his gaze is shooting nails into me, and in the next, it is as though all is well.

Can't help but sneak a look at him once again and my eyes automatically go to his chest where the coffee had spilled. I came away with a very small burn as the Americano was not scalding hot, but I don't know if it is the case for him.

I do not want to bring it up so this very light camaraderie between us isn't shattered but the journey is just over three hours long and we are barely forty five minutes into it. I didn't expect to be in such close proximity and in such a confined space with him for so long, so I decide to just say what I want so that my heart can lighten.

It's a while longer before I finally get my mouth to work. "I apologize for spilling coffee on you," I say and quickly divert my gaze when he turns to me. "I got the two cups for the both of us and it's why I didn't arrive much earlier. I'm sorry and please allow me to launder the shirt you changed out of. Also thank you for lending this one to me. I'll have them both cleaned and returned as soon as possible."

"No need," he replies. "I have a lady that comes in weekly to handle all things domestic. So just return the shirts and she'll see what can be done to them,"

"Oh," is all I can say. I then follow the response with a nod but I'm not at all satisfied by it. I want to do something to at least lessen the weight of my mistake pressing down on my heart. I battle with myself to let it go since it seems that he has but there is just one more question I want to ask, "Did you..." My voice is too low so I clear it and try again. "Did you get a burn from the coffee?"

He turns to me so quickly that I cannot look away, and as a result, I'm forced to hold his gaze so that I don't appear timid.

"No," he replies. "Did you?"

I shake my head.

His eyes rove all over my face and then slowly down my upper body. It is no doubt a somewhat innocent inspection but there is nothing innocent about how that perusal makes me feel. It doesn't help that he is completely aware of exactly what I look like beneath my clothes. I look away before my breath chokes me and try my best to calm the pace of my heart.

The night at the hotel comes back to mind again, and I try my possible best not to entertain it but at his proximity to me, it's nearly impossible. He's too close and his scent of tobacco and lavender is much too familiar.

His phone begins to ring and he takes the call.

I can't help but sneak glimpses at the hand tapping away on his thigh. The fabric of his pants is taut around the muscled flesh and it really doesn't take much to be reminded that they had once caged me to receive his thrusts.

Restless, I run my hand through my hair and almost wish that I could ask the driver to roll the window down. It doesn't help either that the shirt I have on smells completely of him and the heat from his very presence by my side is scorching my skin.

Absolutely nothing is helping, even breathing.

"Let's stop for a rest."

My eyes shoot open to see that he is addressing his driver.

Soon, we pull into a gas station and he turns to me. "Take a little break. We'll leave in about ten minutes."

He doesn't have to ask me twice. I nearly fly out of the car and head straight to the restroom. There I just stop and stare at the tiles. I don't have the actual desire to relieve myself here but I do have the desire to text Jodie.

I'm never having a one-night stand in my life again. It's haunting me... every second and every minute.

Her reply comes almost immediately.

Isn't it a good thing if it haunts you? Most people want to forget their one-night stands.

I reply, *Well, I'm one of those now because he is my boss and it seems neither of us can get past the fact that we fucked each other.*

Well, it's better that neither of you can get past it because it was good. Imagine how much more awkward things would have been between you both if it had been bad.

She has a point and it brings a smile to my face despite my troubled mood. I put the phone down, wash my hands, and adjust my outfit. His shirt on me is not half bad but the scent is a very vivid reminder that I'm almost wearing him is driving my libido wild with lust. This is the last thing that I need today.

I text Jodie back. *We're going out today. I need to get drunk and also remind me to buy a dildo*.

I walk out of the bathroom and head back into the store. I want to pick something up but then I realize I would have to chew it a few feet away from his ears, so I decide against it and pick up a small bottle of juice instead. Then I realize it would probably make me want to pee so in the end, I just settle for gummy bears.

I groan inwardly, as I head off to the counter at how truly exhausting it is being around him. Or perhaps, it's just exhausting to be me.

I stop however when I meet him there. He's on the phone but his eyes are locked on me as I approach. I place the pack of gummy bears on the counter and reach for my card to pay for it but he signals to the cashier to add it to his."

"*No, don't worry about it,*" I mouth my refusal but he ignores me and continues with his call. So as not to make a scene, I accept the purchase and we return to his waiting Mercedes-Maybach GLS.

We both get in, and the journey continues.

CHAPTER SEVENTEEN

Grady

The event in Breckenridge is just about to begin when we arrive.

We're shown to our seats just as it is in full swing and my keynote is soon called upon. It breezes by and afterwards, there is a storm of salutations and networking that we have to work through. Five hours later however, we are done for the day and begin our return back to Denver.

I shut my eyes, needing the rest more than anything and it leads to me sleeping through the rest of the journey until I feel a small tap on my arm.

"Mr. Abbott?" I hear a soft voice call repeatedly. I'm awake enough to respond but I listen to her for a few more seconds before my eyes come open. I turn, and the light of the setting sun through the window covers her in a beautiful, mesmeric light. I can't look away from her and once again, it is slowly beginning to dawn on me that we cannot work together. Not with me constantly on the verge of an incapacitating arousal. I straighten and loosen the knot of my tie.

"I'm sorry for waking you but earlier on, I got a call from Bloom. They have signed the contracts we sent over yesterday, so can I quickly hop off anywhere here? I'll take a taxi to collect them before they close for the weekend."

I give it a thought and make my decision. "No need. Let's just drive over."

"Oh, okay," she says.

I give Andrew the needed instructions.

I wait in the car as she collects the contract and immediately, begin to peruse it the moment she hands it over. They have agreed to all our stipulated conditions. Twenty one million in projected revenue and direct access to all of their users. It is quite a pleasant end to the week. I hand the document over to Blair. "Send that over to customer success management so that they can start working on it next week."

"Yes, sir," she replies and slips the folder into her briefcase.

I want to head straight home so I drop her off at the office. Before she leaves however, I want to tell her that she did good today. I watch as she gets out of the car and shuts the door. I take a deep breath and before she walks too far away from the car, I roll the window down and call out to her, "Blair."

She turns around, the light evening breeze is blowing her hair all over her face. It's not in a particularly cinematic way and most probably half blinds her. "Yes, sir," she answers as she struggles to push the hair out of her face. Her face is flushed and almost pained.

"You did great today."

She goes still.

So as not to linger, I roll the window back up and the car pulls away.

CHAPTER EIGHTEEN

Blair

I break down in the taxi.

I can't stop the tears from flowing and by the time I arrive home, my eyes are puffy enough to warrant Layne's concern.

"What's going on?" She runs over to me.

I throw my arms around her for a much needed hug. For the longest time I don't speak and she just lets me be.

When I'm finally able to pull away from her, the first thing she notices is my outfit. "You look different. This isn't what you wore this morning is it?"

"No..." I sniff and head over to the fridge. In seconds, I have a strawberry in my mouth and a handful of grapes in hand.

"What happened?"

"I spilled coffee on my boss and almost burnt him. This is his shirt."

Her mouth forms a little 'O' as her eyebrows rise. "Is that all?"

I think of how to explain to her just how that seemingly simple incident was the catalyst to the most tense day that I have had in a very long time. Words don't seem to be adequate enough to properly convey my frustration, so I just plop the rest of the grapes in my mouth and grab a bottle of water.

"You didn't get fired did you?" she asks.

I shake my head. My gaze goes over to the bubbling pot on the stove. "What are you making?"

"Chicken soup," she replies. "I need something brothy to soothe me."

"That's exactly what I need too."

She cocks her head at me, her gaze soft and endearing. "You're not going to give me any details?"

"It's basically the coffee spill incident," I reply. "But trust me, it was more than enough to send me on a self-loathing spiral for the rest of the day. Well, the majority of it."

"If working for him is this stressful, then why don't you just quit? I don't want you to have to go through all of this."

I consider her suggestion as I head over to the sofa, taking my seat in one corner.

She comes over to perch on the arm of the sofa I'm sitting on.

"This is all happening because I slept with him, so now everything seems a bit more personal when it shouldn't be. Don't worry, I'll get over it."

"If it was just any other generic company, I would have pulled you out of there myself, but you've mentioned that they can really help your advancement in your industry, so I'm restraining myself. From nothing to an Inc. five hundred company in five years? And he started right out of college? The information is that he's worth at least a billion dollars."

I am a little bit surprised at her well of information.

At my expression she explains, "I was a bit idle today, so I did some research."

"Did you also see any pictures of him?"

She releases a whoosh of breath. "I did, and I couldn't stop staring at him. If it wasn't too weird to ask, I would have asked you for all the details about your night together."

"Don't ask," I say. "That'd be creepy."

She laughs. "At least, give me some sort of impression."

"Anytime he comes within three feet of me it's all I can think about. It doesn't help that his scent is all over this damn shirt!" I look down at the expensive fabric with disdain and then begin to pull it off.

"That bad?" she asks. "How can you work?"

"I barely can," I reply.

"You need a drink," she says. "I'll make you something."

"No need. I'm going out with Jodie soon. I'll get my fix then."

"In that case, I'll get you some soup to cheer you up. Things will get better. Also remember not to drink too much tonight. Tomorrow's dad's memorial and we need to bring him some flowers in the afternoon."

"I know," I reply, my heart feeling just a tad bit heavier. "Maybe that even contributed to my unusually sour mood today. I probably didn't even realize it."

"It happens," she says and with a soft brush of her fingers down my hair, rises to her feet. "I'm glad you're sticking it out, but don't force things beyond what you are able to bear. This company is not the only company there is. I'm proud of you and Dad most definitely is too, so just take things easy."

This makes me smile sadly. "Well, I doubt he's proud that I slept with my boss."

"Don't worry, he knows the daughter he has. Remember when you took a nail to his Cherokee when you were about four and refused to admit it because you were too afraid to disappoint him?"

I laugh at the memory. "You remember that?"

"Of course, I do. I despised you for getting away with everything. You, with your hair in pigtails and you could do that stupid squeaky laugh with him, he would have torn down the moon and hung you in the sky. I couldn't stand either of you and neither could Mom."

"Aww..." Tears misted my eyes. "He really did let me get away with way too much. And then he would call me—"

She chorused it with me. "My winkle star."

I laugh again.

She places her hand on her waist. "Then Mom would say, it's *twinkle* star Byron! Ugh, she was so irritated."

"I know," I squeal, tears in my eyes. "But then he would ignore everyone and say to me, 'winkles get over here, recite that poem for me again,' and then I would do a whole performance."

"Damn. I hated you both," however she quickly corrects herself and lifts her gaze to the ceiling. "I mean I love you Daddy. She was the problem. Still is." She says pointing at me.

"Hey!" I exclaim.

She blows me a kiss and returns to the kitchen.

Our reminiscing however continues to bring a ton of memories to mind. "Remember when you called me Bla instead of Blair for a whole year?"

She chuckles as she stirs the soup on the stove, and so did I.

"You were so mean." I wipe the tears from my eyes.

"You were like thirteen then right?" she asks.

"Yes, and you were twenty-one. You were too mean."

"You deserved it. You were too bratty."

"True," I agree, and pull her blanket over my frame to dream of my dad that literally had stars in his eyes every single time he laid eyes on me.

My sigh is heavy as my eyes sting with tears one again.

I truly miss him.

And what a truly bittersweet day it has been.

CHAPTER NINETEEN

Grady

I'm reviewing our security culture framework when I hear the voices beyond my door. The sounds are muffled so I can't hear a single word until the door is slightly pushed open.

"You failed the test? A mere baseline test?"

I lift my gaze from my screen as silence fills both rooms. Allen still has my door slightly ajar, his intention to come in completely halted by the news he has just received. I hear her soft voice mumble some form of a response, and a low laugh rumbles from his throat.

My door is left ajar as he goes back out to the reception to speak to her, but I don't miss her haste in coming over to close it shut. I'm not sure though if it's because she doesn't want me to be disturbed, or if it's because she feels shame at the progressing conversation.

More muffled laughter follows from beyond the door, before it is eventually pulled open once again. Allen walks in with eyes sparkling with amusement, and shuts it behind him. "Do you know about this?" he asks in a lowered tone.

My brows furrow with partial disinterest, especially since I can already guess what the jesting is all about. "About what?"

"That Blair failed the simulated phishing test? The fact that she works in one of the biggest Cybersecurity companies in the country and she's your secretary makes it a hundred times funnier and tragic."

"You hired her," I respond, although I feel a slight prick at my conscience for the indirect jab at her abilities.

"Are you saying that I erred in choosing her?"

"Erred? Really?"

He takes his seat. "What can I say? I am ah, sophisti-cat."

Despite the difficulty, I'm somehow able to hold back my smile at his rendition of Theodore Bagwell. I return my gaze to my screen, but I do however consider the question.

Before I can reply, he slams a folder on my desk. "Four hundred and thirty two new corporate accounts and more than eighty percent of these are from the conference you two attended last week."

I meet his gaze. "And?"

"She had a hand in that by suggesting the email spyware demo. Previously your headlined speeches have only had at most, a sixty-five percent conversion rate but this time around, it shattered our five year history, because of her suggestion."

I take my hands off my keyboard and lean back into my chair. "So the point you're making is that I'm not a good salesman?"

"Oh, you are." He smiles, enjoying himself a bit too much in my opinion. "But you have to acknowledge that even though she failed the phishing test, her value to the company is already gaining traction and she's only been here like what? Two weeks?" His grin is wide and his bearing pompous.

I don't want to talk about her, especially with Allen because things are sure to be dragged into murky waters. I can't help but shake my head. "Where did you get these numbers from?"

He scoffs. "Of course, David handed them to me to process. I know you're aware of the math, so how can all of this be brought in without my involvement?"

He is right but I don't foster his already untamable ego.

"All in all, you have to admit that she is a great hire and this brings me to the main reason why I'm here. Vasiliev just called."

At the mention of the CEO of the biggest digital solutions provider in the country, my attention is completely seized. "What does she have to do with Vasiliev?"

"Well first of all, the Vasiliev that called is not Harold Vasiliev, but the chairman himself, Sasha. Apparently, their VP was at the Breckenridge event last week and after your keynote address, he returned to them bearing good tidings. They want to sign with us, but his father still has a stick up his ass, so he wants to meet with you first."

I take a few moments of silence to process all the information. "Who did he call? And why wasn't it immediately forwarded to my office?"

"I have no clue. Your secretary should know the answer to this."

The inefficiency bothers me immensely, so I immediately pick up the intercom phone. "Blair, why didn't the call from Cognizant come directly to my office?"

The line goes completely silent, so it's clear to me then that she is probably not even aware of whom Cognizant is. "Fix this," I say and end the call.

"Could you be a bit more polite when you speak to her?"

This commentary completely takes me by surprise. At first, I feel concern that my curtness to her borderlines on rude but when I realize just how much anxiety this concern stirs inside of me, I immediately check myself. My irritation is then directed at Allen. "Are you kidding me? Is this kindergarten?"

"No, sir," Allen replies with a smile, completely unfazed.

I wonder how he almost always remains so carefree. I have only ever seen him gloomy once, and that was when his father passed away. At the time, it had immensely worried me that his loss would keep him in that state permanently but thankfully he had bounced back. Thus, I have learned to appreciate his cheer as a part of who he is, where once I used to be somewhat irritated.

I'm about to return to work when I realize that he still has not answered my question so I repeat it, "What does Vasiliev have to do with her?"

"Oh, that. I just thought to bring up the idea that perhaps you should allow her to play a major role in this one. Sasha is notorious for being especially difficult when he's dealing with men, but I hear that when women are involved, he folds like a cheap chair.

"That can't be right," I say. "A man who is that easily affected cannot have built Cognizant."

"Exactly. But Cognizant didn't rise to its current status until a few years ago when Harold took over as CEO. I've heard though that regardless, he still gives Sasha a hard time, hence the infamous moniker of him having a stick up his ass."

I go silent again to think.

Allen watches me for a little while. Then with a tap on the desk, he rises to his feet. "I hope you'll consider her, but of course, no pressure."

"No pressure? Didn't you come in here ready to hold a gun to my head till I agreed to let her participate? But now that you heard she failed her test, your confidence in her is shaky?"

He turns to face me. "You know you instantly lose fifty percent of your coolness when you make things up, right?"

I harden my gaze on him, but still can't help but ask, "Why do you like her so much? You've been her advocate from day one. Is there something that I don't know about?"

"She's hot," he says.

My response is simple, "Say that again and I'll fire you."

He laughs loudly.

For his sake, I hope that his 'hot' comment is a joke.

"I'm playing with you. I just like her because she's a goofball, just like I am while everyone else around here is walking around with a stiff neck and a frozen face." He holds out his hand to point at me. "Case in point, she's a breath of fresh air that I appreciate."

"She's a goofball?" My mind goes back to the serious faced and somewhat awkward woman that I have reached the extent of physical intimacy with, but I just can't picture the image of cheer and playfulness that he is conjuring. This can only mean then that she is either excessively tolerant with him, or she is especially cold towards me. I'm not sure though which of those scenarios makes my stomach churn more.

"Yes she is, but I figure that you'll soon chase that warmth out of her with your chill. Just a note of warning though, if I see that start to happen... I'll immediately transfer her to a different department."

"You figure? And why not just make her your secretary then? Right now? Why wait?"

"You can't get rid of her that easily and Meredith would murder me. We made a pact a long time ago that I can only have unattractive male secretaries."

"Why do the male secretaries have to be unattractive too?" I ask.

He raises his brows in a suggestive expression. He then proceeds to explain what I can't even fathom, "In a past life, I may have been bi, until I met Meredith of course."

I'm sure he's joking but the shock on my face is as set as concrete.

"If I hear a word of this from any other soul," he threatens. "I will hurt you, and then resign."

I finally get over some of my shock and I can't help teasing him, "You're joking? Is that why you're always hanging around me? I used to wonder what your constant pull towards me was all about but now I think things are beginning to make sense. For the record, I'm flattered."

Allen rolls his eyes at me as he takes his leave. "With all due respect sir, shut up." He exits the office.

I can barely suppress my amusement.

CHAPTER TWENTY

Blair

I have nearly wrung all the blood from my hands by the time Allen comes out of Grady's office. The moment he appears, I immediately jump to my feet but still try my best to compose myself. "Did he ask? About the test?"

Once again, he mocks me with a smile.

"I swear, I still don't know how I failed the test. I didn't even realize what it was until it was over."

"Forget about the test," he says. "There's a new account that might be coming in and it's a big one. I just suggested to your boss to have you on it, but I don't know if that'll do anything. You were able to get yourself on the last one, so perhaps you have some tricks up your sleeve?"

"Oh," is my response, at the sudden information. "This is about Cognizant right?"

"It is."

There's a knock on the door, we both look up to see who has come into the reception.

I immediately recognize her as one of the receptionists from the ground floor. She is incredibly tall, hoisted up almost to Allen's height of 6 ft 2 on six inch heels that I can't understand why she's wearing at work. She does appear comfortable in them though so I immediately check my jealousy. Her hair is a shiny wavy brown, and the nude wrap dress she has on is clinging to her body like a second skin. She looks naked.

Staring at the dress, for a moment both myself and Allen are speechless.

"I have a message for Mr. Abbott," she says in a silky, breathless voice.

Even her smile seems too bright for me to take in.

Mr. Allen recovers before I do, "Shoot your shot," he says as he takes his leave.

I can't help but think that perhaps this is exactly what this woman is trying to do. My query immediately begins after the brief introductions, "I'm sorry that you come all the way here, next time please just give me a call."

"Sure," she says but her gaze is no longer on me. It is on the door leading to Grady's office. Her gaze is twinkling with excitement.

I honestly can't blame her. But there is no way in hell that I'm allowing her to *shoot her shot* at the man. It is of course not personal, but during work hours, it is my job to man his territory. She can do whatever she wants afterwards.

True to form, she takes a few steps towards me and whispers excitedly, "Do you mind if I hand this over to him personally? I can say that you stepped out for a bit and that this is kind of an urgent delivery. I heard that Cognizant would be a very big client for us."

My eyes widen in amazement. "So you want me to come off as incompetent, so that you can hit on the boss?" It is not my intention to be this crude but I honestly can't believe she hasn't thought this through and has only considered her interest in this intended ploy.

She immediately becomes defensive, all the light and elegance in her eyes and frame disappearing. "Who says I'm hitting on him? Sheesh, take it easy."

I keep my gaze neutral even though I am subjected to her sharp eyes, until she hands the folder to me. Then she turns around and storms out of the reception.

I eye her retreating frame and pull the folder open to look at the one page memo. Cognizant has indeed become a massive IT consultant and digital solutions provider with about fifteen billion in yearly revenue. So, there is no doubt that I stand to learn a lot and gain some exposure from the deal. I quickly study the memo and after memorizing what I need to about the company, I knock on his door and walk into his office.

He is however on his feet and putting on his suit jacket.

My heart lurches seeing that he is about to leave. His gaze meets mine and I momentarily freeze.

"What is it?" he asks.

This is the cue that I need to get myself back together. "T-the memo came from the ground floor. On the call from Cognizant?"

"I don't need it," he says as he grabs his phone. He starts to round the desk and I take several steps backwards as though I'm the one he's approaching. It's only at the slight confusion on his face that I halt my steps. My mouth then immediately blurts out what I want it to, "Can I come along? Please?"

His face goes blank.

Cold chills begin to crawl down my arms. *Why are you so goddamn intimidating? I* cry inwardly. If it isn't for the fact that he has been inside me, I'm not sure that I would have been able to take the pressure of working for him. "I apologize if I'm overstepping but I—"

"You are," he says. "You are overstepping."

"I-I'm sorry," I stutter and step away from him. I focus on calming my state as he walks to the door.

He stops at the door to look at me. "Do you know how to play golf?" he asks.

"Uh, no but uh, I can do everything else." My mind goes blank at the utterance. I *can do everything else? What does that even mean?*

"Everything else like what?"

"I can uh... uh, I c-can get your drinks or uh... help carry the bags. The golfing bag I mean."

He stares at me.

I squirm like a worm under his piercing gaze.

"Can you at least drive the golf cart?" he asks.

This is not a question to ponder on as I can see that he is already getting impatient. "Yes sir! I can! Most definitely."

"Alright. Come along then."

At his words, my spirit nearly leaps out of my body. "Yes! I mean... thank you."

He continues on his way out.

I do a quick, little girly swirl before going after him.

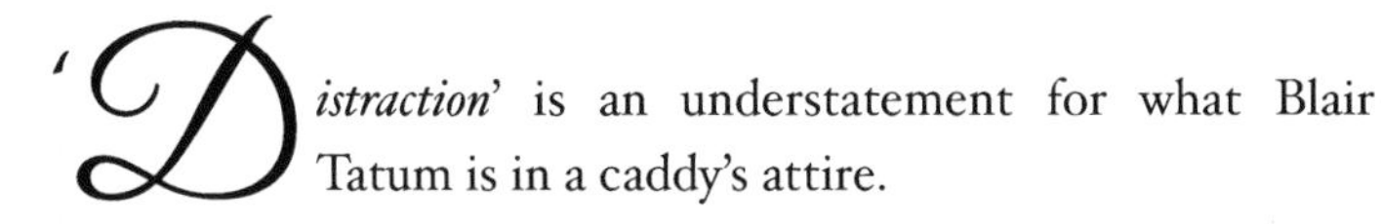

CHAPTER TWENTY-ONE

Grady

'*Distraction*' is an understatement for what Blair Tatum is in a caddy's attire.

I truly didn't expect her to change into the outfit since this is still a business meeting regardless of the location. But on a positive note, Sasha Vasiliev took one good look at her and lit up like a bulb.

Therefore, before I had the chance to inform her that she didn't have to be too friendly to the older man, she took it upon herself to indulge him as much as he desired. He couldn't take his eyes off her and neither could I for that matter, except of course when she is looking in my direction.

We have an official *caddy* assigned to us, but she insisted on driving us herself.

Her skills with the cart are jerky and bumpy at best, but not much else can be fully noticed with how short her plaid skirt is. It just barely rests above her ass. The creamy length of her legs, disappearing underneath the material to converge at a place I am no stranger to is more than enough to set my blood boiling. The skirt is complemented with a tight white shirt that hugs the fullness of her breasts, and on her head sits a white baseball hat.

"So, Miss Tatum, how long have you been working for Mr. Abbott here?"

"About two weeks," she replies with a dazzling smile.

I pause at the smile that I do not think I have seen on her before. It is sweet and bright and against my better judgement, pulls at something in my chest. I almost can't look away.

It sure brings to mind what Allen said about her being a goofball. *So is this a confirmation then?* I wonder. That she is full of light but then when it comes to me, she becomes withdrawn and somewhat timid?

"Do you enjoy working over there?" Mr. Vasiliev asks her. "How does the highly acclaimed Mr. Abbott treat his staff?"

She glances back at me, and then slightly purses her lips at the older man. "My title is the executive assistant, sir, but I'm sure we can all see exactly what that entails, seeing as I'm the caddy for the afternoon."

He throws back his head to release a booming laugh, while I on the other hand can't think up a response.

So, I just rest my gaze on her but she seems too shy to look at me.

Soon, we arrive at Sasha's putt, a tricky, downhill 20-footer. We both stand to the side as he readies himself for the hit but I can see already that he is going to miss the hole. True enough, he swings the club and it breaks about four inches to his right. The ball rolls right past the hole and stays out.

"Fuck me!" he curses.

Blair sends me a worried look.

I hold her gaze for as long as she has the guts to do the same, unmoved and relaxed.

"I'm missing some good luck today aren't I?" He laughs.

Blair sends a sweet smile over to him.

It makes him stop and myself too, for that matter.

The short, balding older man just stares at her. "Thankfully, these are the only times when I sometimes have trouble getting my stick to fill up a hole."

At the comment, shock instantly flashes across her face.

I move my gaze from her to meet the slimy grin on his and it takes every ounce of my self-control to keep from swinging my club at his head.

"You've been doing quite well, sir," she replies. "There's just four more holes to go and I'm sure you'll certainly win."

"Hey! You can't say that in front of your boss. He has ten thousand dollars riding on this game."

"I believe in you, sir," she says.

He turns to me with unconstrained delight. "Abbott, you just might have the greatest secretary of all time." Then his gaze roves down her body. "And they most definitely do not come like this anymore. All curvy and lively, and willing."

Blair excuses herself to go over to our assigned caddy.

I can overhear that she is speaking to him about replenishing our refreshments. Her phone suddenly falls from her hand so she lowers to retrieve it and as she does, neither myself nor Sasha can look away from the jut of her ass against the material.

At first, I didn't think much about this outfit but now, I'm strung between ordering her away to change, or finding somewhere secluded so I can fuck her brains out.

I'm slowly losing control of my mind and this is a problem given the nature of this meeting. I return my attention to Sasha but he too, doesn't seem to be in the mood for discussing business either. I resolve to bring all of this to an end as quickly as possible.

"If you hire them like this at your office Abbott, then I'm ready to sign everything to you right now, just so that I can pay visits to check up on my investment." He winks at me.

I nod in response.

He then slaps me across the arm with a grating laugh.

I can't help but to glare at him.

"You don't talk much do you young man?"

"I don't," I reply and walk ahead with my club to attempt my putt on the green. My strike pushes the ball right into the hole and as a result, I hear a little clap from her. To preserve my sanity, I ignore it and continue on my way.

Half an hour later, we're at the last hole and the scores clearly indicate that I am in the lead.

Given that I'm here to discuss a very important business collaboration, it wouldn't be wise to let the man lose so outrightly. But at the same time it wouldn't help his ego either for me to pretend to fall back, just so he can win. So I turn to him and say, "I'm going to win this one. So how about we double the initially agreed pot, so that when we have a rematch, you'll be extra motivated to win your money back?"

He regards me coolly. Then the light changes in his eyes and he bursts out into laughter. "You're not even going to try to lose so that you can get my business?"

I position the head of the club at the ball, as I get ready for my strike. "Those kinds of antics are for people that have nothing to offer."

"But having something to offer young man, isn't the only thing at play in these dealings."

I hit the ball and it rolls straight into the final hole.

The game is over.

There's a smile on my face as I straighten and turn around to face him. "It should be because that's what truly matters. For instance before I left, I told my team to attack your system with a maze ransomware. Your internal security is currently battling with the service disruption to your banking and logistic clients."

At my revelation, the shock that creeps onto his face makes the base of my stomach curl with excitement.

"What?" he asks.

Before I can respond, the calls start coming in on his phone, which he promptly pulls out of his pocket. He turns away with a malicious look at me and quickly responds to one. He begins shouting instructions in Russian.

I return my club to the kit and by the time he's ready to face me, I have a smile on my face too.

"What is the meaning of this?" he asks.

"Not to worry," I reply. "I'll order them to exit your systems soon. They didn't steal nor encrypt your data, so you're fine but I just wanted to show you exactly how vulnerable you are. If someone else had been behind this, you would have been battling a ransom disaster right now.

A smile begins to spread across his face. "I invited you here to prove that you're worthy of my business, and you've done exactly that."

"No, Mr. Sasha, you invited me over to lobby you for your business. But again, as I said, those antics are for people who have nothing to offer. If you still feel after this short demonstration that you don't need us then of course, I'll respect your decision and look away which will of course leave your company vulnerable to such a potentially devastating threat. And as for our game, I will always be ready to answer your call for a rematch, regardless of whether we proceed to work together or not."

He walks over to me with his hand held out.

I then proceed to accept.

After the firm handshake, he once again hits me across the back.

I don't like the way he keeps doing that, so I'm about to open my mouth to tell him this.

Before I can make things very uncomfortable for him however, Blair steps in and completely distracts him. "Thanks again for the invitation, sir. It was a great game and it would of course, be such a pleasure for our two companies to collaborate."

"Yes, I am sure that it will be." With his gaze on her akin to someone eyeing a steak they wished to devour, he brings the hand she held out for a handshake over to his lips and presses a kiss on it.

I watch her do all she possibly can to hide her irritation at the gesture, and it is incredibly impressive just how she is able to maintain a friendly demeanor until the end.

Soon, we all return to the club house.

He goes on his way while Blair and I head off towards the changing rooms.

Just as we are about to go into the respective areas for the sexes however, she stops and turns to me. "You know, you could have given me some sort of heads up," she says.

I stop and turn to face her. "What do you mean?"

"I know it's my job, but seeing how you handled things in the end makes me realize that I didn't have to butter him up as much as I did. Especially, since he was..." She stops and inhales deeply. "Anyway, a little heads up that you have things under control next time would be great."

"I always have things under control and for the record, buttering him up is not your job. You chose to do that all on your own."

I watch the hurt flash across her eyes, so I decide not to drag the matter on any further. I can't deny though that I feel somewhat conflicted. As to why exactly, I'm not sure so I turn around and head into the changing room.

"You might fire me," she calls to me. "But I'm going to say this; I think you're a dick. And I don't know if you're doing it on purpose, but intimidating and belittling the people around you, doesn't make you look cool, just so you know."

Silence.

I turn to face her. "What did you say?

She turns around to leave, the fear back in her gaze but it is too late.

I grab her hand and pull her with me into the changing room. In no time, she is pressed against the tiled wall and my heart is racing in my chest.

"What are you doing?" she asks.

My voice lowers dangerously. "What exactly do you mean by I'm a dick? Are you saying that you didn't enjoy the attention that he gave you all afternoon or are you pissed off because it didn't draw mine?"

She smiles. "Well, apparently it did."

The jibe is brutal, but it's also undeniable that I'm hard and have been for the better part of the last few hours, unable to control the rage of my libido at her appearance. My gaze runs down the glistening sheen of perspiration on her neck, and all the way down to the opening of her shirt that exposes her ample cleavage. "Well maybe I did," I admit. I am spiraling too much out of control so I shut my eyes and fight to regain my restraint. It works so I'm able to move away from her.

Before I can get too far however, she grabs onto my shirt.

I stare into her eyes looking for answers but I find nothing. All I see is a similar rendition of the fire that is raging in the pit of my stomach. "We work together," I remind her. "We can't do this."

"Okay," she says, and slowly lets go of my shirt. "You're right, I'm sorry." She walks away.

Somehow, I find the strength to let her go.

CHAPTER TWENTY-TWO

Blair

I cannot believe myself.

I almost made the same damn mistake with him again, and I can't believe it. What's worse is that I don't even understand how things progressed so rapidly. One minute I was at his throat and in the next, I was fisting his shirt.

All I recall is feeling hurt and somewhat mocked, and then his response translated those feelings to anger. Then it all boiled down to the vehement need to either kill him or fuck him.

A few minutes later, I'm changing back into my corduroy slacks and silk blouse when his message pops up on my phone.

You can take the rest of the day off. I'll return to the office with Andrew.

I stare at the message and before I can stop it, my eyes burn with tears.

I most definitely have a problem. I look around in despair, not knowing how I'm going to be able to go back to work with him in that office. I know that our crossing the line is not completely my fault but at the same time, he is my boss and I shouldn't have made any advances whatsoever.

At the ball of anxiety scorching me from the inside, I release a heavy breath and make up my mind then to resign. This decision seems to bring me some element of peace, so I wipe the tears from my eyes and make my way out of the club.

I head straight to Jodie's diner, since for once I'm not yet ready to face Layne, and secondly I need someone to drink with.

Four Bahama Mama's later and a long narration of my woes and plight, and all she does is stare at me in confusion. "Um... again, you're resigning because?"

"Can't you imagine how awkward it'll be between us?" I wail. "I don't even know how I'll be able to face him tomorrow."

"But what did you do that was so wrong though? Be attracted to him?"

"We're supposed to be professionals."

"Oh, I get it now. You're at fault for coming onto him even after he rejected your advances, several times. I get it. Yeah, you should resign."

My face is straight as I glare at her.

She's not moved. Instead, she rolls her eyes and continues, "Do you know what is wrong with your kind of demographic; the goody two-shoes, do everything proper type? You all still feel shame. And shame my dear is a buzzkill. You need to get rid of that shit and do what you fucking want."

Her words resound inside me but at the same time, it feels so very wrong and almost foolish, so I scoff it off, and drain my cocktail. "How can you live life without feeling shame?"

"Well, that's how I'm living right now and I'm having a blast. That's why I didn't slave away like the rest of you and incur thousands in debt, just to attend some fucking college. "

"No shame Jodie," I respond. "You know I love you but, we need to talk about your hopping around. From jobs to places to people. Isn't it exhausting?"

"It isn't," she replies. "For now. But when I eventually get tired of it, I would have gathered a lot of insight into just exactly what I want to do with my life. My point is that none of you can do this because you're still afraid of being judged for being a loser... still afraid of feeling shame, so it stagnates you and keeps you in a box. I say embrace that crippling inner judgement and discomfort and soon that bitch will disappear. Then you can start truly living your life."

"Really?" I ask dryly. "So how would you handle this situation if you were in my shoes, and missing your shame nerve or bone or whatever.

"I would walk into his office and fuck him. Then put my clothes back on and get back to work."

I stare at her, dumbfounded. "Wow. I thought that coming here would console me, but now my headache just tripled in size. Thanks a lot Yoda."

"Anytime," she beams at me.

I push her face to the side as I rise to my feet and grab my purse.

"Hey! Where are you going?" She calls at my exit. "We're not done. Blair!"

I wave at her without even bothering to turn around, too weak to even speak.

It's almost midnight when I return home and thankfully, I find that Layne is asleep. After turning off the light in her room, I return to mine and reaffirm my decision to quit. It's either this or my still very present ability to feel shame will kill me.

The next morning, I'm a little late to the office so I know he has already clocked in.

However, I do not go in for a quick greeting. I do however want to get this whole resignation thing sorted out so the moment I'm done with my letter, I knock on his door. Without waiting for a response that I am certain will not come, I go in and stand in front of the desk.

A moment later, he pulls his eyes away from his screen to regard me. "Do you need something?"

"No, I brought you something," I reply, and lean forward to place the white envelope on his desk. From my handwriting on it, he can immediately read what it is. I don't even bother looking at him and instead stare at the panoramic view of the city behind him. "It's been such a privilege working here and I want to thank you for the opportunity, but I think that it's best that I move on."

I wait for a few seconds and when he doesn't say a word, I meet his gaze and force a tight smile to my lips. Then I turn around to take my leave.

When I got to the door, he eventually spoke, "Is this because of yesterday?"

This question has so many layers and I don't know which one to peel first so I decide to just leave it untouched. "No it isn't," I lie and continue on my way.

"So what's the problem?" he calls to me.

I turn to face him. "It's just some personal matters that I need to attend to."

"I wanted to fuck you yesterday," he says.

My heart stops in my chest.

The door is still closed but it almost feels as though the entire building is listening. My instinct is to hurry away in order to quell the discomfort making my blood curl, but I find myself unable to move.

He continues, "I sent you home because I had reached my limit, and I knew that there was no way I would have gotten through the day without giving in and touching you."

I'm stunned by his admission because my assumption all along was that he dismissed me because of the advance I made towards him.

As I am trying to process his response, he rises to his feet.

Once again, I want to retreat but my feet remain fixed to the ground as though I have been nailed to the spot.

He arrives at the front of his desk with his hands in the pockets of his slacks, and then takes a seat on the edge of the table. His gaze is locked on mine.

This time around, I refuse to look away. "You shouldn't say that."

"I wasn't going to," he replies. "But since you're quitting, I might as well say exactly what I want to. Blair, I can't stop thinking about our night, and trust me, I've tried."

I feel the strength begin to seep out of my bones so with a rasp, I clear my throat and shift my weight from one leg to the other. "Well, I didn't know that," I say. "I just thought you didn't want me here."

"If I didn't want you here, then I wouldn't have hired you."

"Well, you didn't want me at first."

"With good reason," he replies. "For instance, look at the point we've arrived at."

I immediately correct him, "We're here because you don't talk to me. Because I never know what you're thinking or how..." I catch myself at the passionate outburst.

"Go on," he says.

Still, I take a deep breath and try to stabilize my tone and emotions. "Mr. Abbott, thanks for the opportunity but I'm still convinced the best thing for the both of us is to part ways."

"Alright by me," he says.

I can't help the sharp jab of pain in my chest at his words. I turn around to leave.

"But there is one thing..." he says. "Since we're going to part ways anyway, how about one for the road?"

I return my gaze to his and see that he is not for even a second, joking. "Are you asking me to have sex with you?"

"Yes. That is exactly what I'm asking."

I'm stunned and as a result, the first words that rush to my lips are to express my incredulity. Then, what Jodie said the previous day at the diner on the art of being shameless comes to mind.

Quitting this job is not an easy or desired decision by me and as I've come to also discover, neither is restraining myself from being physically attracted to him. She said that she'd come into his office to fuck him and then return to work, so why couldn't I do the same? The truly, most preferred answer that I can think of comes to mind, but I am too ashamed to spit it out.

"... shame my dear is a buzzkill. You need to get rid of that shit and do what you fucking want."

My hands become restless by my sides, especially since I know he is watching me intently.

"I will," I reply. "I will have sex with you but I have my own conditions too."

"State them," he says.

I cannot believe what is about to come out of my mouth, "I will have sex with you, but I still want to work here."

CHAPTER TWENTY-THREE

Grady

I'm almost convinced that I have misheard her.

So I wait a few more moments for her to correct herself. When she doesn't, I cock my head at her, now expecting some sort of explanation or clarification.

"I know I just technically resigned but i-if you accept my terms, I think that we can make it work." Her gaze falters from mine, and it shows that her courage to say all these words is running out.

At another time, her shyness would have been somewhat endearing but right now... it is not. "I don't think that's going to work." I see the determination on her face but I can also sense the incoming resistance. Her features darken and somehow it turns me on even further.

"Why?" she asks.

"Allen says you're a goofball, but I have yet to see that side of you."

She is immediately confused at my statement. "What?"

I straighten and move away from the desk. "Blair," I begin. "The person I am in my private life is not the same person that I am here in the office. And I want to keep things this way. Heading the company requires me to constantly make very strategic choices, and I don't want anything that will cloud my judgement."

"Alright," she says and walks away, pulls the door to the office open then shuts it.

A second later, the crippling silence of the room engulfs me. I watch the door, the tension in the pit of my stomach churning and my breath becoming harsher. Before I can stop myself, I march towards it. I pull it open and meet her at her desk. She turns around at my sudden arrival but before either of us can process what is happening, my hands are on her.

I pull her into my arms and take her lips in mine.

The first draw is long and deep, and by the time the intimate contact is broken, livid lust is blazing through my system.

Slanting my head, I slip my tongue into her mouth and her response is a mix of a cry and a whimper. I'm just as affected myself, the vivid reminder of what it truly means to melt into a puddle coming to mind.

I can't see, smell or feel anything beyond her delicious warmth and her intoxicating scent.

"Grady," she breathes into my mouth, needing to speak to me but at the same time almost unable to break off contact.

"I'm not ready," is all I can say, and whether it's for the kiss to end or for us to properly set the parameters for our relationship, I'm not certain.

Somehow, she finds the strength to pull away and her hands immediately grab my shoulders to hold me at bay.

With her head lowered to the floor, all I can do is watch her as I try to catch my breath. Her hair has fallen down the sides of her face and I can't help but lift my hand to move the thick mass out of her face. I need her to look at me, and I need us to connect beyond the reservations that my brain is blaring through my head as to why all of this is a terrible idea.

"Grady," she says. "You can't keep doing this."

"I know. But how the fuck, am I supposed to let you go?"

She lifts her head.

The determination in her eyes strikes me in the chest.

"Let's not think," she says. "Right now. I think we're both past the point of allowing the other to leave anyway, so let's just get this over with. We can choose whether to continue or discontinue this later on."

Immense relief washes over me, but it is bitter sweet. "Okay," I agree, and bend my knees so that I can wrap my arms under her ass. She crushes her lips to mine and a moment later, I'm slamming the door to my office shut with my leg.

With a swipe of my hand, I clear off whatever is in the way on my desk and seat her on it. Her legs automatically spread apart to invite me forward and I don't waste a single moment longer before settling my hips between her thighs.

She is wearing a pair of striped cotton pants which I proceed to peel off her, and in no time my hands are on her bare and lustrous skin. And the very fact that I get to touch her this intimately again, fills me with so much excitement that I can barely contain myself.

Her arms are around my shoulders as she buries her face in my neck, her pants are soft and her need acute.

I'm just as desperate to bask in her, and the avid reminder that I was contemplating giving this up barely a few minutes earlier squeezes my chest with fear. "Why do I feel like this with you?" I find myself muttering as I plant a kiss on her cheeks, then my lips begin to follow the curve of her jaw.

With a low whimper, she unlocks her arms from my shoulders and instead cradles my face in her hands. Her lips lock on mine and we both melt into the desperate kiss. "*Fuck...*" Her voice trembles into my mouth. "...the way you taste, Grady."

I know exactly what she means, and I can feel the force of the aphrodisiac that she is seeping into every nook of my being. With a sharp tug, I jerk her even closer towards me until the rock hard strain through my pants is digging aggressively into the soaked dark lace covering her sex.

I grind my hips into her and it earns me a long winded gasp. Her head falls into the crook of my shoulder as I increase the intensity and frequency of the strokes and soon she's holding onto me for dear life.

"Grady... Grady," she breathes, and her call sends a shivering thrill down my frame. The urgency at which I want to take her spikes to dizzying heights, so I can no longer bear the constraint of my dick in my pants. I grab onto the buckle of my belt and in no time, my pants are unzipped.

She then grabs the edge of my briefs and with clumsy amusing attempts, she moves to rapidly pull them down my hips. "I need you," she rasps. "*Fuck me*, as hard as you possibly can."

I don't need any further cajoling so with a sharp tug on the strap securing her underwear to her hips—the material is ripped apart, unsheathing her pretty pussy for my perusal.

Much to her protest, I move slightly away which removes my cock from her adoring hands, but I need to taste her. To devour as much of her as I can before my cock takes the stage. With a slight push, I spread her legs even further apart and the intoxicatingly musky scent that is so uniquely hers welcomes me into bliss.

I have missed this, much more than I realized or even expected. I lower my head. My tongue first of all, digs into her opening, spurring a fresh flow of heated arousal. I lap it all up and then proceed to cover as much of her entire sex as I can with my mouth. I'm completely consumed by this delight in devouring her, so it is only as my lips move to suck hard on her engorged clit, that I faintly register her half-hearted struggle to pull me away from her. The torment I know is overwhelming, and at the rake of her fingers down my back, I can't help but smile.

When I finally lift my face from her sex, she pulls me forward to deliver her gratitude with a heart melting kiss. I know that she can taste herself in my mouth and it heightens the entire act to an excruciatingly erotic degree.

I can't pace myself any longer so my hands immediately move to the buttons of my dress shirt. Unfastening them however is taking too long, so I rip the shirt apart and tear the material down my arms, needing her hands on my skin as I ready myself to fuck her.

She doesn't even wait and in a breath, her head is lowered and her lips closing around the hard disk of my nipple.

My entire pelvis goes numb at the contact and when she sucks hard on it, her soft heated hands caress across every bit of my skin.

My knees go weak. "How can we give this up?" I find myself asking in disbelief, my entire body burning with a crazed yearning.

"Well, you're the one who doesn't want to consider my conditions," she accuses as she bites into my nipple.

With a strained laugh, I pull away. One hand softly holds her chin so she can face me directly and look into my eyes, while the other palms her soaking slit. Her eyes flutter shut as my fingers thrust in and out of her and then my hand comes away with her slickness to be slathered all over my cock. "Look at me," I order.

She manages to pry her eyes open. The delight on her face is infectious and at the smile she flashes at me, my heart nearly stops.

I gaze at her, slightly dumbfounded once again at why I'm holding myself from letting this woman in. From letting anyone in for that matter. Maybe it's because I've gotten so used to being alone over the years, I'd succeeded at convincing myself that I prefer it.

She licks her lips in anticipation as the broad head of my cock nudges at the lips of her sex. And the moment the first inch of me slides into her, her lids clamp shut. "*Oh God,*" she quivers.

I suck on her bottom lip, unable to shut my own eyes. I just want to watch her, every expression and emotion that appears on her face, as I possess her. In these few moments, she is mine, and the notion is as terrifying as it is exciting.

She grabs onto my arms as I continue to plunge repeatedly into her, and the hungry sheath of her heated walls around my cock is beyond exhilarating.

"*Harder*," she buries her face in my neck. Her hips are restless and frantically jutting forward to keep up with the maddened rhythm we are both exploiting.

However, I'm not satisfied, so, with a firm grip on her thighs, I pull out of her to just the right extent and then slam back into her.

The hard plunge sends her back arching and her nails digging into the skin of arms. Her neck is now fully exposed and trembling with groans, so I nibble on the sensitive flesh, tasting the slight dampness and sweetness of her skin. There's nothing about this woman that doesn't arouse me. As I withdraw and drive into her once again, I feel the screws in my brain rapidly coming loose.

Her moans ring out so loudly across the room that I have to crush my lips to hers in order to muffle her, vaguely aware that at any moment someone could walk in on us. A part of me can't help but worry about this, but at the same time, the rest of me doesn't give a fuck.

In this moment, nothing beyond the crippling sweet tension and the wild grating of her walls against my cock is producing is as important.

Soon, even I can no longer afford to stay quiet, so I allow the release of suppressed, tortured groans from the back of my throat.

Suddenly, jerking her hips even closer to bury every single inch of me inside her makes her almost lose her balance but she quickly regains it. Her body is twisted at just the right angle and the grind of her hips into my thrusts makes me shudder from the top of my head to the tips of my toes. It doesn't take any longer for me to come, but noting that she is yet to fall apart, I force myself to hold on just a bit longer. I pull out of her.

The loss of contact rips an agonized complaint through her lips.

"Calm down, baby," I assure her with a rough kiss and then with my hand around her waist, I guide her off the table. Before she can comprehend my intention, I turn her around and ensure that her hands are firmly placed on the desk. "Hold on," is the only warning I give to her before I once again spread her thighs apart and position the head of my cock at her opening.

With my hands holding the curve of her hips, I slam into her and go deeper than I ever have before. "Fuck," I groan aloud while her nails scrape down the table.

"*Grady*," she whimpers uncontrollably.

For a moment, I vaguely register that she is close to tears. I continue pounding voraciously into her and she throws her ass just as frantically backwards to meet my thrusts. I don't think that I have ever fucked any woman as hard before.

My libido is out of control as my thoughts and memory recall all the countless nights since our first time at the hotel that I have dreamt of doing this again with her.

It's even better than I remembered, and I want this to last forever.

Eventually however, it comes to the most gratifying end. An orgasm blasts through her body like a seizure, and it simultaneously triggers my own release. For a second, I consider pulling out since it occurs to me that I have failed in using protection but in this moment, I'm not capable of any sense whatsoever. I empty myself into her and keep coming until finally, I collapse on top of her, barely able to catch a single breath.

We're both heaving and panting, filled with amazement at the rolling aftermath of the orgasmic waves that have completely engulfed us.

CHAPTER TWENTY-FOUR

Blair

The next morning, an alarm is not needed to wake me up.

My eyes are wide open and have been for the better part of the night, so when the blaring begins, I immediately pick up my phone to shut it off.

My gaze is fixated on the barreled ceiling above, the lines of its trim now solidly committed to memory.

The world seems tilted to me, as though everything is out of balance and incredibly foreign.

And I know it's just me because once again, and against my better judgement, I have allowed myself to be fucked senseless by my boss.

There is absolutely no way that I can go into the office today. I don't want to and my lack of sleep has already guaranteed that even if I did, I would be nothing but a sloppy, exhausted mess.

My hands tighten around the phone in my hands, as the guilt of irresponsibly calling in sick when we both know that it is not the case, haunts me. The slight patter of rain on the roof reminds me of how cozy my day could be if I succumb to just remaining in bed, so I turn to my side and pull the blanket over my head. I still have an hour to make up my mind.

Three hours later, I'm jarred awake by my ringing phone. The moment I read the time to see what my initially intended ten minutes nap has extended into, I jump out of bed swearing, "*Fuck! Fuck.*"

I see that it is Allen who is calling, and it terrifies me more than anything. I quickly answer the call as I hurry to my closet to pick out the first item of clothing that I can find. "I'll be right there. I'm so sorry I'm running late. There was an emergency."

"Um, calm down," he says. "I'm just calling to find out why neither you nor your boss are at your desks? I thought you both went for a meeting somewhere. So none of you are in yet?"

I halt at his words, and take the few needed seconds to calm myself. "He's not there?"

"He isn't."

"Um, have you tried to contact him?"

"I can't. His phone is switched off. It's a Tuesday morning and he can't be reached. I'm pretty sure there's a problem."

"Um, what do you want me to do about this? I mean, what can I do?"

"Do you have his house address?"

"I don't think so," I respond. "Or maybe I do but I have to search for it."

"I'll send it to you. Head over to check on him."

This instruction doesn't sit too well with me but before I can work up a complaint or excuse, the call disconnects. I stare at the phone, my entire mind in a complete muddle and soon, the message with Grady's home address comes in.

I stare at it and wonder at the force that seems to be pushing me so desperately towards him.

Suddenly, there is a brief knock on my door so I turn around to see Layne come in.

"You're still here?" she asks in surprise.

"I slept past my alarm."

"Yikes," she says. "I didn't know you were still at home or else I would have woken you up."

"It's okay," I say. "My boss is late too, so I think we're both just not ready to face the world today."

She's amused at my statement. "Why? Did something happen?"

"Nope." I shake my head and keep my face as expressionless as possible.

"Okay," she says. "I'm about to make some oatmeal. Grab some before you leave."

"Alright," I reply and once again, I am left alone in silence.

I immediately search for his phone number to dial it and just as Allen said, it is indeed unreachable. I have a few meetings scheduled for him today which I have to quickly cancel and reschedule if he truly isn't going to be coming in. Anxious, I rush to dress myself then head to the bathroom to brush my teeth. It's as I am brushing my hair into a ponytail that another message comes in. I quickly lower my gaze to my phone and see that it's a message from him.

My heart slams against my chest in alarm, as I let go of my hair and dive for the phone.

His message is very simple. *I won't be coming in today. Please reschedule my meetings.*

I stare at the message for a long time, wondering what the problem is. And then it occurs to me that I myself need the day off too. So I head over to my bed to take a seat.

After plopping down on the soft mattress, I send him my response.

Are you all right? Is there a problem?

I'm nervous because the words are too endearing but I don't know how else to phrase them.

His reply soon comes in. *Everything's fine. I just need the day to handle some personal matters.*

I don't want to say anymore but I know that I need to ask permission to also be away from the office. Just as I'm thinking about this, another message comes in.

Take the day off too. I think we both need it.

My sigh of relief almost deflates my entire frame.

Sweeter, more appropriate words have never been spoken.

With a heart nearly bursting with joy, I fall back onto my bed, beyond grateful that I don't have to go through the hassle of becoming a functioning human for the day. So I pull my dark, creased slacks off, along with my camisole and bra then crawl back underneath my blankets.

But then I remember that I have to reschedule his meetings.

With a groan, I throw the covers off, grab my laptop and in an hour both his and my schedules are clear.

After Layne's delicious breakfast banana and blueberries garnished oatmeal breakfast, I return to the haven underneath my covers and slide into a long, exhausted slumber.

CHAPTER TWENTY-FIVE

Grady

I get the call at about 11 AM that morning and it immediately throws me into a frenzy of anger. "What?"

The Douglas County sheriff sighs heavily into the phone. "He was spotted walking downtown. He had a hip flask in one hand and his shotgun in another. Then he stopped at the park near the Cherry Creek School and fired a couple of shots into the trees."

I immediately rise and grab my keys. In no time and with the phone pressed to my ear, I'm reversing out of my driveway. "He's detained now?"

"Yes, he is," the sheriff replies. "We know him around here so to an extent, we have been lenient in letting him get away with a few misdemeanors but the parents from that school are coming for my job. Especially with that Walmart shooting in Cali last week. The kids all thought that he was going to attack them."

My heart grows heavier at his report. "He said he was chasing a raccoon?"

"Yeah, that's his story. He said he found the creature messing around in his trash can and got his shotgun to chase after it. Then it ended up in the tree. We've still not sighted it though."

"I'll be there in thirty minutes, Mark," I say and end the call. I step on the gas pedal and speed my way towards Aurora.

The moment I arrive at the police station, I can hear my father all the way from his cell at the back.

The sheriff, Mark Liu greets me with a handshake and I listen to the man that I have known for almost twenty years.

"He's a respected veteran in our community," he says as he escorts me. "So, we've constantly tried to be as lenient with him as possible but things are getting out of hand. Especially with the drinking. If this happens again, we're going to have to charge him."

"I understand," I reply and turn away from the sheriff to watch my father.

He takes off his boots and slams them against the iron bars of the holding cell in annoyance. "I know my fucking rights," he slurs in his deep cowboy drawl, rubbed off from his earliest days growing up on a ranch between Fairplay and Jefferson. "How you gonna lock me up for holding a fucking gun? I've been handling guns since before you fuckers could walk."

My head lowers as I wish it would be possible to turn a blind eye to all of this, and to him, to just walk away. Especially since, he isn't going to welcome me let alone, listen to me.

The sheriff proceeds in releasing him while I head over to wait as he's processed.

He gets out cursing and hollering at the men to return his gun to him and when none of them budges, he throws his boots at one of the officers.

"What the fuck!" the officer yells.

I rise to my feet to keep him from getting into a fight that his raggedy old bones cannot take. "Dad," I call.

At the sound of my voice, he stills. Then he turns around to meet my gaze.

I haven't seen him in seven months and in that seven months he's lost so much weight and it pains me to see it. His back is hunched, the faded t-shirt he has on plastered to his body like a saggy second skin, his jeans are dirty and in tatters. His balding head still has some sparse density of white while the thick mustache under his nose is immensely stained with yellow.

"What the hell are you doing here?" He asks as he sees me.

"It's nice to see you too, Dad."

He immediately starts to limp away, his hands waving in the air. "I don't want you here. I didn't call for you. Mark, you did this? You called this son of a bitch over?"

"Hey! Gary! That's no way to talk to your son. You should be damn proud of him"

"I've got nothing to be proud of. I thought I raised a man but then he turns out to be a pretty weak ass metrosexual. I want nothing to do with him."

I roll my eyes at him and ten minutes of aggravation later, he is strapped into the front seat of my SUV.

For more than half of the ride home, he remains fairly quiet. He of course, doesn't miss the chance to let out grunts of disdain and disapproval on what I suspect is my driving, but I ignore it all. All I want to do is to ensure that he is home safe and sound and be on my way back.

He however, cannot help himself. "Cars like this... is why you rejected the army?"

I inhale deeply, and do my utmost best to reign in my irritation. In the past, he was an incredibly loving father, but after the years and following the death of my mother, he has just degenerated into someone so bitter that I barely recognize him.

We are all aware that it has to do with a past trauma suffered during his time as a Navy Seal, but as to the details of the incident that nearly took his life, but most definitely claimed his soul, we are not aware.

So, I have grown to accept this version of him that he has agreed to share, but the deterioration almost into a killer, is getting out of hand. "'Your plan is to go out massacring middle school kids?" I shoot back. "That's how you want to be remembered?"

This stuns him silent, and reveals to me that his mental state is still cognizant despite the alcohol still in his system. His voice once again becomes calm and controlled, and it allows me a glimpse into the indestructible man that I once nearly worshipped, "'I served for forty-five years," he says. "Gave my life and soul to protect this country... little kids? How dare you say that to me, you bastard?"

I glance at him. "Then what were you doing firing a gun near their school?"

"I was hunting that bloody raccoon!" he roars. "It's been hollering and making a fucking racket every morning and you want me to just let it go?'

"So, you took a shotgun and chased it down?"

"Why the hell not? I'm more qualified to handle that weapon even if I had my two eyes blinded, than any of those under qualified officers over there. I could take them all out in a flash, without breaking a sweat."

His madness is back but thankfully, we have just pulled into his trailer park in Denver Meadows, so I let out a deep sigh of relief.

I don't say another word as I drive over to the trailer that he insisted on moving into almost a decade earlier, and which I have refused to even spend a night in. And that was the beginning of our animosity towards each other.

"You don't have any food?" It's another twenty minutes later and I'm moving through the filth that is his trailer. Clothes are strewn everywhere as well as endless plastic bags and styrofoam plates of stale or even rotting takeout food. I cannot believe that this is how he is living as every time I have come over, he has seemed fairly okay.

His refrigerator is also empty, only containing some cans of beer and a long expired jug of milk.

"You can go now," he says as he walks over to his arm chair and plops down into it. I don't need anything from you."

"I'm not offering anything," I retort as I slam the refrigerator door closed.

Pain is reverberating through my entire body at the state that he is currently in, and the most frustrating fact is that he keeps refusing any help whatsoever in doing something about it.

He is a bit taken aback at my outburst and for the longest time he just stares quietly at me.

It's in these moments that I usually hope he has regained his senses and that the next word out of his mouth would be even slightly reasonable.

However yet again, he disappoints me.

"I will never be proud of you," he states. "I raised you to be a man that would need nothing and would instead give and serve. Imagine the honor and respect you would have if you had joined the Seals. I wanted to pass down that legacy to you."

I turn to him. "Dad, I'm worth a billion dollars. You can keep your legacy to yourself. I'll create mine."

His laugh is bitter. "Money," he says. "That's all you've ever cared about and that's why I refuse to take a single dime from you."

This is my cue to leave.

I can't endure any of these pointless arguments anymore, so I begin once again moving through the filth so I can get to the door. I pull it open but just before I leave I stop and take one last look at him. "All I did was refuse to go down the same path you walked. I'm still waiting for the day that you'll be able to convince yourself and me that I deserve being excommunicated by you for that choice."

With that, I shut the door behind me and return to my car.

For the longest time I sit in the driver's seat, unable to leave. I mean, how can I leave him in this state and return back to the safe, abundant life that I live? But on the other hand what can I do, when for the longest time he has refused to listen to anyone apart from himself? It seems then that until he somehow comes to his senses, I have to accept that this is the father I have to deal with.

CHAPTER TWENTY-SIX

Blair

The next morning, I can't deny that I have put a little bit more effort into my appearance.

This has required a little forage into Layne's closet and the most suitable but still fairly decent find is a collared gingham dress. The goal is to feel as confident as possible since things are still in limbo between us.

He arrives a little later than usual at 10 AM and coupled with his absence the previous day, it all serves to fuel my worry.

I have no idea what is going through his head and I can't imagine that it's good. It does seem though that our brief tryst together may have truly affected him in some way, if it was enough to make him take a day off and come in late.

I hide my face behind my desktop and only give a small greeting.

"Come see me," he says and pulls his door open.

I take a few moments to process the request and to calm my racing heart. Then I get up and head over on wobbly four inch heels. "Yes, sir," I say as I shut the door behind me.

He is settling in, but he has his eyes on me. Just as he is done hanging his jacket, he begins, "Let's talk about what happened two days ago."

My heart skips a beat. "Sure."

Just as he is about to continue however, there's a knock to his door. Before either of us can respond, Allen walks in.

For once, I'm incredibly disappointed to see him.

He immediately notices my expression and of course is concerned. "What's going on? Is this a bad time?"

I instantly return a smile to my face. "No it's not, we were just having a quick meeting." I turn to Grady. "Sir, I'll come back after you're both done."

"No need," Allen says with a smile on his face. "I'm here for you too." He heads over to take a seat in front of Grady's desk. He then places a folder on Grady's desk which he then proceeds to open. "You both were out of the office yesterday. Was it something that you both planned?"

There is no expression on his face so I quickly hurry to explain myself. "I uh, felt a bit ill so Mr. Abbott permitted me to take the day off too."

"You were ill?" Allen turns around to face me and I quickly nod.

He continues, "So sorry to hear that. Are you better now? What was wrong?".

"Um..." I clear my throat as my brain goes into overdrive to think up an excuse.

Grady however, and to my surprise saves the day, "What's the folder for?"

"I obtained a brief from over the weekend. It was Meredith's brother's birthday and he had ABAX executives present. They've long heard about us, so they want to look into a collaboration. I've already scheduled them to come in for a meeting later on today."

Grady leans forward for the folder as Allen hands it over to him.

We all remain silent as Grady goes through the brief and then with a nod, he shuts it and places it on the table.

I take the chance to watch him and notice for the first time just how unusually tired and gloomy he seems. "What manager are you going to hand this over to?"

"That's why I'm here," Allen responds. "I'm hoping that you'll let Blair take the lead on this one."

My heart drops into my stomach.

Grady's gaze moves wordlessly to me and so does Allen's.

Under the attention of these two men, all the hair on my body begins to rise. I want to also advocate this opportunity for myself but I'm not even sure if I'm still going to be working here at the end of today.

I open my mouth to speak but Grady cuts in, a frown across his brows, "Why are you passing this off to her? She doesn't have the experience to handle this."

"Well, I'm hoping you'll work with her on it so that she can learn the ropes and be able to hold her own weight. It will most definitely take a lot of the burden off you."

"Where are you getting this idea that I'm burdened?"

At his question, the room goes silent.

Then Allen smiles. "Meredith's expecting. She's about three months in and she's held back from giving me the news because she was worried about how I would take it, since I wasn't exactly excited about the idea when she brought it up a few weeks earlier. I also wasn't really there for her when she was pregnant with Alexa, so I don't want the same thing to be repeated this time around."

Grady sits up then, his eyes a bit brighter now with understanding. "Congratulations, man."

"Thank you," he says. "But you know what this means. Last time we were in the midst of that dreadful quarter because of Softcat, so I couldn't be with her as much as she needed me. This time around, things are a bit more stable here, so I'm going to have to take some time off. This will mean early evenings and sometimes late mornings for a little while till things settle for her."

"I understand," Grady says. "I wouldn't keep you from that. And there's no need to worry about me, I have a thousand employees available if I have too much on my plate. You seem to forget this fact a lot these days."

Allen laughs at the jibe. "I know but I can't help noting the potential in Blair, so I want to do my best to show off her talents before I'm no longer round."

My laugh is nervous and awkward. "There's no need for that Mr. Allen, I'll be just fine."

He doesn't even acknowledge me. "So, what do you say?" He stares at Grady.

"Well it's your account," Grady says. "And I don't have jurisdiction over it. All I demand is good results, so you can assign it to whomever you please."

Allen turns to me. "You heard him. So, are you ready to take on the challenge?"

My lips part but the only word that can sound from it is a dumb and contemplative, "*Uh*."

"*Wow,*" Allen mouths. "I can't believe that I just boasted to my boss that you could potentially be my Trojan horse."

My mouth immediately snaps shut in embarrassment but I'm surprised however to see that when I turn towards Grady, his lips are slightly curved in amusement.

I eventually manage to work up a response, "I uh...I'll take a look at it to see if I'll be able to handle it."

"Good enough." Allen says and picks up the folder to hand it over to me.

I walk over to pick it up and immediately turn on my heels to exit the cramped office.

CHAPTER TWENTY-SEVEN

Grady

I know that I shouldn't be too concerned about this but she has her first meeting with the ABAX clients in twenty minutes and I'm worried that she might not be able to handle it. Since Allen's departure, the lead position on the account handed over to her along with a limited time of three hours to get ready for the initial pitch meeting, I have watched her through the surveillance utility on my computer as she has tried to make the needed preparations.

Soon, 2 PM arrives and she rises to her feet. A brief knock later and she comes into my office to inform me of her departure. "I'm on my way to the meeting with ABAX, sir," she says. "So if you need me, please send a message and I will find a way to promptly respond."

I watch her, hoping she will be bold enough to request my assistance but she doesn't. Instead, she turns around and walks away. She is ordinarily not meant to handle a first sale alone and it's not very impressive that she has chosen to most probably blow it rather than admit her incapability. Or perhaps, she is overestimating herself?

I try to push it out of my mind but then a few minutes later, I can't help but tune in. A short call to the security department and in no time, I'm able to listen in on the dynamics of their meeting down in the eighth floor's conference room. She starts strong with a healthy knowledge of the company.

Then it doesn't take long before the thorough clients begin to reveal the chinks in her armor. "We receive forty thousand emails a day and at any time an employee could misclick on something and cause a devastating breach to the entire system. 1,300 employees and 13,000 customers spread across three countries... this threat is real and it eats away at my peace of mind on a daily basis."

His companion is the next to speak up, "We can even to an extent, relax on the threat from outside sources but what concerns us the most is the threat from our third party contacts. They could suffer a phishing attack which will automatically give the bastards access to us and then an unsuspecting employee could fall victim to that. We heard about the recent breach at Telkcom and we're no longer able to take this lightly."

"Um," she says. "I understand these concerns and this is what we're especially able to—"

He cuts her off, "What personalized service can you give to our sales staff?"

"Uh..." There's a ruffling of papers. "We will ensure that they, along with all the other employees will get the in-depth training that—"

"No that's not what I mean. The sales staff works within a restricted environment, so their administrative access is not as expansive. I'm fucking worried that they'll be overburdened with the exhaustive training."

"T-then we can speak to them in order to figure out what depth of training will be most appropriate for them."

"It doesn't need to be conventional right? It just needs to be relative to their sphere of access."

Silence.

Blair releases a shaky sigh.

At this, I rise to my feet. In minutes, I'm riding the elevator down to the eighth floor and I soon arrive at the conference room. I go in and see her shuffling through the stack of papers on her lap.

The moment I introduce myself both men's eyes widen with delight. "Grady Abbott? We've heard so much about you from Allen."

"Same here," I say and take my seat by Blair's side.

She hasn't turned to me.

I can see that she is becoming increasingly nervous, so when yet another sheet of her papers floats to the floor, I bend along with her to retrieve it. My hand closes around hers as I try my best to whisper as rapidly and discreetly as I can, "Calm down," I tell her. "I'll support you. You're doing great."

Her gaze is on me as she straightens, and it doesn't feel like she believes me, but I do notice the rise and fall of her chest becomes comparatively easier.

She begins to speak again and her tone is also more stable, "I understand that what you are pushing for is a seamless implementation that will become more of a culture than a hassle to the employees, so we will ensure to customize the service to meet all your employee's needs."

They don't seem convinced of her statement and so both men turn to share a look at each other.

They are both bulky with one in a tan suit and a slightly protruding belly, while the other is in a simple black shirt, jeans, boots and a shaved head.

"What are the departments you currently operate through?" I ask.

The bald one turns to give me his response, "We have finance and IT."

"And they face greater risks than for instance sales right?"

"Yes," he concurs. "And that is why we don't want a one size fits all service."

"I understand that," I say. "For instance, shorter training videos that have the key messages should be fashioned for sales while others with more administrative involvement should have a more in depth training, but at the same time none of this should be a burden that everyone is constantly more than willing to skip?"

The room goes silent for a few seconds.

Then his partner in the suit responds, "Exactly."

I turn to Blair and wave a hand, giving her the signal to go ahead.

"Our training content comes with customizable features," she says. "For one, frequent reminders can be sent for the employees to go through these brief spurts of training, and that will be followed with constant phishing campaigns that will be able to monitor their progress and reduced susceptibility to these attacks. For example, we have our popcorn training which takes about three minutes to complete, and regular surveys for your employees so that they can give the necessary feedback on the efficiency of the service. The only thing set in stone is our quality but as to the approach we will continue to tweak things until your employees' engagement is earned. We even have a gamified tutorial that can teach them essential cyber security awareness in ten minutes and our phish alert buttons that can tune them into actual threats. Basically we won't stop until they become human firewalls."

The men burst into laughter and I cannot help but crack a smile either. I watch as she straightens her back, and confidently brushes her hair over her shoulders.

Both men turn to each other and it is then when I notice the tattooed legs of a frog peeking out from the edge of the bald man's short sleeve shirt. "You were a Navy Seal?" I ask.

His attention turns to me. "Yes I was. Retired about seven years ago. You?"

"No, my father. At some point, I was to go down that path but I sat down to watch a BUDS documentary one evening and almost shit my pants."

His laugh resounds across the room. "I went through it," he says, "and I shit my pants. That fucking training. You know I had to go through it twice."

"Twice? Why?"

"I almost died the first time. I was negative buoyant as hell and during one of the drown proofing classes, I don't know if you know what those are about."

"Of course. They tie your hands and feet and tell you to find a way to survive in the water, right?"

"Basically," he says. "Well, I drowned. They sent me to the hospital afterwards. I would have returned to the training and I wanted to. I kept arguing with them that I didn't strike that fucking courtyard bell, so they couldn't kick me out but turns out they could, since I had missed several weeks already. What a hell of an experience."

"Sure sounds like it. My father always told me his stories from that time, especially during his hell week. He never stopped talking about one of his instructors especially-Morty? Do you know him?"

"Fuck me," he almost jumps out of his chair. "That bastard. He passed away last summer. I attended his funeral and although I hated his damn guts, I have to admit that he was one of the best goddamn instructors we had. Tough as a nail, but he was good people."

"My dad said the same things."

"What class did your father graduate from? I was in 235."

"Oh, much earlier than yours," I reply. "I think 198?"

"Ah. Wait a minute isn't that Marcus's and Tyler's class? What team was he assigned to?"

I already know where he is going with this. "Seal Team 5."

"Fuck," the man curses.

The reminder of the attack that killed off the members in that team and about a dozen more pilots and rangers except my father, darkens the mood of the room.

"Your father is Gary Abbott?"

"He is."

"Wow," he says. "I should have made the connection. You do look like him. What a pleasure it is to meet you man." He holds out his hand again.

I accept the firm handshake. "Pleasure's all mine."

"How's the old frogman doing?" he asks. "I haven't laid eyes on him in at least a dozen years."

"He is doing all right," I reply. "Saw him yesterday."

"Well, next time you see him, let him know that the entire brotherhood misses him. He's still a living legend amongst the rest of us but after that incident, he sort of checked out."

I smile at the compliment, but it makes my heart ache at how different this testimony is to the broken, rampant man I just saw the previous day. "I will," I reply.

Both men got ready to take their leave.

"After that trip down memory lane, I guess our collaboration is established." His partner laughs and the meeting is concluded.

Both clients go their way.

Blair and I on the other hand, ride silently back to my top floor office.

CHAPTER TWENTY-EIGHT

Blair

"Did you know he was a Navy Seal before you came over?" I ask. We are on the elevator together and although, I would normally avoid speaking to him in such a confined space, I can't help it since I'm aware that once we arrive back at the office, we will both be distanced again.

He turns eyes to me that seem quite troubled, so I'm not surprised when it takes him a few more seconds to respond.

"No," he says. "I did not. But I did know though that he was in the army. It's on his bio page on their company's website."

"Yeah," I say, feeling slightly inadequate. "I found that interesting when I saw it and thought that perhaps I could bring it up but I don't know enough about the army to hold a decent conversation. I didn't want to say anything foolish or insensitive."

"Why would you want to bring up the military?" he asks.

The elevator dings its arrival on our floor. "My father. He was ex-military too, a Navy Seal too I believe."

"Was?"

"Yeah," I respond as we begin to exit the elevator. "He passed away a long time ago while on active duty."

"My condolences," he says softly

I shake my head in response and we continue walking side by side in silence.

Soon, we arrive back at our office and I head over to my desk. I want to thank him for his help and for not completely taking over during the meeting, but my mind and mouth refuse to cooperate, so I just watch as he returns to his office without a word.

We still have a conversation to tackle which had been interrupted by Allen, and I don't know if and when we will get to it. A few hours ago, the possibility had been huge that I would no longer be working here, but now and after successfully signing my first clients and with him supporting me with the process, I don't think that things will be that cut throat. But then again, this is Grady Abbott–and correctly predicting his actions or trying to decipher his intentions–is as pointless as trying to make a cat bark. So I remain at my desk and soak in the elation of signing my first clients. Then I get to work on collaborating with the available account managers.

About half an hour past closing time however, the door to his office swings open and it's so unexpected that I don't even acknowledge it until I feel the prompt tension in the pit of my stomach at his presence.

I lift my head from my screen to see him watching me.

"Are you going to stay longer?" he asks.

"Yes, I will."

"What about dinner?" he asks. "You don't want to celebrate signing your first clients?"

I go still at his question. "Yeah I do... I mean I will."

"Let's go for dinner then," he says. "Or do you have plans to celebrate with someone else?"

Again, I stare dumbfounded at him and then it clicks as to what he is asking. I rise to my feet. "I don't. I'll be right out."

He continues on his way.

I'm left alone to scramble for my things. When I later arrive at the front of the office building, I see his car running and automatically start to head to the back seat. But then the light comes on and I stop to see that he is the one in the driver's seat instead of Andrew.

"Sit up front," he says and I nod in response.

I head over to the passenger door and slide in as gracefully as is possible.

Immediately after, we are on our way.

I have become quite familiar with his scent and it welcomes me like a returning addict. It's intoxicating to inhale but does absolutely nothing in calming my nerves. I truly wonder when I will start to fully relax around him. Perhaps my anxiousness is due to the professional authority he has over me or for the fact that we still haven't clearly established what we are.

Anyway, we continue to drive silently until we come to a stop at the first traffic light. He then sends a glance my way. "How do you want to celebrate?"

The question is too open ended. A couple of things come to mind but the one at the forefront is the both of us alone in the stall of whatever restaurant we are about to head to.

Instead, I respond, “Some nice food will be a good start. And wine. Definitely wine.”

At my comment, he chuckles.

The soft sound in the small space fills me with a feverish yearning for him. I am burning all over with a sweet warmth and it makes it a little hard to breathe.

“Do you have any specific cravings?” he asks.

I can’t help but watch the fluid movement of his hands against the steering wheel as he navigates the vehicle. His sleeves are now rolled up to just below his elbows, and the slightly bulging muscles in his forearms are delectable to say the least. Before I can catch myself, I hit my hand against my forehead at my roguish thoughts.

It seems to startle him. “Are you all right?”

I’m startled too, but immediately work up a smile. As naturally as is possible, I slide the hand away from my burning forehead to flip my hair over my shoulder. “I’m fine. I just uh... forgot something at the office.”

“At the office? Do you need us to go back?”

“No, no, no,” I reply. “It’s fine. I’ll just get it tomorrow.”

“Okay,” he says. “And again, where do you want to eat? I’m already en route to an Italian restaurant downtown but I can always reroute if you have a place in mind.”

“I’m not familiar with the city yet,” I reply. “So it’s up to you.”

"Alright," he says, and we continue on our way.

CHAPTER TWENTY-NINE

Grady

The clink of our glasses pierces through the somewhat quiet ambience of the restaurant.

Spuntino, although a high-end restaurant, is small and intimate, with weathered wood and glowing copper furnishing and a selection of the best Italian dishes that I have had in the city.

I discovered it upon one of my dinner meetings with a client about two years ago, and is the first place that came to mind when I was pondering earlier on in the car on where to bring Blair to.

There is a lit candle before us, softly illuminating our space and the captivating glint in her eyes.

She is stunning, more than words can express and I can't help but feel the warm effect of this intense attraction simmering through my veins. It especially makes what I have intended to say to her quite difficult, and makes me wonder if perhaps I am deluding myself.

"Thank you," she says shyly. "For helping me out today. You always somehow end up putting out the fires that I start."

"It's my job to put out the fires," I respond. "Plus, you were already doing pretty well. A little more experience and you will be perfectly fine on your own."

"Thank you," she replies, and then after a second of thought, she adds a 'sir'.

It is unbeknown to her the perfect segue into the talk that I truly want to have with her. "Blair."

She lifts her gaze from her half eaten plate of Arborio rice and pomodoro sauce "Yes, sir?"

"When it's just us together, I don't think it's appropriate to call me that."

She stares at me as she chews slowly, and then lowers her gaze so she can swallow. Then she lifts her glass of wine to her lips.

"Do you want to keep working at FireEye?" I ask her.

At the question, she almost completely spits out the wine.

There's a slight spill down her chin so I pass a napkin over which she uses to cover her mouth in amusement.

"What?" I ask.

She quickly tries to compose herself. "I'm sorry," she says. "Ignore me."

I think back to what I said and can't really see why she became so amused. So I lean back and wait for her episode of amusement to pass. When it does, I make a face in demand for an explanation.

“I’m sorry,” she repeats, finally composed once again. “It’s just the way you started that statement... it sounded as though you were about to blackmail me for something. My reaction is silly, I apologize.”

I can’t help the curve of my lips. “Well, maybe I do want to blackmail you.”

Her smile turns shy. “Alright,” she says. “Let’s hear the details of this blackmail. What do you have against me, and what is the ransom?”

“Let’s make this... thing between us somewhat official,” I say. “How far do you want us to go?”

The smile slowly seeps out of her face. “Shouldn’t I be the one asking you that?”

“I need to know what your expectations are, so that things can be managed from the start.”

She lifts her glass and empties the wine. “I don’t have any,” she replies. “In fact, I would prefer that we just maintain a professional relationship. We have slipped up twice but I think we can both come to a consensus that it won’t happen again.”

I’m surprised at her response, but also do not fail to notice that she doesn’t properly look me in the eyes. I realize what’s happening. “What are you defensive about?” I ask. “Did I say something offensive?”

Her smile is tight. “Of course not, sir.”

“Don’t call me sir,” I say. “Not while we’re here. Not while we’re like this.”

She holds my gaze. “What should I call you then?”

"Don't you know my name?"

A heavy silence floats between us.

"Okay," she says and adjusts her posture.

"Relax," I tell her. "We're speaking plainly, like two adults who so happen to be immensely attracted to each other."

"Alright, Grady," she says.

I get straight to the point. "I don't want a relationship, but I don't want us to be strangers either. We work together, and will be spending a lot of time together, so let's make this friendly and simple. How does this offer sound?"

She cocks her head. "Wow, you really are a businessman."

I don't have a response for that so I just watch her.

"I'll think about it," she says. "When I make my decision then I'll let you know what it is."

Heat kindles in the pit of my stomach at the defiance in her tone, whether intentional or otherwise. Truthfully, I'm beginning to suspect that beyond the physical connection between us, what I really want no matter how brief is her intimate presence in my life. Admitting this though causes alarm bells to sound through me but I don't give them any attention. Once in a while, a change in one's convention I believe is beneficial. "Alright," I reply, and we continue on cordially with the rest of our dinner.

CHAPTER THIRTY

Blair

I'm not sure how I feel.

Perhaps this is because his proposition is in an unknown territory for me so at the sudden and now very real possibility of it, I can't help but shrink away or as he caught on, to latch onto his words in search of something to find an offense with.

Or perhaps twice is my mental limit of having a sexual tryst without the establishment of some sort of commitment, because the notion of constantly and intentionally offering myself to him without any affectionate attachments whatsoever is too cheap a trade for me to buy into. In fact, the very thought of it renders me incapable of enjoying the rest of my meal which is a shame because the fettuccine and sauce that comes with my meal are especially exquisite.

Instead of the usually charged thrill of being in his presence, I now feel a certain sort of dread and discomfort that I can't explain so I'm glad when it all eventually comes to an end.

Together, we walk to the entrance of the restaurant and by the time we arrive, I realize that it's raining. I love the rain, so I take the time to watch its consistent stream, and welcome the coolness that its downpour brings to the night.

And that is when I receive the call.

It's Layne, so I'm happy to receive it, near desperate for a quick reprieve from the internal turmoil of my current emotional state. I already have my bone of contention ready to be stated to her. *I want him, but I'm completely terrified of so easily giving myself to him. We would probably both thoroughly enjoy our time together but I have the nagging feeling that at the end of it all, I'll be the one left heartbroken.*

"Hello?" I answer but I don't get a response. "Hello? Layne."

"Let's go," Grady says to me as he accepts the umbrella and keys that the valet has just brought over.

"Layne!" I somewhat yell into the phone.

And then I hear her soft groans and labored breathing.

"Blair," she struggles to speak. "I c-called 911. I don't feel good and I'm scared. Please come to the hospital..." Her voice cracks. "I-I don't want to be alone."

My entire body goes numb with fear. "I'll be right there!" I swear to her, my brain muddled in panic. "Where... w-where is it? What hospital are they taking you to?"

"I'm in the ambulance. We're driving to the hospital. We're going ...." She pauses.

I hear her efforts to inhale. "Layne, what's happening? How much pain are you in?"

“The baby’s fine,” she answers wrongly. “They told me that he’ll be fine.”

“Layne what hospital? Please uh... g-give the phone to the paramedic.”

“We’re going to Saint Joseph,” I hear the paramedic say aloud and that is all the info I need to move. I turn around and only then do I realize Grady is holding onto my arm. I see the concern in his eyes at my panic, but I don’t have the time to address it.

“I need to get a cab,” I tell him. “My sister’s in the hospital. I’ll see you tomorrow.” I start to hurry off into the rain but suddenly there’s a strong arm around my waist. It forces me to a stop and then an umbrella comes over my head.”

“Hey!” I begin to protest as I turn around to meet his dark gaze.

“I’ll take you there.”

It suddenly hits me then that he has a car, but for some reason I never thought to solicit his help. Tears fill my eyes. “Okay. Thank you.” I nod in gratitude and hurry with him towards his waiting car.

Fifteen minutes later, we arrive at the Emergency Room at Saint Joseph and are promptly directed to the multi-patient room that she has been moved to.

We are soon able to locate her amidst the other ER patients and find a nurse administering an IV to her.

I immediately hurry over, trying my best to keep calm but it’s nearly impossible.

"Is she all right?" I ask the moment I reach the nurse. I look down at my sister and see that she's sleeping. "How is she doing?" I ask after introducing myself as her relative.

"She's doing okay," the nurse answers. "The doctor has examined her and says that it's uterine fibroids."

My heart contracts. "What about her baby?"

"Her doctor's ordered a couple of tests and after they come in, then the diagnosis will be made. For now though, her baby is doing okay. Fibroids are not unusual with pregnancy and can be appropriately handled if they are found to be threatening. So for now, he has told her to focus on resting. We have administered a mild pain medication to help her relax, so she will be able to calmly pass the night."

Suddenly, I feel a warm hand on my arm and immediately relax into the body behind it. I don't need to turn around to meet his gaze, so I shamelessly accept the momentary consolation so that I can get myself together.

"She'll be fine," he says softly to me. "Breathe."

Seeing my sister lying on the bed, unmoving and unconscious brings back the devastating memories of the time we had lost our mother.

One minute I was extracting my DNA during science class in the eighth grade, then in the next, I was getting the call that I no longer had her.

The possibility of that nightmare happening again suddenly makes it too difficult to breathe, so I turn around and slide my arms around his waist.

His strong sturdy frame is all that I need right now, and he doesn't stop me. His arms come around my shoulders and hold me close as tears burn my eyes. Soon, I'm able to catch my breath and rein in my emotions so I pull away from him. But I keep my puffy eyes lowered to the ground and hidden as I turn back to my sister. Leaning forward, I place a soft kiss on her cheek and my hand on her belly. I think then of her husband... and wonder if I should call him? But he is so far away and the last thing I want to do is torment him with the news when he can do so little or absolutely nothing at this moment.

Grady's hand interlinks with mine and it makes me turn my attention to him.

"Let's get you something to drink," he says.

I'm reluctant to leave. After reassuring me however that we will return soon, I give one last look to my resting sister and follow him out of the room.

All I can stomach is water and by the time I've consumed two full bottles of it, I feel somewhat consoled.

I don't want to head over to the room just yet, so we find the waiting room and settle down beside each other.

I'm exhausted from the strenuous day, and the emotional toil of the evening.

So, I can't help it then when I accept my body's desperate call for a rest and proceed to place my head on his shoulder. His pats on my arm are gentle and coaxing and soon enough I drift into a restless but exhausted sleep.

CHAPTER THIRTY-ONE

Grady

I listen to the gentle but sometimes restless rhythm of her breathing, and can't help but feel sympathy for her. Her intention no doubt had been to briefly shut her eyes for a quick rest, but instead she had slipped right into slumber. Either way, I am relieved.

It does worry me though that her head is on the muscled edge of my shoulder which I imagine is not very comfortable, but it has been barely half an hour since she started sleeping and the last thing I want to do is wake her up.

As I worry about it, she begins to move uncomfortably and unconsciously, so I put my arms around her shoulders. She is now nestled in my arms and I can see that it helps her to relax a bit better. I turn my attention to my phone and with my free hand, settle into concluding my work for the rest of the day. I go through my urgent emails and manage to respond to all of them before she wakes up again.

She's startled as her eyes flutter open, especially at the position she now finds herself in. "I'm sorry," she mumbles half coherently.

I shake my head.

She takes a moment to regain her wits and then rises to her feet.

My attention is back on my phone but it's quite difficult I realize to fight the impulse to watch her.

"I'll go check on my sister," she says and begins to walk away.

I also rise to my feet and head over to the main desk to sort out her sister's private room. By the time it's ready, my phone begins to ring, so I pick it up the moment I see it's Blair.

"Did you leave yet?" she asks.

"No," I reply. "I'm just downstairs."

"Alright," she says. "I'm so sorry about taking your time tonight. I know more than anyone, just how insane your schedule is for tomorrow.

"That's alright," I reply.

Her response is a long, heavy sigh.

"I'll take you home," I tell her. "Leave your sister to rest. You can be with her when she wakes up in the morning."

"No, I'm worried that she'll wake up in the middle of the night and find herself alone. I'll stay here with her and don't worry about work. I'll make sure to be in on time."

"There's no need to come in tomorrow," I tell her. "I'll get a temp to handle your work for the day."

She takes a moment to consider this. "Just for the morning. I'll be in by 11 AM at the latest, and right before the meeting with West Aurora. You need the report from the DDoS attack and I'm not done proofing it. I will make sure that it's sent to you on time."

I pause for a second before speaking again, this time extremely calmly so that it will somewhat reassure her, "Blair, you're currently dealing with a family emergency. Take the time you need to handle it and then return to work. This doesn't affect your perceived performance at the office in any way, so don't be nervous."

She releases a deep breath. "Okay then. I'll be an irresponsible employee for the second time this week and take tomorrow off. I will still get the report sent to you in the morning, so please check your email for it. I'll call you to also remind you."

"Alright."

"Also, I'll be on standby tomorrow so don't hesitate to call me if you need anything. I'll be here with her but I have my laptop at home, so I'll still be able to get anything that you need done."

"Sure," I reply, and can't help the smile that comes to my face. We both know that I won't contact her but if accepting her diligence makes her feel better, I cooperate with it.

The call comes to an end and I fully cover her sister's bill. I want to stay a bit longer to ensure that they have all they need, but the special consideration feels a bit unsettling to me, so I make up my mind to head home.

Later that night, I can't help thinking of her. I wonder how her sister is doing and if she has settled into her private room. I also wonder about Blair and if the extra bedding and blankets I ordered so that she can pass the night there as comfortably as possible have been delivered.

The light in my room is currently turned off, so the space is cast in a dimness that is only slightly illuminated by the moonlight through the glass doors and balcony beyond.

My gaze hasn't move away from my phone on the nightstand. I have expected it to light up for the last few hours, with the expectation that she would contact me to question or refuse the gesture of getting them a private room.

However, nothing has come in which makes me worry that perhaps the service wasn't given to them? Or maybe she outrightly rejected it?

I turn to my side and wonder about why I feel so restless. The covers are over me, so I throw them aside and shut my eyes to catch some much needed sleep.

However, I can't help but think back to the different sides of her that I have seen today. From her nervousness with the new clients to her initial shyness during our dinner. Then her withdrawal after my proposition and her panic at her sister's illness. She had seemed so terrified that it made me wonder if perhaps she had experienced something like this in the past.

She'd mentioned her father's death so maybe that's it. But then there is also her mother whom I haven't heard a single word about.

Blair herself just seems to pull me in and I acknowledge now that a relationship with her no matter how brief and casual will be rewarding.

Refusing to ponder any further, I put her out of my mind and try to get some sleep, but then the massive bed suddenly feels too empty to me. Then I can't stop myself from imagining what it would feel like to have her in it. To have her under me and her hands gripping my sheets.

The very vivid memories immediately return and although it was not my bedroom, we have slept together on a bed before... the first time we met.

"Fuck!" I curse with irritation at my wandering thoughts. Getting a boner right now is the last thing I need. Lifting my pillow, I brutally bury my head underneath and this time around, I employ all my willpower into pushing her out of my mind.

CHAPTER THIRTY-TWO

Blair

"He got us the room?"

I nod in response as I bite into the McGriddles that Layne and I are having for breakfast.

"I would have rejected it but he'd already left, and it was just too late to put up a fuss. So I'll just reimburse the cost to him."

Leaning forward, Layne grabs my wrist so she can guide the last bite of my breakfast to her mouth.

"Hey!" I frown at her lifelong habit of stealing my food but can't exactly get truly mad, given her current state. With a sigh, I clean my hands and hers with some wet tissues. I take all the emptied packets and bags to the trash can in the corner.

Then I return to sit on her bed. "How are you feeling?" I ask.

"Great," she answers, "but back to your boss. Why do you have to reimburse him? Did he ask you to do that?"

"No, but I don't want to owe him. That's unprofessional. He already pays me a salary at work and now, he also has to pay for my sister's personal bills?"

She sighs as she settles a hard look at me. "From what I've heard so far, he doesn't seem like the kind to act so kindly. Is there something else going on between you two?

I try to feign surprise at her mere mention of our possible underlying relationship, but she doesn't fall for my drama. Her gaze narrows until I'm forced to turn away, almost amused.

"Blair."

I immediately get up from her bed, but she catches my wrist. I struggle to break her hold but at the slight wince of pain she releases, I turn around in alarm. "Are you all right?"

Her eyes are shut as she recovers, but then what follows is a slow and mischievous reveal of her perfect pearly whites. "You can't refuse me, especially when I'm in this state."

"Wow!" This antic, I'm most definitely not falling for, so I pry her hold open as gently as I can. "Layne!"

"C'mon," she coaxes, and pulls me back.

I plop down beside her on the bed to reluctantly meet her gaze, but then the warmth seeping out from it encourages me to discuss the situation between Grady and me with her. "He asked for a casual relationship."

And just like that, all of the light from her eyes vanishes. It would have been thoroughly amusing if it didn't feel so tragic.

"He just wants to sleep with you?"

"Well, hearing it like that doesn't make me feel very valuable."

"Fuck him," she erupts, her voice still a little breathy and strained.

I can't resist making a joke out of her choice of words. "Uh, I don't think that's what you actually want me to do."

It takes a moment for her to realize what I'm saying, and when she does her frown only deepens. "What was your response?" At my silence, her eyes widen in alarm. "You didn't agree to it did you?"

"Of course not. But, what would be wrong if I did though?"

She is dumbfounded as she stares at me. "So you mean you're okay with him using your body but not committing to you?"

I shrug. "I'd be doing the same to him."

"But you have feelings for him. And that's what's going to end up giving you the short end of the stick."

"What?" I exclaim. "Feelings?"

The look she gives me is almost sympathetic. "You haven't even realized it, have you?"

"I don't have feelings for him," I argue.

"Sure," she says sarcastically, and resettles her earlier agitated frame back onto the mattress.

"I'm serious," I insist. "Why do you think that I do?"

"Because you speak and act like you do."

"How?" I ask.

She begins to shut her eyes.

I lean forward to grab her shoulders. I shake her lightly and it forces her to open her eyes.

"You just do," she groans. "Don't you want him to feel the same way?"

"Stop saying that," I complain. "You're going to make things complicated."

"They already are, Blair," she says.

I glare at her and she glares back. Then I rise to my feet. "Isn't it time for them to send you back home?"

"I need a final checkup from Doctor Kelly to be sure that everything is okay," she reminds me.

"Right."

"Blair," she calls softly. "Don't you think that things can work out between the two of you?"

My nerves tighten. "Layne, we work together and if you keep hammering on this, it's going to affect my performance."

"Because you like him."

"*No,*" I almost scream out. "Layne! Stop!"

"My bad," she concedes.

I give her a harsh look and head out to inquire on the details of her discharge.

However as I go along, I can't help thinking about her words concerning Grady. I would be lying to myself if I say that I have never thought along these lines, but occasionally having a thought about something and voicing it out loud are two very different things.

Now that it's been plainly stated, things feel a little more established and it agitates the hell out of me.

With a sigh, I focus on requesting for updated details of Layne's condition and discharge, then try my best to push him out of my mind.

CHAPTER THIRTY-THREE

Grady

"How about we have lunch at the cafeteria today?" I ask over the phone.

The other end of the line goes completely silent.

I tap a pen on the table and at his continued lack of a response, the tapping pace goes even faster. "Hello?" I call. "Why aren't you speaking?"

Allen clears his throat. "Um, I always get my lunch from the cafeteria. That's nothing out of the ordinary but you... have you even been there before? If you just show up, you'll give people quite the scare and unless you're going there to fire someone or for some administrative meeting then please just head outside to eat your usually overpriced lunch or get Blair to handle a delivery for you.

My sigh is heavy at his teasing. "There's only thirty minutes left for lunch. I'll be in your office in five minutes." I rise to my feet and consider putting on my suit jacket. But I wonder if perhaps the extremely formal look will further make me seem unapproachable. So after a bit more consideration, I let it go and also leave my folded sleeves as they are. Soon, I step through my door, and just as I expect, she's not at her desk but it also stops me for a moment to reconsider my intention to have my lunch in the cafeteria today. I eventually decide against it but just as I turn to return to my office, the door to my reception is pushed open.

Allen appears in his fully suited attire, with a bright smile on his face. "You said you'd be at my office in five minutes. This is ten minutes after."

"I changed my mind," I reply. "I think I'll just order something in."

"No," he says and turns around to head out. "You need to eat with the peasants that you milk daily for your company's progress. And that includes me."

I frown at his use of the word 'peasants.' "Do you usually eat at the cafeteria?"

"Of course. They make the best pecan dumplings I've ever had. Even Meredith forces me to bring some over to the house for her."

We soon arrive at the elevator to wait for its arrival, but when I look over at him, there's a massive smile on his face that makes me uncomfortable. "What are you so happy about?"

"It's been about two years since we last had lunch together."

I'm a bit taken aback by the statement. "Didn't we have a lunch meeting with CMNDi two months ago?"

"That's a business meeting," he says. "This is different, and I want to know what's prompting it."

I turn away from his excited face because there is no way in hell that I'm going to admit anything to him. I don't even dare admit it to myself so the moment the elevator arrives, I step into it without a word.

"It's a good thing we're having lunch together. I was going to come over to notify you of something."

"What is it?" I ask.

"Meredith," he begins. "She's having twins."

I turn to him in surprise. It wasn't that long ago that he was adamant about not wanting anymore kids but now, he's expecting twins?! The almost cruel turn of events is incredibly amusing to me, so much so that I laugh out loud at how forlorn he looks. "Why do you look like that?" I ask. "Isn't this celebratory news?"

"You know why my face is like this. She won. Women control everything, man. From now on, I won't even bother voicing an opinion because I've realized that there is a noose around my neck and that she is the one that decides where we should go and what should happen."

"You're happy about this," I say. "Sure, you weren't necessarily expecting it right now, but even your dad has mentioned how much you love kids and wanted a big family, especially since you were an only child."

"You're right." He smiles. "I'm just a bit edgy because when I asked her how all of this even happened, she acted like she didn't know what I was talking about. The woman is more meticulous than even you are and if she didn't want a baby, she wouldn't have gotten pregnant."

"True, but it's definitely not her fault that she's now pregnant with twins. That's on you."

"No arguments there," he agrees.

I shake my head in amusement at the interesting but yet endearing relationship that he has with his wife.

Our elevator soon arrives on the ground floor and as it pulls open, we meet a handful of employees waiting for it. They immediately recognize Allen but it takes a few more seconds for my face to register and when it does, I don't miss the shock in their eyes. Resonant and excitable greetings immediately follow and I don't blame them. Except in company gatherings, it is usually rare that they come into contact with me. Their bosses report directly to me and I come in earlier than most of them. I also probably leave later than most of them too, so there are very few chances to run into me.

"Wow," Allen exclaims as we walk away from the surprised group. "You're like a celebrity. One would think that you didn't even work in this building."

He's amused at this but I'm now all the more worried about going to the cafeteria because if I show up there, wouldn't it make Blair uncomfortable?

"Anyway," Allen says. "I want to give you a heads up that I'll be taking about a week off at the end of next week.

Rest assured that I'll still be productive enough at home. I'll handle my workload and ensure that my presence is not missed."

"Aren't you meant to be helping Meredith?" I ask. "She's going to give me a call if she finds that you're still working when you're meant to be helping her."

"Well if she does, then tell her that I need work to keep me sane."

"Alright, that is exactly what I'm going to say."

We arrive at the cafeteria then and walk into the massive air conditioned space.

"I'm kidding," he says. "If she calls you to complain, don't ever tell her I said that."

"I'm going to," I remain adamant as my gaze takes in the room. Employees are sitting together in clusters at different tables and in the middle of the hall is the huge buffet.

The heads that turn towards us gradually begin to increase and maybe, it's just my imagination but it also seems as though the room has become significantly quieter.

Allen leads the way to a pile of clean plates.

I walk with him. "How are the meals in general?" I ask. "You've only spoken about the dumplings."

"The meals are great and it better be given the millions I release to Culinary at the end of each month."

I turn to him with a frown. "Millions?"

"I'm exaggerating." He grins. "It's thousands. Mere thousands."

I give him a suspicious look as he hands me a tray and I proceed to fill it up with a flat plate and bowl. Then we join the line but those who have recognized us immediately step out of it, so that we can go right ahead to the buffet. It brings it all to attention, especially as about a dozen people are now displaced and standing out of what was a straight and civil line mere seconds earlier.

"Thank you," Allen accepts the gesture.

I have no choice but to walk with him as we head straight up to the buffet.

I receive countless greetings from the serving staff which I am quite happy to respond to. I even begin to strike up a conversation with one of the bubbly ladies that I recall personally interviewing for the position almost a decade earlier when we were just starting out.

But then in no time, the executives come running out with an entourage of about four suited staff with them. I recognize the leader Aaron and his deputy Marisa who are the duo that run the department.

"Sirs, Mr Abbott. Mr Canter." They welcome us excitedly.

I had held the small hope that we would be left alone but I can see now that until we take our seats, it will probably be impossible.

"Sir," Aaron speaks. "We have a private room for you and Mr. Canter. You also don't need to get your food from here. Just come with me and I'll ensure that you're properly served."

"This is fine," I reply but when I see that he's about to argue and insist, I immediately give a clear directive, "Please leave. Mr. Canter and I just want to have a quick meal together before our next meeting. And there's no need to treat us with something special since I've heard that the meals in general are great. So if it's good enough for the staff, it should be good enough for me too, right?"

"Y-yes sir," he replies.

I turn my attention away.

They soon retreat but then Aaron refuses to leave our side, choosing instead to remain by us with a nervous smile on his face.

"It sure is great to own and run a company," Allen says. "I come here several times a week and they don't give me half as much attention."

"You're familiar to them," I say and pick up my tray of served dishes. A plate of squid ink rice, diver scallop and maitake mushrooms, some chicken salad and a bowl of leek soup. It does look quite appetizing so I am eager to get into it.

We pick up our trays and, for the first time, I allow my eyes to scan the room for a table. *Her table.*

I soon spot her, but her back is facing us.

"Sir, we've readied a table for you," Aaron says, his hand gesturing towards my right.

"No, thank you," I respond. "We already have a place to sit." I then turn to Allen to see the surprise on his face

"We do?"

"Over there," I say.

His eyes follow the direction I'm nudging towards. "Oh," he says. "Blair." And then he sighs. "She's still sitting by herself."

"She always sits alone?" I ask.

"That's how I always meet her. She doesn't have many opportunities to interact with other staff anyway. Her position only puts her in contact with you and senior management."

We begin to walk over as I listen to Allen, and I know that she doesn't realize we're approaching. Her back is to us so when we arrive and Allen pulls out the chair by her side, she is startled. And then her eyes nearly pop out of her socket as I take the seat right in front of her, and focus on arranging my tray on the table while Allen is already chatting her up.

"Hello, sir," she greets me.

My gaze finally meets hers. I haven't had the chance to speak to her since the start of the day as early meetings outside the office kept me away till 11 AM. Upon my return, it had been with a guest, so all of those had kept me preoccupied until now. "How are you?" I ask and she nods shyly in response.

Allen is watching us, so the moment she lowers her gaze from mine, I do the same.

"Sir?" Allen asks. "I expected that you both would be a bit more casual with each other by now. Mark calls me by my name."

"He's two decades older than you," I point out but then my nerves tighten. My words imply that because Blair is younger then she shouldn't address me so informally but this is not my reasoning at all.

"Fair point," Allen says.

"And besides, I've told Blair to call me by my first name but she still refuses to. There's not much I can do about that."

. . .

Allen smiles. "I suspected as much." He's dabbing some hot sauce into his Pho broth when he realizes that he's forgotten to bring a pair of chopsticks with him. "Damn it," he says and rises to his feet. "I'll be right back."

CHAPTER THIRTY-FOUR

Blair

I have become quite intimately acquainted with Grady for a little while now, but in this moment I can feel the beads of sweat beginning to gather across my forehead. I can also feel the gazes of certainly everyone in the cafeteria on us. For one, I have heard that it's rare for the CEO to visit the cafeteria and since I've been working with him I've rarely seen him even eat lunch.

I have offered to handle this for him, but he has always refused with his reason being his lack of preference for eating lunch except when he has lunch meetings with his clients outside the office.

But now, he's right before me and although I realize that no one will think too deeply about why the two topmost executives of the company are sitting with me since I am one's secretary, it does nothing to dispel the self-consciousness and anxiety that I feel.

"How's your sister?" he asks as he slides his fork into his squid ink rice.

"She's doing great," is my response. "I spent yesterday taking care of her, so she has fully recovered. Thank you again, for being so lenient with me."

He isn't looking at me as he eats and I'm perfectly okay with it. Although, I'm unable to stop my heart from melting in my chest as I watch him. His motions are unhurried and calm, his lashes fluttering softly and his shoulders encased in a crisp white shirt that brings memories to mind of just how appealing his skin looks without the clothes.

Sometimes it's almost impossible to believe how far that I have gone with this man.

He suddenly looks up and before I can move my gaze away, he catches me staring. I freeze for a moment but then thankfully, a comment comes to mind. "Thank you for getting us a private room. I wanted to say this to you in the office but you haven't been available all morning."

"It's okay," he says and returns his attention to his food.

I look at his crisp dark hair, neat and swept away from his face, then at his clean shaven face and sharp jawline. Then I take in his familiar addictive scent. I want him, right now and so badly that it's almost too painful to breathe or to sit comfortably for that matter, given the pulsing bud between my legs. "I'll pay you back," I say.

He keeps eating and is silent for a while. And then he asks.

"Why do you want to pay me back?" He puts his fork down, and with both elbows on the table, resting his chin on his interlinked hands. His electric blue gaze is now directly on me.

It is exactly this kind of attention that he should not be giving to me while in the presence of so many people. I look briefly around and lo and behold... we are the focus of so many eyes. I have never wanted for Allen's presence as much as I currently do. "Let's talk about this later, sir," I reply.

He relaxes his pose and picks up the bottle of water by his side. "I don't need the money," he says. "But if you really want to pay me back, then come to my house tonight." Once again, he holds my gaze.

I'm all out of responses. Allen returns then so I focus my gaze on my half-finished salad bowl.

"What did I miss?" Allen asks.

I dare not answer the question.

The instant I return to my desk, I pull out my phone and text Jodie. *He invited me to his house.*

A few minutes later, her response pops up. *And?*

He's never done this before.

Did something happen between you two? Before this?"

I tell her the truth. *He proposed a casual relationship. No commitments.*

And?

I refused it. Well, I told him I'd think about it.

Well, his message is clear then. You're taking too damn long.

I throw my phone aside and try to return to work, but as I stare at my computer screen, I can't help but ponder on what is truly holding me back. Perhaps it is fear, just like Layne said; the fear that I would be the one broken... this is very likely.

We have crossed a lot of lines so far but it's still possible for us to work together. If I agree to this however, and things end badly then it will be the end of my career in the company. I make up my mind then, and hope to God that I can stand by it.

So when he comes out of his office later that evening to head home, I rise to my feet and give him my response, "My answer is no," I say.

He stops and turns to me.

I don't wait for him to respond. "I think that we work quite well together," I continue. "And I don't want that to be jeopardized. We have already crossed several lines... I know, but I'm sure that if we both agree from now and forward to keep things strictly professional, then everything will be fine.

The frown that furrows his brows is deep. Suddenly, his jacket falls from his arms.

My gaze follows it in surprise and when I look back up, I see that he is marching towards me.

I immediately begin to retreat and it isn't until my back hits the wall that I realize I have nowhere else to go. My heart nearly flies out of my chest. "Sir," I croak out.

He doesn't stop until his chest is pressed against mine and it turns my legs to jelly. I hold his gaze but my hands are against the wall to support me, because the way he's currently regarding me, with both hands in his pocket and his gaze darkened with desire is enough to melt me into a puddle.

"I don't want to keep things professional between us," he says through gritted teeth. "I want to fuck you. Over and over again." His hand lifts to rest on my waist.

A small, treacherous gasp escapes my lips. I'm too susceptible to this man, too impressed, too aroused, too attracted. He's a raging fire and I feel as weak and dumb as a moth about to fly into the midst of the inferno, seeking its own death.

My head turns as I lean away but it only gives him more access to my extremely sensitive neck. Of course, he knows the spots that drive me mad, and he takes full advantage of it... the bastard. His lips linger along my skin, just shy of making contact with the heated flesh. "How can you not want this between us?" he asks, his voice raspy and low. "You've experienced how it could be, how close we come to driving each other crazy, every single time. How can you not *fucking* want this?"

His tone is strained with frustration and desire and it makes me literally quake from the tip of my toes to the top of my head. With a heavy sigh, I move my hands from the wall and place it against his chest. The intention is to push him away, but he grabs my wrist and refuses to let go until I look up at him... until I stare into his eyes.

"Come home with me," he says.

"Give me more than you're offering," I reply. "I want to mean something to you beyond the assistant you fuck when you feel like it."

He goes silent... and continues to watch me. "I can't remember the last time I was in a relationship, Blair," he says. "I don't do them well. The expectations that come with it becomes a burden and when I'm not able to meet it, it will feed resentment. And then we'll truly have to end things. I'm not ready to deal with complications like that."

I give his explanation some thought, and then twist my wrist from his grip. "Let go."

He releases me and steps backwards.

I check to ensure that all the blood has returned to my legs, before heading to the space beneath my desk. I retrieve my purse and my phone and then proceed to walk past him. "Let's go," I say, and the pit of my stomach does several little flips.

CHAPTER THIRTY-FIVE

Blair

I know where he lives, as I've handled quite the number of correspondence that contains his personal details.

However, arriving and taking in the grandiosity of his building complex is a different matter.

A uniformed valet takes his car from him at the entrance, and it almost makes me ask if this is a hotel. His apartment is on the topmost floor which is the penthouse unit. I realize the moment he gets into the elevator and taps a key card to it that the only one with access to his floor is himself and whomever he allows.

"Maybe we don't have to be in a relationship," I say. "But for the duration of our time together, we must be exclusive."

"Of course," he agrees. He then begins to retreat to the wall and I turn around to see what he's doing. After leaning against it, he beckons to me so I also step backwards until my frame settles into his. His warmth wraps around me like a shield, and shamelessly I turn my face to the side, reaching up on the tip of my toes to inhale his intoxicating scent. "And," I say softly. "I'm going to need a card."

He gazes down at me. "What card?"

"The one that gives private access to your floor."

He watches me for a moment.

I'm not daunted. "What? You don't want to?" I ask defiantly.

His lips begin to spread into a wide smile. "You're usually much more timid at the office."

"Well we're not in the office and right now, I'm not your assistant."

"I'm not complaining," he says. "I immensely enjoy this uninhibited side of you."

"So do I get the key or not?"

He turns around with me and before I realize what he is about to do, my feet are off the floor.

"Grady," I laugh just as he presses me to the wall. I hook my legs around his waist while his hands settle and support me under the curve of my ass.

Before I can say another word, his mouth covers mine, and I crumble.

His flavor... of intimacy, longing and sweet desire puts me in a state that I never want to wake up from. I'm only aware of the ding of the elevator as we arrive on his floor and the next time I'm coherent, he's shutting the door to his apartment. Our lips part and the soft smack that sounds at the separation severely shakes the wall that I have erected to put my emotions in check.

My eyes flutter open to stare up at his face, and I can't help but reach up to brush his slightly disheveled hair back into place. His chest is slightly heaving and so is mine, the need to devour each other at the foremost of our minds but tonight, I want to take things somewhat slow. So I press a kiss to his cheek and whisper to him to let me down.

He does so and my limbs slide down his body. It is only then I realize that somewhere along the way I have lost my purse. I look around to see that I am no longer holding it.

He is able to immediately guess what I'm searching for. "I'll check the elevator," he laughs and turns around. "Make yourself at home." He shuts the door behind him.

I'm left alone in the massive apartment. It could have however passed for a house if it was located on the ground rather than at the top of the high rise building. The ceilings are incredibly high and right in this foyer is a magnificent chandelier that extends to hover just above the massive bouquet of Asiatic lilies that sit upon the center table.

I know that he is extremely wealthy, but seeing this magnificent display of extravagance is quite intimidating. I walk further into the space to meet a massive living room with windows that cover the entire length of one wall and also extend several feet above me.

There is a huge television embedded into a brick wall north of me, and on the second floor above, I can see an impressive array of bookshelves filled with countless titles. My eyes run down the winding staircase till it returns back to the floor, and then I turn around to head towards the kitchen.

It is immediately my favorite space so far, with its steel appliances and white cabinets. Again, there is a bouquet of fresh white lilies in the middle of the island which makes me believe that he has a cleaning service on employ to keep the place as sparkling clean as this. It almost seems unlived in and just a little bit lonely.

I hear the click to the front door signaling his return, so I turn around and head over to meet him.

True enough, he has found my purse which he places on the foyer table.

We are both amused at the occupation that led to its loss in the first place and share a smile together.

"You haven't had dinner have you?" he asks. "What do you want to eat?"

I place my hand on my stomach as I ponder on the question. "I'm still full from lunch but I could definitely eat. Do you have something quick available in your fridge?"

"Absolutely not," he says. "Just some beverages and snacks."

"Hmm, I guess we should order something in then. What do you want?"

"You decide," he says. "I'm not very hungry either."

"Okay. So, let's get down to business then." My hands goes to the button of my blouse, and I begin to undo the buttons there. I watch him beneath my lashes and relish the intensity of the gaze he has on me.

He doesn't move and given my very clear understanding of how he is perceived to the world, I'm completely floored by how much I am able to hold the attention of a man that most others don't even dare approach.

The moment my blouse parts, revealing the swell of my full breasts, encased in a sheer bra, I can almost hear his breathing briefly hitch.

"Let's eat something first," he says and begins to head over to the elevator. "We might not get any sleep tonight and the last thing I need is you collapsing on me."

"Oh no," I disapprove. "Your schedule is maxed out for tomorrow. Of course, we have to sleep."

He ignores me and continues on his rummage through the double doored steel refrigerator. Soon, he emerges with some apples, a packet of bacon, and four eggs. "What can we make with this?" he asks.

Kicking my shoes off, I head over to him immensely amused. "Not much."

"So we should just order something in then?"

"I think that will be best," I say and grab an apple from the bag. I head over to the sink to wash it.

He pulls his phone from his pocket. "Chinese fried rice and chicken good with you?" he asks.

I nod in response and then take a bite out of the apple. He connects with the restaurant so I go over to him but then something occurs to me. Excited at my intention to be naughty, I place the apple on the counter and move silently until I'm behind him. My hands slink around his waist and quickly proceed to unbuckle his belt.

CHAPTER THIRTY-SIX

Blair

He remains still as he listens quietly to the speaker on the other end, and even when I slip my hand down his now released fly to the inside of his briefs, he doesn't flinch.

However, when I grab the width of his fully aroused cock, I feel the slight jerk of his frame. The reaction spurs me on, so I tighten my hold around the sensitive flesh to stroke it in a fluid and precise motion. I know that he is severely affected by what I'm doing, which is why it's beyond impressive that he is still able to maintain a somewhat stable tone as he continues his conversation over the phone.

At some point however, I feel his body slightly shudder and then his words become rapid, and inpatient. It amuses me so much knowing I'm going to be in trouble with him when he eventually ends this call.

So I tighten my hold around his stomach and pump him ever harder. The moment, I sense him begin to turn around to get me, I try to pull my hand out of his briefs. His hold around my scrawny wrist however sends an excited panic through me. I squeal out as I struggle with him, pulling with all my might to be released from his hold.

Eventually, I'm able to free myself and instantly hurry away.

His call comes to an end then, so he slips the phone into his pocket and turns to me. "Come here," he says.

My pelvis goes numb with desire at the command in his tone. "I don't want to," I reply and continue to back away.

His eyes are locked on me as he begins to approach.

Then it's not long before I realize I have nowhere to go but up. So I hurry up the stairs, not even aware of where I'm going.

He follows at a leisurely pace and when I look back to see the quiet fire burning in his gaze, I know that I'm in a lot of trouble. The moment I reach the top of the seemingly endless stairs, there is only the hallway to head down, so I do but soon realize that this chase will be coming to an end in no time. I hit a dead end, so I turn around to watch him beginning to unfasten the buttons of his shirt.

"I'm sorry," I say half-heartedly, as I suspect that I will be ruthlessly albeit deliciously ravished the moment those hands of his get to me. "I just wanted to tease you. I won't be that naughty again."

This doesn't work, as he doesn't stop and with every step he takes that wicked glint in his eyes gets darker and darker.

"Grady. Grady!"

The shirt slides off his shoulders and falls to the floor just as he reaches me.

I'm thrown over his shoulder like a weightless sack and can't contain the laugh bubbling through my system. "Grady!"

I'm gently thrown on the bed and before I can even sit upright, his beautiful warm body is on mine. Every word thereafter is stolen from my mouth with a deep kiss, his tongue coaxing mine in long languid strokes.

My core tightens painfully as he rubs the bulge of his erection against my crotch, so much so that I'm soon writhing helplessly on the bed needing more but yet completely engrossed by what he is already doing to me. I want to do more for and with him so I open my eyes, and try to turn with him.

Realizing what I want, he allows it and I straddle his chest. "I'm in control today," I say to him.

He moves his hands behind his head to settle in to enjoy the show. "Are you?"

"I am," I respond and reach to caress the skin of his now exposed cock.

"Then why are you still dressed?"

He has a good point so I shrug the shirt off my shoulders, and soon after, my bra is flung aside. My breasts are now fully exposed and open to his perusal... it warms me when he can't seem to take his eyes off them.

He suddenly straightens and before I can stop him, one breast is in his mouth.

"Grady," I shriek at the jolting sensation but I don't want to stop him just yet. With my hand still pumping him from behind, I let my head slightly fall back as he devours my breasts.

He sucks greedily on my nipples, his tongue and teeth flicking while lightly grazing the hardened buds as his hands mold the soft mounds from beneath.

It is only then that I register where we are, and all I see is that it is a well-furnished, well lit room decorated in white and beige accents.

I return my attention to the man I'm on top of and wrap my hands around his neck. I realize then that I'm mere seconds from getting completely carried away and handing the reins over to him, so I summon all of my will, to push him away from me.

He's reluctant to move away from my breasts but soon complies and falls back to the bed with a harsh groan.

I laugh softly at the torment on his face, but soon lower to place a sensual kiss on the skin beneath his pulse in his neck.

A harsh breath escapes him at the contact and I'm spurred on. I place another kiss on his shoulder, on his nipples and continue to trace kisses across his skin, tasting every inch of his flesh until I reach his navel. I thrust my tongue into it and it causes his entire frame to jerk.

"'Blair!" He laughs.

I'm equally as amused as I continue the assault till my lips reach his groin.

For the first time I don't feel hurried, although there is an intense sense of urgency for us to get the other off. Today however, I'm going to take my time to enjoy every bit of him. Since I'm already somewhat selling my soul, then I'm going to enjoy every second of the perks.

His cock is soon in my mouth and at my hard suck of the wet damp head, his hand finds its way to his hair.

I absolutely love how restless he's becoming under my touch, his hips jerking and jutting as I proceed to lick and plant kisses up and down his shaft. Then I return to the head and take him into my mouth as deeply as he will go. I have to stop when he hits the back of my throat and then with my lips firmly closed around his thick column, and my teeth lightly scraping the sensitive skin, I pull off him. Next is his balls which I suck greedily on and then the feasting begins.

"Fuck," he curses aloud as my mouth and hands settle on a frantic rhythm in milking him. "Blair..." His body shudders as my tongue laps up the arousing discharge from the head. Then I return to bobbing my head and hands up and down his shaft.

Not long after, he is spilling completely into my mouth and I'm lapping up as much of him as I can. His deep groans echo endlessly in the room and it fills my chest with pride at just how intensely the orgasm affects his body.

"Fuck! Blair!" He growls as he throws one hand across his face to hide his expression from me.

I watch in amusement as he recovers as I take off the rest of my clothes, relishing just how almost magical it is to be able to make a man– who is so used to being in control– completely lose it.

With my knees digging into the mattress, I lower my ass and grab onto his already hardening cock to impale myself onto. My body quivers at the sensation of him filling me up, stretching me tight and soothing an ache deep within that nothing else can.

My hands are all over his rock-hard torso as I clench and unclench my walls, relishing every thick inch of him.

I sense him begin to rise, and when he brings my hand to his lips for a kiss, my eyes flutter open. His muscled arms band around my waist and they meld my body to his. This position is staggeringly intimate. Every rise and fall of my chest in labored breathing is synchronized with his as his ocean blue eyes bore into mine. We're so close that I can trace the specs of gold and grey in his irises and almost count the lashes along his lids.

Down below, our bodies are so deeply connected that it's as though we have melded into one.

My eyes sting with tears as I move him in and out of me and I can't understand why. Also, it's not helping that he's watching me, enthralled as though he's committing every single feature of my face and expression to memory.

Then he leans forward to press a kiss to my lids and my entire body quivers. "You're so fucking beautiful Blair," he whispers to me.

I feel a surge of anger fill my chest. Violently, I push him away from me until he lets go and falls back to the bed. Then with my hands pressed to his torso, I lift my ass off his groin and slam back onto him. A few moments ago, we were making love, but right now this is nothing beyond the primal act of fucking. The maddening need to pound viciously into the other for the sole purpose of chasing a release that we both desperately crave. I clench my eyes shut, so I won't see him and he wouldn't be able to see that deeply into my eyes again. It made me feel too exposed and too vulnerable. So I pound my hips ruthlessly against him.

My orgasm this time around, is crippling. It arrives as a fierce wave of pleasure that slams into me and steals the breath out of me. My cry rings out across the room, drowning out all else but I'm aware that he too has climaxed. I feel the spill of his seed deep inside me, and the warmth and heat of it all, makes me dizzy.

I'm no longer able to sit up straight, so I collapse on top of him and then eventually, find the strength to roll off to the side.

I immediately curve my body into a fetal position, still trembling from the endless waves of the shattering experience. I want to go home so I can manage the turmoil of emotions currently barraging through me, but I'm certain I won't not be able to walk for the next few minutes. So I proceed to wait until I feel him sling an arm around my waist. Before I can complain, my naked body is brought possessively against his. My ass settles in the crook of his groin while his arm curves over my breasts, positions that are very effective in making me once again, lose my mind.

All I want is to soak in the heat and scent of his skin, but this depth of intimacy is too dangerous. So I somehow find the strength and try to pull away from him.

But he refuses to let me go. He buries his face in the crook of my neck and begins to drift off to sleep. "That was fucking amazing," he whispers into my ear.

CHAPTER THIRTY-SEVEN

Blair

I can barely respond. I realize now that this will be the second time I'm encased in Grady's arms, and it is messing with my ability to breathe normally.

I know I'm playing a very dangerous game by still remaining here like this with him, but I don't want to extricate myself from the sheer pleasure of this.

I do however want to hear it from the horse's mouth. That he's even a little bit as affected as I am. So before he falls any deeper into sleep, I part my lips and speak, "I should leave."

It takes moments before he responds, and I don't dare breathe until he does. He tightens his arms around me. "Why?"

My heart jumps in my chest. "Well work, tomorrow"

"I'm your boss. You can come in late."

My lips spread into a stupid smile that make my cheeks ache. I nestle even further into him.

He growls into my ear, "Stop. Unless you want to cancel our entire day at the office tomorrow."

I muffle my laughter and it's thereafter the easiest thing in the world to settle into his embrace and fall asleep

I listen to the gentle rise and fall of his chest against me, and it isn't long before I join him in bliss.

We are however rudely awakened by the sudden shrill of his phone, late into the night.

His movements fully rouse me, as with a groan he leans away to reach towards the nightstand for his phone. It is however not there, which is understandable since our clothes were discarded at the entrance to the bedroom

He pulls away from me and I instantly feel the chill of his absence. Sitting up, I reach for the covers to pull them up my body and watch as he retrieves his pants by the door. The call disconnects before he can respond to it but he soon redials the number, and places the phone to his ear. I look around the dimly lit room solely and softly illuminated by the soft glow of the moon from beyond the balcony. I think of where my own phone has been discarded needing to know what the time is since there is no clock present.

"Sheriff?"

I listen to him speak, and that immediately gets my alarm bells ringing. *Sheriff*? I listen more attentively and although I worry that it's a little intrusive, I assume he would have taken the initiative to move into another room if he truly needed the privacy.

Grady releases a deep sigh. "How is he now?" he asks. "*Fuck,*" he curses.

I'm a bit taken aback by the frustration in his tone.

"Just a second, I want to check what the time is." He starts to pull the lit screen away from his ear but then immediately returns it. "Alright, I'll be there in about an hour. Thank you, Sheriff. Please keep an eye on him for me." He ends the call, and for a few more seconds just stares straight ahead. Then he turns around to find my gaze in the dimness.

"Is everything all right?" I ask.

He comes over to me, gloriously naked and sits on the side of the bed. "It's just ten minutes past 6," he says. "Do you want to stay longer to sleep in or do you want me to give you a ride back home?"

"I'll leave," I immediately say and start to rise. "I'll get a cab home, don't worry about it."

Then before I can move too far away, he grabs my arm and pulls me back towards him. For a while, he just stares at me, and I hate that the light is not enough to show the true emotions on his face.

"Grady," I call softly. "Is everything okay?"

With a sigh, he brings my hand to his cheek. "No," he says. "My dad was found passed out drunk next to a highway in Aurora."

My heart seizes in surprise. I don't know what to say to this so I instead lean forward and throw my arms around him for a hug. This pulls the fabric off my body as a result and leaves the both of us once again, skin to skin.

This time the heat we generate is mild but no less sweet and heart wrenching. "I hope he's okay."

"He might not be," he says. "After the scolding I'm about to give him."

I smile but do not produce an actual laugh. Then I move away from him, but before I can think up my next action, he slants his head and begins to nibble softly on my bottom lip. This amuses me so I take the initiative to demand a complete kiss. Our tongues tangle against the other in a slow, sensual dance that has me reeling in no time. My heart begins to pump faster and my core tightens almost painfully as he has immediately awoken the need to have him inside me once again.

He soon breaks it off, but it results in a whimper from me. I place my hand on his chest and hide my face in his neck. I can't get enough of this man and it makes me truly wonder if I will ever be sated.

"I have to leave soon," he says. "Sleep in, and come to work a bit later. I'll do the same."

I shake my head and mutter into his skin, "We have Elaine's new module presentation at 9 AM."

"Move that to the afternoon," he replies. "I'm sure I have a free hour somewhere."

"You do," I respond.

"Tell her to just turn in the documents before then, and also to send a copy via email. I'll study them when I get some free time during the day.

"Yes, sir," I reply, and lift my gaze up to once again meet his beautiful blue eyes. Our voices are soft and low, and I'm certain that if someone else were in the room, they might not have been able to hear a word we have said to each other so far. This level of intimacy and closeness is staggering and enthralling. And it especially makes me wonder how I'm going to navigate speaking professionally to him after this. We both are truly playing with fire or—maybe it is just me.

"I'll order some breakfast for you," he says.

I shake my head and move to the edge of the bed. "No, I want to take a shower. This is usually when I get up anyway so that I can be in the office before eight."

"Alright, let's take one together then," he says.

My heart leaps into my throat. "I don't think that's a good idea."

"Why not?" He asks and rises to his feet.

"You have to be out of here. If we get in that shower together you will be late."

"You're right." He smiles. "But I'm still not going to pass this chance up. Let's go. We'll try our best to be quick." He pulls me along with him and we head towards his massive bathroom. In the space is a shower stall made entirely of marble and glass, and a large four legged bathtub in the corner.

I can't help but stare, the dream of one day soaking in it with him taking shape in my mind.

He notices my gaze on it and laughs softly. "Not today, Blair. We have shit to do."

"I know," I reply. "I know. Do you have a spare toothbrush?"

"I do," he says and we both head over to his vanity sink.

The warmth of the bathroom lights are so flattering that I'm not too ashamed of being naked. I do however pick up a towel from the rack in a corner to wrap around myself.

He grabs it and pulls it away before I can cover up.

"Hey!" I protest.

He hands me the toothbrush and throws the towel across the floor. "When we're together, let's be completely exposed to each other. I want this to feel as natural as possible." He squeezes some toothpaste onto my brush.

I stare at it. "But this isn't natural though," I say, unable to stop myself.

"It is," he says as he runs his brush under the gushing faucet. "Let's make it so. When we're together let's forget everything else. The past and the future. Let's just live in the present and just be with each other. Uninhibited."

That's a lot to ask, is my final thought on the matter but I don't voice this one out loud.

CHAPTER THIRTY-EIGHT

Grady

She clings onto me as I quickly regulate the temperature for the shower's cascade and in no time, we are both submerged under it. The soothing water however is the least thing on my mind.

My father's present arrest and hold in a jail cell is incredibly grievous, but as she wraps her arms around my neck and begins to kiss me deeply, a huge chunk of that worry and frustration seems to be washed away along with my coherence. Suddenly, she stops and I almost follow her lips like a hypnotized man.

She laughs at the involuntary reaction, and brushes my wet hair out of my face. "We can't spend too much time in here. Incredibly busy day ahead. And your father..."

I can feel the concern in her tone as she no doubt feels sympathy at the situation. But somehow, it feels in that moment like I won't be able to go through the rest of my day without one last joining with her. So without warning, I pick her up from the floor and let out the order, "Wrap your legs around my waist."

I see the shyness in her eyes as she laughs at her sudden disconnection from gravity, but still she does as I have said and also throws her arms around my neck. "Grady, we don't have time," she warns.

"We have just enough," I say and turn with her till her back is against the tiled wall.

The cascade's pressure is heavy, so even when we step aside a huge chunk of it is still beating down my back which as a consequence also keeps her drenched.

After making sure she is properly balanced against the wall, I set one of my hands free and slide my thumb through the slickness of her sex.

I absolutely love how she is already immensely wet and willing, constantly open and responsive to my touch.

Her eyes are boring into mine as the pad of my thumb circles her clit, and it causes an almost pained expression across her face. Her breathing is now harsh and particularly loud in the confined space while her body is writhing and grinding to the rhythm of my strokes.

Her arousal is released out to my fingers and I want nothing more than to taste her. So I release her, and after making sure she is stable enough, lower my body till my head is between her thighs.

"Grady," she calls out in warning but any further words freeze in her throat when my mouth covers her folds. Her agonized cries as I suck hard on her clit is so satisfying to listen to and so is her grip on my hair, though painful. Her hips are writhing uncontrollably with her body jerking to the wildness of my tongue and lips as I ravish the most intimate part of her.

It isn't long before she's quivering from the release of her orgasm and I make sure to lap up every bit of her before rising to my feet. I pick her back up, press her somewhat limp body against the wall, and slam into her.

Our fucking this time around is hard and fast as we are both aware of the time constraints of the day and its responsibilities have imposed on us.

I bury my face in her neck to hide the near crazed, euphoric expressions that I know is on my face. I'm grunting and growling like a bull while she is just as overtaken, her hips pumping furiously to meet the depth and intensity of my thrusts. The smack of flesh against flesh and the squelches of our discharges are so erotic that for a few minutes I'm certain that my mind goes blank. Never, have I felt so close or so connected to a woman before.

She nearly squeezes the life out of me when she eventually climaxes, while I on the other hand, hold on just as desperately to her. I empty every bit of my seed into her, slightly aware that once again I have forgotten to use protection. Only after a few minutes of recovery have passed, and her legs are sliding down mine to the floor that I remind her of it.

"I know," she mutters still without the energy to speak. "I'll take care of it."

With my hands digging into her ass to press her as close as is possible to me, I give her a deep kiss and we further melt into each other.

CHAPTER THIRTY-NINE

Blair

After our somewhat lackadaisical wash in the shower is completed, out of the need to force ourselves out of each other's arms and the stall, he turns the faucet off and carries me out of the bathroom. He sit me gently on the counter and I'm riveted by the pampering as he grabs a towel.

He begins with my hair, and I can't help staring at him as he softly rubs it dry.

Most enjoyable is the way he runs his fingers through the strands to untangle the wet mass, and then leans in to take a good sniff. I smell like him; of his shampoo and body wash... the feeling is just divine. "You're spoiling me," I warn him. "Very soon, I'll be telling you that I can't walk anywhere and then you'll have to carry me around."

He responds with an amused smile but I can see that his mind is not completely with me. I understand this of course and want him to quickly get to his father. "Why don't you go dress?" I ask. "The Sheriff is—?"

"No," is his response as he grabs the dryer. "We have time. I want to do this."

I want this just as much as he does, so I wrap my legs and arms around him, and shut my eyes to enjoy his pampering.

As he works the warm air into my hair, the strands slide through his fingers and occasionally, he includes a soft massage to my scalp that leaves my toes curling. My eyes peep open once in a while and each time, I meet his gaze completely focused on the task at hand, but I know his thoughts are still with his father.

It makes me wonder what the story is between the two of them. The only thing I know is from what my ex-military client from ABAX shared with him during our meeting. I want to pry, so he can share his heaviness with me but I know that it's not my place and that it will shatter the unexpected level of affection he is showing, despite our otherwise physical agreement.

I soon sense that my hair is about halfway dried so I hop off the counter.

"I'm not done," he says.

I shake my head and take the dryer from him. "I'll do the rest at home." "Let's do yours."

To my surprise, he agrees and turns to lean against the counter. He shuts his eyes as I find a comb and begin to smooth out his light waves with the dryer.

He's still as gloriously naked as I am, so I can't help but to feast my eyes on him. The hard ridges of his torso; the dips and contours of his flesh and how taut it all is across his frame. My eyes lower to trace the slight dusting of hair past his navel and then of course past his groin to my now favorite part of his body.

I quickly retrieve my gaze when my hands slip and move from drying his hair to his forehead.

Thankfully, he doesn't reopen his eyes at my clumsiness and I bite my lips to hide my smile. As he enjoys my service, I take the time for the first time up this close to properly examine and appreciate his beautiful face.

Shaved clean, his skin is soft and supple, like a newborn's. His brows are groomed, leading down to a high arched nose, and dipping into soft, plump lips. Then there is this jawline of his that turned what could have otherwise been solely soft features into a severe attack on every woman's brain cells.

I turn the dryer off and although I try to talk myself out of it, I can't help but reach forward to place a soft kiss on the tip of his nose.

This immediately brings his eyelids open and for a moment he stares at me.

I feel a bit nervous at the intensity of his gaze. It seems dark and more piercing than usual and it makes me fear that perhaps I've crossed a line.

"Let's get dressed," he says and before I can respond, he takes the dryer and replaces it on the wall.

"Do you have any lotion I can use?" I ask, but then change my mind. "Don't worry about it I'll be heading home soon."

"Of course I do," he says and opens up a cabinet beside the mirror.

It holds a very simple collection of about four bottles and I quickly find what I need. I take it with me but can't help noticing the way his gaze has changed once again. He stares at my naked body and it makes me incredibly self-conscious. "Grady, I'm not wearing any clothes, so if you keep looking at me like that my skin's going to melt off."

He laughs as he follows me out of the bathroom. "You can't blame me. You've got to be the sexiest woman that I've ever seen."

I can't help but feel equal parts pleasure and displeasure at the statement which I appreciate but is also a reminder that he has of course been with others apart from me. I grit my teeth, thankful that he can't see my face as I head back into the adjoining room that serves as his walk in closet.

"What I want to do right now is work that lotion into your skin, but I know that if I start that, there will be very little chance that either of us will get out of this house today."

"I know." I smile and turn around to hold the lotion up as a weapon. "Don't come close to me. I'll take you up on the offer next time." I take my seat on the stool in the center and begin to rub the scented lotion all over my skin. I could have indeed waited to get home but I'm glad for the chance to have something of his smeared all over my body for the rest of the day. Hopefully, no one else will be able to detect and connect this scent on me to him, but he will. He most definitely will.

I turn around to see him putting on a pair of dark boxer briefs, and wonder if I can borrow one of those.

He turns to see me looking at it and instantly guesses my thoughts. Lifting a rolled one from the stack in the drawer, he throws it over to me.

Of course, I miss the catch to his amusement.

"Did you play any sports in school?"

"Of course not," I reply and grab the briefs off the floor. I'm glad to hear his laughter especially since a few moments earlier he had seemed gloomy. "What about you?"

"Track," he says. "I used to run a lot then. It cleared my mind. I still do from time to time but it's hard to find the time during the weekdays because of my early schedule."

"Nice," I say, but then something occurs to me. "Wait, but if you don't exercise that often how is your body like this?"

"Like what?"

"You know."

"No, I don't know," he says.

It makes me sigh. "Now you're fishing for compliments?"

"I don't deserve any?"

I throw my head back and sigh aloud. "Fine. Your body's amazing. Sick. Brain damage inducing... fine."

He's just shrugged his arms into a shirt but a deep rumbling laugh overtakes him at my comment. "Really? Brain damage inducing?"

"No further comments," I say and head off into the bedroom to find my bra. The rest of my clothes are there too, so I pick them up, shaking my head at what a passionate breathless mess we were last night. I want to see him dress though, so I take what I need and head back into the closet. I put on my bra and even though I'm aware he's watching me, I don't indulge him by turning it into some show. I just give him knowing glances from time to time and relish the soft smile on his face. He really is too good looking and that is just one more ingredient for this recipe for a disaster that we're both currently putting together.

I want the chance to button him up but I suspect that this will cross yet another line, so I let the fantasy go, and instead ask about something fairly neutral. "Your dad," I begin gently. "Did you get to see him enough when you were younger? With him being a Navy Seal and all?"

He is quiet for a moment which makes me think once again that I have stepped across a boundary. All of this double checking and contemplation is truly stressful to deal with. "I'm asking because of my own experience with a military father."

"I did," his response comes. "And we were once very close but then about the time I turned twenty he got into an accident while on active duty."

I stopped at the sudden revelation, all sorts of damning consequences coming to mind.

He notices my concern and instantly calms me. "He didn't sustain much physical injuries but the damage to him emotionally was severe. Since then, I don't feel like I've had a father. He retired voluntarily, and he's never been the same. Our relationship has since soured."

"I'm so sorry to hear that," I say.

"Things can be easily mended in my opinion but he is the most stubborn prick to ever exist, so we're still constantly at odds."

I want to go over to give him a hug and struggle with holding back. Eventually, I give in and go over. Lifting myself on the tips of my toes, I place a kiss on his cheek and then quickly take my leave.

A few minutes later, he emerges from the closet to see me getting my things together and announces that he's heading downstairs.

In no time, I myself am ready to go, so I hurry down the stairs.

My stomach growls from hunger and it makes me think of the dinner we'd ordered the previous evening before things got out of control. So, I head straight to the front door and pull it open to check if perhaps it's still there. I'm beyond excited when I see that the brown paper bag is indeed still there. "It's still here, oh my God." Delighted, I lower to pick up the food and bring it into the house. It seems to take forever but soon, I arrive at the kitchen.

Grady is brewing a pot of coffee. "I'm having second thoughts about eating that," he says.

I ignore him and plop the bag on the island. "Let's see its state first," I insist, and retrieve the packaged meals. First comes the rice, and then the chicken. Afterwards is the fried dumplings and shrimp. After inspecting them, I find to my relief that they're all still very edible. "They're still great," I say, "I'll heat them up. Where are your plates?"

Putting his mug down, he turns around to head over to the cabinet behind him.

I can't help but admire his appearance; the new pair of slacks and crisp olive green shirt that he has on. Dressed like this, he has reverted to the almost unapproachable executive from the office but as he turns around to hand the plates over to me, there's a warmth in his eyes that heightens the burning pressure in my chest.

I quickly look away to hide just how affected I am by him. Soon, our meals are heating up in the microwave so he passes me a cup of freshly brewed coffee. The aroma is wafting all across the kitchen, the perfect accompaniment to a surreal morning. "Do you usually brew the ones you come to the office with?" I ask.

"No" he replies. "Andrew gets them for me when he picks me up."

"Ah," I say. "No wonder you never let me get them for you."

"I don't want to trouble you."

"It's my job you know," I remind him.

He nods his head in agreement. The microwave announces its completed run, but before I can go over to retrieve the plates, he's already turned around to grab them. He lays them out on the island and then passes me a fork. He munches lightly on a few pieces of chicken and rice and teases me about the carrots and broccoli that I keep picking out. "You eat like an eleven year old," he says and places his fork down.

"Hey!" I complain, to his amusement.

He takes his drained cup to the sink and then grabs his keys from the table. "I'm already late," he says. "I'll see you at the office. Tell Andrew to take you home, he's already waiting outside."

"Oh no, he doesn't—"

He cuts me off with a wave. He soon disappears around the corner.

I can't help but feel a bit sour that he doesn't give me a kiss at his departure. I hit my fork to my head at the thought. "You're just fuck buddies," I remind myself. "Don't dig a pit for yourself with impossible expectations."

With a sigh, I finish up my meal, clear what I can of the dishes and then hurry out of the magnificent apartment to start my day.

CHAPTER FORTY

Grady

Upon my return to the office later that morning, I can't believe just how eager I am to see her. Especially after the quarreling and rants from my half-drunk father, having to wrestle him back to his home and discussing with the Sheriff on how to perhaps hire someone in the park to look out for him.

I feel emotionally drained and want to lean against the elevator but as I've come in at a busy hour, there are other employees in the space. They all get out at their various floors taking the time to send me greetings before they do and soon I arrive on mine.

She is however, not in her seat.

I stop in the middle of the reception and just stare at the empty space, not even realizing what I'm doing until there's a sudden knock on the door. I turn around as it's pushed open to see that it's our course development leader, Elaine.

"Grady," she calls. "Good morning." She seems quite taken aback to have met me in the reception since I'm usually always in my office. "I just came by to drop off the course list for Blair. She requested it earlier."

I nod in understanding.

She proceeds to place the document on the desk.

"Do you know where she is right now?" I ask. "I just got in."

"She's probably down at client management. Do you want me to contact her for you?"

"Don't worry about it." I shake my head. "What I need is not urgent."

"Alright then," she says. "Have a great day." She heads out.

I continue on to my office. I can't stop thinking about my father and his deteriorating mental state, and the fact that he isn't even aware of it enough to seek or allow any help being offered to him. It puts me in an incredibly sour mood, and it's not until there's a knock on my door a little while later that I finally look up from my computer screen.

My heart slightly jumps in my chest at the probability of who it is, seeing that they came straight to my door. "Come in," I call out and the door is pushed open.

It's Allen, and the degree of disappointment I feel is too heavy to hide.

It even makes him stop in his tracks at what is probably an incredibly unwelcoming look on my face. "What's wrong?" he asks, slightly alarmed.

I quickly rearrange my expression and lean into my chair to take a little break. "Nothing," I respond. "What's up?"

"It's either there's something really bothering you or you were incredibly disappointed to see me," he says as he approaches.

I don't bother responding, so I just watch him as he takes his seat.

"So," he begins. "I'm here to remind you that I'm taking about two weeks off from the day after tomorrow. Meredith's really struggling with the morning sickness so I'm on duty to help out with Alexa."

"Sure," I respond. "Do what you need to, but be available for emergency situations. We need to be able to contact you at all times."

"I'm aware, sir." He laughs.

"Why don't we do something together tomorrow. Maybe catch some dinner? Go to a bar?"

He seems stunned at my suggestion. "Wow, you must really have a lot on your mind."

I try my hardest to keep from rolling my eyes at his quite accurate speculation.

He goes on, "And you know, there's no way I'm going to say no to that."

"Alright then, I'll get Blair to set it up."

CHAPTER FORTY-ONE

Blair

I'm a tad bit nervous as I return to my desk.

It's now lunch time and I'm not certain if Grady has returned from his emergency call from this morning. I want to ask him how things went and if his father is doing much better but as expected, I'm considering this might again, be too personal given the nature of our current relationship.

Still, I want to know if he has returned, so I head to his door and give a little knock.

There is no response and it makes my heart sink just a little.

Just when I'm about to turn around however, I hear his call. "Come in."

My heart lurches. *He's back?* I brush at the creases in my blouse from running around all morning, and let out a deep breath pushing the door open and walking in confidently.

There's a pen in his hand as he seems to be pondering over some files on his desk, but his gaze is solidly fixed on me.

"Hello," I greet. "I just wanted to check if you had returned."

"I have," he answers.

I nod in acknowledgement. "And how are things? How's your father?"

His gaze on me seems to narrow and it's only after a few moments of silence that his response comes, "He's okay. Things are under control." His tone is cold, his gaze is cold, and so are his words.

It hurts because I can remember the warmth that he basked me in the previous night and earlier this morning. "Alright," I turn around.

I'm almost at the door, when he calls me, "Blair."

I immediately turn back to face him, hopeful, but for what exactly I'm uncertain. "Yeah?"

"Allen is going to be taking some time off after tomorrow, so I offered to treat him to an outing tomorrow night. Perhaps dinner and some drinks? It's preferable if they are both in the same place, so the hassle of moving around is eliminated."

"Of course," I reply. "I'll handle it."

"Thank you," he says and there is a bit of relief in his tone.

With that, I take my leave and get on with my task. Knowing both of their personalities to a certain degree, I select a restaurant downtown that isn't too formal. The moment the reservations are booked, I send the itinerary to both men and focus on my meeting with my new clients the next morning.

On the evening of the following day however, I'm alerted by the restaurant that neither of them have shown up and that their table is about to be given away if any more time is wasted.

My report is immediately dropped as I jump to my feet.

Grady is out of the office for the inspection of a video production company that he has an interest in acquiring. While Allen, well I have no idea what he is up to. Slipping into my loafers, I grab my purse and hurry from my desk. A quick visit to Allen's office shows that he too is not in his seat, so I resort to immediately driving over to the restaurant myself to hold the reservation for them.

Allen is the first to arrive and he quickly apologizes for the inconvenience.

"That's okay," I respond, and rise to my feet to leave.

He stops me. "Hey! Stay. Why don't you join us?"

I'm a bit perplexed as to the invitation. And also how I wish that Grady would be this open and as cheery as Allen. "I don't think that's appropriate," I say. "My boss wants to spend the time with *you*."

"You're making it seem like we're lovers or something," he replies with a shudder and a corresponding dramatic shake of his shoulders.

It makes me laugh.

"Relax," he insists. "At least until he arrives. I'll get you something to drink for all your trouble."

Before I can reject the offer, he signals to the waiter and the uniformed older man comes over. "Just a Moscato will do," I go for the least expensive option as I plan to shoulder the expense myself instead of leeching off both my bosses.

"You have a sweet tooth?" he asks.

"Somewhat," I reply with a smile.

"Okay, and how's your project with ABAX coming along?"

"Great. We're sending out the first round of phishing tests to their employees tomorrow."

"Nice," he replies and heartily lifts his glass to me.

I do the same and they both connect with a clink.

All of the agitation that I've been nursing all day almost seems to wash away with his presence, and I just can't help but to thank him once again for all his help.

With a wave of his hand, he brushes my praises away. "It's nothing," he says.

Then my mind goes to my moody boss. Ever since his return from bailing his father out from the Sheriff, his mood has somewhat reverted back to the initial, withdrawn state it had been when I first met him. He is courteous to me but beyond that, one would never be able to guess how intimate we've been with each other. I consider that this might be inappropriate to bring up to Allen but since they will be spending the evening together, I decide to give him a nudge so he can find out if all is well.

"Getting along better with your boss?" Allen proceeds to ask.

I'm grateful for the timely segue into my agenda. "We are, but lately I've sensed an unusual withdrawal from him."

"Do you know why?"

"I most definitely do not," I say with a laugh in order to make things seem as light as possible. "It might not be related to work and if this is the case, then I'd love to be able to help him out with it but I've not yet found the courage to ask."

Allen smiles. "Don't bother," he says. "I've known your boss for almost seven years now and I know very little to nothing about his personal life. I've never heard him speak about his father or mother and most definitely who he's dating. For all I know, he could be married and I wouldn't have a clue."

"Oh," is my only response to the disheartening report.

"Yeah, he's an incredibly private man but I will extend my hand to him if it's something that he truly needs help with."

"Thank you," I reply just as I sense someone approaching us. I lift my gaze and lo and behold it's my aloof boss. I immediately rise to my feet but Allen doesn't.

"Sir," I say.

Grady greets me with a quiet nod.

I however do not miss the way that his gaze lingers on my body.

First of all he stares into my eyes, and then moves his attention down along the fitted jumpsuit that is molded to my body.

I feel naked and exposed and it causes an excited shiver to shoot through my body.

He takes his seat.

I turn to face both men. "I'll be leaving now," I say, but Allen stops me. "Blair, c'mon just join us."

"Oh no, I don't want to intrude."

"We're not on a date. Grady, do you mind?"

I glare at Allen and for once, I do not appreciate his carefree personality. With every single word out of his mouth, he is unknowingly digging me into a hole.

Grady lifts his gaze from his phone. After a quick glance at me and Allen, his lips part to respond.

I quickly cut him off. "I need to get going," I insist. "My sister needs my help tonight and I have a very early day tomorrow. Goodnight, sirs." Without waiting for a response from either of them, I hurry away from their presence, my cheeks flushed and knees wobbly.

CHAPTER FORTY-TWO

Grady

"You scared her off," Allen says.

I watch her hurry away and don't bother giving a response to the statement. "How are things?" I instead ask him as I put the phone down and pick up the menu to peruse. I don't realize how my gaze moves one more time to catch a glimpse of her leaving.

This action, Allen most definitely does not miss. "Has my plan worked even a little bit?" he asks.

My brows furrow. "What plan?"

"To get you to notice her brilliance and wit and be even a little bit attracted to her?"

I gaze dazedly at him.

His hands immediately lift in defense. "Hey, don't attack me. Meredith came up with the idea."

"What?"

"She said something along the lines of 'If Grady won't go to the girls, then you have to bring the girls to Grady."

I'm speechless for a moment. "So you decided on the choice of my executive secretary, not based on competence but based on whom I would be most attracted to?"

"Hey, don't get me fired," he says. "Of course not. Competence was at the forefront of my criteria but unlike you, it wasn't the only thing on the list."

I shake my head at him, a slight smile tugging at the corners of my lips as my gaze returns to my menu. "Why are you so concerned anyway about finding me a partner?"

He goes silent for a few minutes and it catches my attention. Before even speaking, I'm able to guess who the culprit is. "Your father?"

He laughs at the very fond memory of the harsh abrupt man, who somehow still managed to radiate the most warmth whenever he was around.

I'm equally as amused and warmed as I lean back in wonder. "Really? What exactly did he say?"

"When he was in the hospital he told me, 'make sure you get that boy married. If we allow him he's probably going to spend his whole life at that desk, forever trying to prove himself.' "

"Ouch," I say, albeit warmed by the concern.

The waiter arrives then to take our order and it gives us both the much needed quiet time to reminisce.

After the waiter leaves, I decide to admit some degree of truth. "Well, your efforts haven't completely failed. I would be lying if I said that I haven't felt any attraction whatsoever towards her."

His eyes light up like a brand new bulb. "I knew it!" He exclaims as his hand hits the table. This violently jostles the ceramic and glasses on it, along with drawing the attention of other patrons at the sudden bang.

"Calm down," I say through gritted teeth.

He manages to rein in his excitement. He does however sit up to lean towards me. "So, what's holding you back? Why haven't you made things official yet?"

I'm honestly confused. "Is that how things work with you? You feel a bit of attraction for someone and then you swear yourself to them for life?"

"Of course!" he replies. "That's what I did with you."

I can do nothing but stare at him in wonder.

CHAPTER FORTY-THREE

Grady

Spending time with Allen is as delightful as expected, however my mind is still unable to move away from my father, especially at the disconcerting news I received today on his health.

Andrew has been dismissed for the night, so I'm behind the wheel, alone with the silence of the night and a very contemplative heart.

It makes me think of Blair and of our morning together. I wouldn't have minded her joining Allen and me but it most definitely would have made her uncomfortable.

I've already seen in her eyes the eagerness to leave the restaurant, so I left the decision up to her. Allen however was the one being problematic. No doubt, he had intended to turn this into some sort of forced date with the intention to leave midway through by citing some sort of emergency. This would have left Blair and me alone together... and I would have liked that.

The SUV comes to a stop at a red light and I turn to stare out of the window. Then I pull my phone out of my pocket and attach it to the dashboard cradle. Her speed dial is set to the number two so I press it and connect the call to the car's speakers. I feel somewhat anxious, so I begin to put together what I want to speak to her about in my mind.

I'm not fast enough as the call soon connects. "Hello?" Her soft voice resounds in the vehicle.

"Sir?" she calls again when I don't respond.

"Did you get home safe?" I ask.

The car goes silent for a few seconds.

"Yes, sir," she eventually responds. "I hope the dinner went well, and the food and ambience was to your liking."

"You did good Blair. Everything worked out well."

I hear her smile, and then notice how her surroundings are a bit noisy. "You have company?"

"Uh... not really," she replies. "It's just my sister and her husband. He's just returned from his work trip, so they are catching up. There's a lot of talking and laughing in the kitchen, so I moved to my bedroom to give them a bit more space to reconnect."

"That's great," I say, ready now to end the call. No doubt, she's wondering about the sudden contact, and wants it over with.

She then stops me with, "Do you need something done?"

My immediate response is to indeed use work as an excuse, and although a part of me is hoping that it will not be the case, I still latch onto it. “No, but I did want to check on your plans with ABAX tomorrow. You mentioned it in the restaurant.”

It is a few more seconds before she speaks again, “Grady,” she calls and I’m a bit taken aback. “It’s after hours, so I’m allowed to call you by your name, right?”

I start to contemplate this but she speaks before I can respond, “I’m guessing that’s a no, so in that case I’m extremely sorry, sir. Please don’t fire me.”

I can’t help my amusement. “It’s fine. You can call me Grady.”

“Alright. Grady! Are you asking me about the project tomorrow because you don’t believe I can pull it off or because it’s my first time and you’re just concerned about me?”

“I’m concerned,” I reply, “because it’s your first time.”

“Alright,” she says.

By her tone, I can tell that she is not pleased about something. “What is it? You don’t want me to be concerned?”

“It’s not that, it’s just... it doesn’t feel very good to be micromanaged, especially by a senior executive, which could throw feelings of incompetency into the mix.”

“I don’t think you’re incompetent.”

“I know,” she says. “Or at least I hope so.”

I release a sigh. “I called you tonight Blair because I wanted to talk to you, about anything even if it’s just for a few moments.”

The line goes silent, and then a panic stirs in my chest. "It's because of my father," I quickly add. "I received bad news today about his deteriorating health and at times like this, what one really needs is a distraction."

"Oh," she says. "I'm sorry to hear that."

I know she wants to ask about the details, but is probably considering that it might be too intrusive. "You can speak freely with me."

"Okay," her tone is breathy and uncertain. "How bad is it?"

"Cirrhosis, and if he doesn't listen and keeps drinking, he's going to end up needing a liver transplant soon."

"I'm sorry." Her tone is heavy.

"No need to be," I respond. "With all his drinking it was inevitable."

"You sound like you need a hug," she says.

The audacious comment makes me laugh aloud. What surprises me even more is my response, "I do need one."

"Should I come over?"

I ponder on the question a little bit, and although the proposition sounds quite attractive, I realize that what I really want after this is to be alone to think. "There's no need," I reply. "I'll be fine. I just need some time to rest."

"Alright," she says.

I don't miss the disappointment in her tone. "Spend some time with your family."

"You too," she replies.

I disconnect the call.

CHAPTER FORTY-FOUR

Blair

"*You too*?" I mutter in disbelief. "You too?"

I can't scream out loud, especially since Matthew is home, so I grab my pillow and soundlessly scream into it. It's at this point that a knock sounds on my door.

Layne immediately pushes it open and this is the state she finds me in.

"Blair?" she calls, alarmed. "Are you okay?"

Dejected, I throw the pillow aside and brush my hair out of my face. "I'm not. I'm really not. In fact, I think I have a mental problem. I just gave the most stupid response to my boss."

She completely walks in then and shuts the door behind her. "Why? What did you say?"

"You too," I respond.

She is immediately perplexed. "What?" She comes over to sit on my bed.

As I stare into her eyes, I wonder if I should say any more given the relationship I'm currently in with Grady, which is one that I'm very aware she does not approve of. I have already mentioned him however, so I know that she will not leave until I spit out what had me screaming into my pillow. "He has a... difficult relationship with his father. Anyway, today he got some bad news about his father's health, so he mentioned it to me and I... uh, I tried to console him a bit, but he told me not to worry about it but to spend time with my family. Guess what I said in response. Layne. Guess."

"You too?"

"Yeah. I said you too."

"That's normal." She chuckles.

"No," I groan as I stare at the wall opposite me. "It's not normal. It's just dumb."

"No, it's human and automatic and he won't think about it, so stop attacking your pillow, and come share the cake with us."

"It's time?" I ask excitedly and jump off the bed. "Yes!"

The treat is a delicious sangria cake bought for Layne but it couldn't be touched till after dinner. I'd blended some kiwi's and poured them into popsicle molds to be frozen, so I retrieve those and share them as well.

The three of us hang out in the living room, debating baby names, and predicting personalities, so it's a happy time. I can't stop thinking about my boss though, who is having a difficult time on account of his father. I had mentioned to

Allen that he seemed a bit withdrawn, with the hopes that he would be able to find out what is wrong, but I can now see what the major problem is.

I want to go to him, but I'm quite unsure of how welcome I will be. It would also be a little difficult to speak to Layne about this and besides, I can also predict what she will say and it would be absolutely nothing in favor of my idea.

So I go to bed, turning my plan for the next day over and over in my mind.

The next morning, I awake and refuse to contemplate. I put on a pair of leggings, a pair of sturdy hiking boots then pack some quick sandwiches and sliced fruits into my backpack.

A little while later, I arrive at his apartment building and give him a call so the front desk can let me in.

In no time, I'm standing in front of his door, wringing my hands in anxiety.

He opens it and is shirtless, with nothing on but the unbuttoned, dark tailored trousers I'm certain he wore the previous day to work and his hair is a disheveled, sleepy mess.

He looks so rustic and beautiful... it makes my blood simmer with excitement. But I'm also nervous because I have shown up unannounced.

This sudden visit I can see doesn't make him particularly excited. "Is there something scheduled for today that I forgot about?"

I lift up the backpack I have in hand. "There's something in here that's very special, but we can only both receive it after going for a short hike up Mayflower Gulch.

He watches me silently for too long, before his gaze slowly moves to the bag. “What’s in it?”

“I can’t say. You can only find out after the hike.”

“Then I have no interest,” he says and turns around.

“Grady!” I call sharply and follow him into the house. “C’mon, just indulge me this once. What’s in the bag is really amazing. You’re going to be so thrilled.”

“I am indulging you,” he says and heads over to his refrigerator to grab a bottle of water. “I just need to know what I’ll be climbing up a mountain for.”

Well, peace of mind is a start, I say to myself but of course, I don’t voice it out loud. I finally give my answer, “Pancakes. The most delicious, fluffy pancakes that have ever been made. I promise you this. After having these pancakes, you just might cry.”

He watches me as though I’m the most peculiar girl he’s ever seen. “Pancakes. You want me to get dressed and go hiking for pancakes that are currently sitting in your backpack?”

I’m about to hesitate but since I have chosen to go this route, which I can see is slowly crumbling from underneath me, I decide to play it out to the very end. “Yes,” I reply. “The hike will clear your mind, and the pancakes will soothe your soul. Trust me.”

Another long silence floats between us as he once again, lifts the bottle to his lips and drains it. “Alright,” he agrees.

I’m stunned. “Alright? You mean...”

“I’ll be ready in ten minutes.”

CHAPTER FORTY-FIVE

Grady

I seriously doubt the existence of the life changing pancakes in her backpack, but her proposition for a hike doesn't seem like a bad idea.

I can't however help but shake my head at the sneaky tactic she is employing to get me to go on the hike with her.

I know why she's doing this, especially since I mentioned my father the previous evening. Her sudden presence does seem intrusive, but I appreciate it more than I would have expected to. I drive her to the copper mountain and we are soon on our way.

She offers me some pieces of sliced apples, and a grilled chicken sandwich which I accept for the needed energy.

Soon, we are hiking up the trail.

At first, we are both silent as we take in the serenity of the place and it isn't until twenty minutes into our climb that I speak, "Thanks for this. I think I needed it."

The smile that curves her lips in response immediately draws one out of me.

"I know you did," she says.

"So I'm guessing that the pancakes are not in the bag? Because so far, I've only seen the sandwiches and fruits."

"Of course not!" she feigns indignation to my amusement. "I'll get them for you the moment we're done."

"You're going to make them?"

"Maybe," she replies and increases the length of her strides up the weedy path.

I can't help but chuckle at her mischief and somehow it turns me on. Just watching her in fact is having the most strenuous effect on my libido. Her hair is held up in a loose ponytail, which leaves the shiny blonde mass a little less tamed than it usually is in the office. It's somewhat wild now with soft, escaped tendrils from her temples and the nape of her neck, effecting a softness to her that warms my heart. Then there's the way her leggings and tank top hug every curve of her body. She is–come to think of it–just the perfect distraction.

Our hike takes us a total of three and a half hours, and in that time we are mostly quiet, content to just be beside each other. We hike through the trail in the forest, take in the fields of wildflowers and old mining cabins. She asks me to take some pictures of her with the wild flowers and is so shy in posing that I almost can't stop laughing. She frames her chin with her hands, makes peace signs over her head and even rabbit ears.

It's all delightful to watch but when she suggests that I be the one to pose for a picture, I keep walking.

"Hey! Grady" she calls.

I keep up with my pace.

Then she catches up with me. This earns me a soft hit on my arm. "Why don't you want to take one?" she asks.

I ponder on the question for a little while and then give her an honest response, "I don't know. It's been a very long time since I indulged in things like that."

She watches me for a few minutes before she speaks again, "When was the last time you went on a vacation?"

"I don't think I've ever been on one. I've just always traveled for meetings and conferences."

"Hmm." She nods. "Come to think of it I haven't been on one either in a while. The only one I can remember is from ten years ago. It was the last vacation I had with my dad. We were still living in Houston then, so we went on a trip to SeaWorld in San Antonio. I remember the dolphins and their water show and popsicles and the heat and of course, these monster turkey legs."

"What?" An amused snort escapes my lips.

"I'm not joking. I still think about them. We didn't have the time to get any and maybe they weren't actually that big, but because I was still so little then, I remember them as being gigantic."

I smile at her story, but then it brings memories to mind of my own father. "When you lost your father," I ask. "How did you take it?"

She contemplates the question silently before responding, "I was devastated," she says. "I was quite close to him, and he was always on my side when my mother and sister weren't. At the time, I think that was what hurt the most. I felt like I was truly alone and would forever be because the one person that was always in my corner was gone."

"Was that how it played out?" I ask, not missing the sadness in her gaze.

"No." She laughs softly. "My sister came to my side. Before then, we were at odds but after he died, she for some reason saw it from then onwards as her responsibility to make sure I was always protected. And it's been that way ever since."

I retreat into my own mind and thoughts about my own father.

"I know you're very worried," she says. "About your father. But he's still here and there's still hope. So don't despair just yet, if that is why you feel so forlorn."

"My biggest fear," I tell her. "Is that one day, he'll be gone and I'll forever feel like I didn't do enough to help him. And at the same time I'm scared that I will forever resent him for not letting me."

CHAPTER FORTY-SIX

Blair

We soon reach the top of the trail at the Gold Hill Peak and are gifted with the magnificent views of the Clinton Creek watershed which descends north-west and forms a reservoir in the valley below. We are both silent as we take in the views over the ridge of a wide expanse of meadows backed by sawtooth peaks.

It is breathtaking, but it's just as impressive as the man standing tall and staring at it with me in a silent wonder.

This is a beautiful moment, and I realize that I don't want to let it pass. So I pull out my phone and before he can complain or catch my intention, I quickly take a picture of him.

He soon notices what I'm doing and instead of a stern reaction, he smiles.

"Am I going to get fired for this?" I ask.

"Let's take one together," he suggests

My heart nearly stops in my chest. "Okay," I respond, and cautiously go over. We turn our backs to the beautiful horizon, and our faces to the glow of the sun. He slips his arm around my waist and we both smile somewhat awkwardly for the very unexpected photo.

Afterwards, all I want to do is to stare at it, but he's right beside me as we get back into his car to return to the city.

The pit of my stomach however is churning out butterflies and it makes the fully air conditioned car still feel somewhat too warm for me.

"What about my pancakes?" he suddenly asks.

I turn to look at him, unsure for a moment on how to respond to this. Then I bite my bottom lip to hide my smile at the major disappointment that I'm about to deliver. "Um well..."

Just then, he comes to a stop at a traffic light, and turns to hold my gaze.

I'm incredibly intimidated by that stern gaze but equally just as amused. "My plan was to get you some delicious ones at IHOP. Have you ever had their Cinn-A-stacks? Absolutely nothing else beats that."

He stares at me without blinking.

I try my best to keep a straight face but it's too difficult. My hand covers my mouth to hide my smile.

Grady shakes his head and returns his attention to the road. "We'll go to the store instead," he says. "I'll make *you* pancakes."

A half hour later, I'm still somewhat dazed as I sit on one of the island stools and watch Grady crack eggs into a bowl. In goes the milk then the baking powder and I'm mesmerized.

My expectation was that he would be struggling to figure out a recipe gotten off the internet but instead, he's working as though he's done this a hundred times in the past. "You know how to cook?" I ask, completely stunned.

"Just pancakes, coffee, and eggs I guess," he says as he begins to measure out the flour. "Plus, this was my dad's specialty and he made it every chance he could get."

I want to ask about his mother, but I'm a bit reluctant since he hasn't mentioned her himself. With Grady, as I'm starting to realize, just the right degree of intrusion per time is recommended. Any more, and he is bound to close up like a clam. Plus, we have taken leaps and bounds in our relations with each other today, and I am more than satisfied with the level of progress attained so far.

"How are you going to serve it?" I ask, almost mesmerized by the effortless motions of his wrist as he works the batter in the glass bowl.

"What do you usually like yours with?" he asks.

"The usual; berries and syrup. Sometimes, I add some whipped cream but we didn't get that from the store."

"Alright," he says. "I'll clean the blueberries. How many of them do you want?" He shakes his head. "I usually have mine like a taco. More savory than sweet, with some bacon, cheese and eggs."

"Hmm, I've had this before too. They're not bad. I still want my berries though, so I'll just have a bite of yours."

With a smile, he retrieves a pan and places it on the induction range. "You know those people that can share anything except their food?"

I laugh, already aware of where he is going with this condition. "Yeah?"

"I'm one of those." He nods.

A little while after, we are both seated beside each other at the island counter and I'm eyeing his appetizing looking taco pancake. "I want a bite," I say.

He purposefully keeps his plate away from me. "Not happening."

With a pout, I ponder on what to do seeing that he is extremely vigilant. So I rise to my feet with my own emptied plate and sigh heavily as I move past him. Just as I'm about to completely walk away however, I pounce onto his back and grab the wrist holding his paco.

He bursts out laughing and tries to pull his hand away from me. Since I refuse to let go however, his strength has me falling on him and it should have thereafter sent me rolling off to the floor but he catches me with an arm around my waist and holds me in place.

Assured of my balance, I still continue fighting for the bite of his paco to his immense amusement.

He soon gives up and I'm able to bring his last forkful to my mouth. The paco is absolutely delicious and especially sweeter, due to my hard won fight for it. I also love the way he's watching me. His eyes are mixed with amusement and wonder and it makes my recent boldness begin to dissipate. I turn away shyly as I swallow, but his grip around my waist tightens. He turns my face to his, slants his head and I'm overtaken by a deep, heart stopping kiss.

This kiss is different and I can feel it in the depths of my soul. He resumes and pauses the kiss like he's savoring a delicacy and one that he incredibly treasures. My face is cradled in his hand, as the warm velvet of his tongue strokes mine in a sensual dance, while his other hand gently caresses my waist, sending currents of mind numbing pleasure through my body.

When we finally part, I'm completely breathless and almost frozen in place. I'm still not ready to open my eyes but I do sense him softly brush my hair over my shoulder.

"Thank you," he whispers and then begins to straighten my posture.

My eyes come open then but I don't dare ask exactly what the thank you is for.

Without a word, I take his plate and mine and we both head over to the sink.

We both rinse them in a comfortable silence, each contemplating our own thoughts especially at the depth of affection that had been packed into that kiss. He helps me load the dishwasher.

Now, I stand around almost confused at what to do next. "I'm going to go," I eventually say. "I think I've given Layne and her husband enough time to themselves today."

"Ah," he says. "We finally hear the real reason behind forcing me to go on a hike and to make pancakes for you. Expertly played."

I'm not even apologetic as an appreciative smile just for him, curves my lips. "Thank you," I say. Then I turn around and head to the foyer to grab my things. He escorts me to the door, and even though I want to stay a bit longer, I am reminded of the clam that he is. That kiss no doubt shook him as much as it did me, so I know it's time for the both of us to take a little step away from the other before the flight mode is activated on both sides.

He pulls the door open.

I'm just about to leave when I stop. I turn around and give him a hug. "Your dad will be fine. Let's hope for the best." I soon let him go and begin to head towards the elevator, but then suddenly he calls out to me.

I turn to see him watching me from the door.

"How about tomorrow?" he asks. "Don't you still need to give your sister and her husband some space?"

My heart jumps at the proposition. "I do. I was planning to spend it with a friend of mine at a bar or something." This response immediately brings to mind our first time ever together at a bar, and I don't know if it is imagined or not but his tone thereafter sounds a bit harsher.

"Spend it with me," he says. "Let's watch a movie here together."

I have absolutely nothing to consider or think about, so I immediately give my response, "I'd love to."

CHAPTER FORTY-SEVEN

Grady

"How do you get through to people?"

Blair is nestled in my arms as we lounge together on the couch, her head in the crook of my neck. The movie we are watching is about a female temporary worker who is hired to tap into her manager's phone in order to get information damning enough to get him fired. Somehow, that insight into his personal life reveals a part of him that she empathizes with and it changes her agenda from hurting him into saving him.

Blair inclines her head to glance at me. "You're referring to the manager, right?"

"Yeah," I reply. "The temp girl is so ... unlikeable, and they're not even in the same age bracket. He's twenty-five years older than she is. So how were they able to connect that deeply?"

She turns away to contemplate the issue as we continue watching the movie and I do the same. "Kindness?" She suggests. "He was kind to her when others weren't."

"Is it that simple?" I ask, my mind on my father.

"Empathy," she says. "I think that's what it is. By tapping into his phone, she realized that they were both quite similar."

"Because of their similar struggles in taking care of their families?"

"Yeah," she says and glances back once again to stare into my eyes.

I love it when she does that. It's very rare in the office that she is this bold, but when we are together like this, she completely unravels and becomes as intimate with me as she wants to be. I study the streaks of hazel in her eyes and can't resist the urge to lean forward to plant a kiss on the tip of her nose.

Blair affectionately wrinkles her nose at the contact, and we both return our attention to the movie. Soon however, I note she is moving against me. Her movements are sneaky and suggestive but the effect on my libido is clear. "I thought you wanted to watch the movie," I say to her.

She laughs under her breath, well aware of what she is up to. "I do," she says. "But must that be all that we do?" She glances back once more to meet my gaze.

I see in it, exactly what she wants. She's wearing a short leather skirt today, which I begin to undo the buttons of all while our gazes are still locked on the screen. Her zipper soon follows and then my hand gains full access to her silky folds. I slide in past her lace covered crotch and grip hard at her sex.

The small gasp that escapes her lips spurs me on. My hand, slightly damp with her arousal, slides in through her underwear. My fingers sink in between the lips of her sex and at the hard stroke of her engorged clit, her body slightly jerks.

I no longer have any interest in the movie, so I shut my eyes and rest my head against hers, solely focused on delivering the most sensational of releases to her.

One finger slides into her and then another, and my thrusting begins.

She can no longer remain quiet, her soft whimpers are encompassing me and drowning out the sound of the still playing movie. My thumb joins in the assault, stroking the bud of her desire in a gentle circular rhythm that soon has her writhing uncontrollably against me. My hands are completely soaked as they oscillate between thrusting hard and fast into her, and stimulating her clit to heighten the sensation.

"Grady," she breathes and arches her hips with her eyes clenched shut and her hand gripping my thighs. "Oh God..." she continues to moan as she nears her climax.

I chase it down vehemently. She climaxes with a violent shudder that I feel just as powerfully against my body. Her release is coming in a heated, steady rush down her opening into my hand and I slick it all over her sex. I continue to stroke her gently to wring out every inch of pleasure still left within her and it's an absolute delight to watch the heavy rise and fall of her chest gradually settle.

Blair turns to glance at me then with glazed eyes. Slanting her head, she captures my lips in a passionate kiss that leaves my head spinning so much that I don't even realize my phone is ringing. When we part, I just stare at her until she nudges me slightly.

"Your phone," she laughs.

I glance over at the coffee table, where it is. "Ignore it," I say to her and yank her skirt down her legs.

"It might be an emergency," she reasons while giggling.

I struggle to get her underwear to follow next. For a second, that rings an alarm through me but I force myself to ignore it. A few minutes later, she's astride me on the massive couch and riding me with a near crazed ferocity. The room was just a little while earlier cool enough for the both of us, but right now I can feel the dampness of our skin, wet with the perspiration generated from our uninhibited fucking.

Our chests are heaving and our breaths wheezing, her lips are whispering the naughtiest, lust crazed words to me. "Holy fuck, Grady... you're so fucking... nngh... this is so fucking good. Right there... right t-there... mmmm."

I've never been much of a talker during sex and neither have I particularly favored it from my partners, but I have found that with Blair, her incoherent moans and cries of just how powerful the sexual torrent I'm stirring within her is, is one of my absolute favorite things in the world to listen to.

My hands dig into her soft, luscious ass as I lift her into hardened, vicious thrusts that rattle her entire frame.

A small scream sounds from her throat, and I capture her lips in mine to savor much more of her essence and passion. I curse as everything tightens and boils within me, nearing its desperate release and I feel the same restlessness within her. "Come Blair," the harsh command sounds, as the ability to keep up my pace and hold back my release begins to diminish.

It is almost automatic. Her cry is thready, and filled with a beautiful anguish that expresses perfectly just how I feel. It seems as though everything in my body and life unravels, the storm of pleasure inside me exploding like fireworks.

She collapses onto me and it's quite a while before either of us feel the need, or are even able to move.

"Is it just me," I ask. "Or does every time with you just seem to get better?"

She shakes lightly in laughter, and it causes me to tighten my arms around her body, so she doesn't fall off. I'm almost drifting off to sleep when she reminds me of my earlier missed call. Since I'm reluctant to move, she peels herself off me, much to my protest. My cock slides out of her and the discharge that follows, spilling onto my thighs and the sofa, is so erotic that for a few moments I can only stare at it.

She soon returns with the phone.

I grab at her waist to pull her back to me. I unlock the screen and it's the Sheriff. The very sight of his name immediately drives away the bliss and contentment I was just experiencing, because it can only mean one thing; that my father has once again, stepped out of line.

CHAPTER FORTY-EIGHT

Blair

Watching Grady's face fall so drastically, is so disheartening to see.

And as I have come to learn now, this call could only mean his father is once again in some kind of trouble.

He listens quietly, nodding his head and then he says. "I hear you. I'll be right there." He ends the call and then stares straight ahead at nothing. He rises to his feet and begins to put his clothes on. Quietly.

I don't know what to say at first and don't want to intrude with questions, so I also gather my clothes and begin to dress myself.

"Blair, I have to go to Aurora," he says. "You can remain here if you want to, or go home. I'll give you a call later on."

"I'll go home," I say and turn to grab the remote so I can turn the television off. I'm then reminded of the movie we were in the midst of watching before we got preoccupied. I also remember the question he asked me earlier on.

What moves people?

An idea occurs to me, so without thought, I turn around to face him. "Let me go with you."

He is just about to head towards the front door when my words sound across the room. I know that I spoke lightly, but in the expansive space and given the delicacy of what I'm saying, my voice seems to have been amplified a hundred times.

"Thank you, but—"

"Grady, remember the movie we just watched? You never know. It seems unlikely but maybe there might be a difference if he sees you with me."

He studies me. "It's not that simple."

"Maybe," I say. "But maybe it is. My father was in the military too. I know what it's like to lose one and I don't think your father would want that to be the case for you. This might be a start and if it doesn't work, then you just brought your assistant along. Not much of a big deal there."

He releases a heavy sigh at my words, and then nods his head.

I almost don't believe he has agreed to it. Quickly, I get myself together and we exit the house.

About forty five minutes later, we arrive at the station and I walk in with Grady to bail out his father. I stand aside but I'm soon able to hear from the Sheriff as he speaks to Grady about what transpired.

Apparently, his father was rude to a woman in the store, pushing her roughly aside to get out of his way in one of the aisles. Her husband watched it happen and confronted

Grady's father, telling him to apologize. His father resulted to using his fists and at the end of the day, both men were severely bruised and injured. The woman's husband is insisting on pressing charges, especially at Grady's father's unapologetic behavior.

I watch as Grady goes silent at the information, and then looks towards the cell where his father is being held. A little while later, he comes over to me and we both turn to watch an older man released from the cell.

He has an ugly purplish bruise on the side of his face, disheveled hair, and stained clothes. He's limping just a bit and muttering curses under his breath. He stops the moment he sees Grady, and the both of them glare at each other without a word. Then his father turns and yells, "Mark! Why the fuck do you keep calling him? Is he paying you for this?"

"I wish he was Gary," the response comes. "I wish he was."

"They're going to press charges," Grady says to his father who is almost as tall as he is albeit slightly overweight.

"Let them do whatever the fuck they want," the older man snaps and heads out of the building.

I head over then but he more or less swats me out of the way without even caring who I am.

Grady holds on to me and I can see the concern in his face at letting me come along.

With a small rub down the side of his arm, I console him not to worry about me and to instead, focus on his father.

A few minutes later, we are all seated in Grady's car, and it's quiet.

Grady's gaze and attention is completely focused on the road as we drive, but I keep trying to sneak looks at his father through the rear view mirror.

He is staring outside the window, deep in thought. I want to ask if he's hungry so we can stop before anything else to get him some food, but between the father and the son, I don't know whom to address. I'm beginning to think that perhaps insisting on coming was a bad idea, when my gaze goes to the rear view mirror. It meets the eyes of Grady's father; cold and piercing just like his son's from our earliest encounters.

My reflex reaction is to take my eyes away but then I realize just how much of a bad move this is, especially since my intention is to establish some sort of rapport with him. So I send him a smile that I know is excruciatingly awkward.

He seems to be glaring at me so my gaze turns sheepish.

"Who are you?" he asks.

I feel a little jolt at his attention. I share a glance at Grady but his mood seems to be extremely sour. I don't think I'm going to be getting much help from him, so I just focus on his father. "I'm Grady's assistant. I mean uh- Mr. Abbott's assistant. It's a pleasure to meet you, sir." I've turned around to face him, but I don't bother offering my hand as it's very likely that he will not take it.

"You work on Sunday's too, Mr. Hotshot?" His father asks.

A snort escapes my lips before I can stop it.

Grady sends me a brief look of part confusion and betrayal.

I bite my lip to control my smile. I turn my face away from them both, but still sneakily try to meet his father's gaze in the rear view mirror.

He is still watching me intently, and his gaze no longer looks so cold anymore. "Where are you from?" he asks.

I clear my throat. "Houston, sir."

"So what are you doing out here?"

"My sister lives here. I came visiting and found the job at FireEye, so I decided to stay."

He continues to watch me but I'm not bold enough to hold that gaze, so I pull my eyes away and fix them on the road. Then I remember that I wanted to ask him if he had eaten. So I turn back around to face him, my heart beating a little too fast in my chest. "Do you want something to eat, sir?" I ask.

"You want to buy me a meal?" He asks.

I'm a bit stumped, as his tone is still somewhat harsh, so I'm not sure of the spirit in which the question is asked. "Um, of course, sir."

"Alright then, let's go. At least one person here as some manners."

My eyes widen in shock at the outright snide, and I see a muscle twitch in Grady's temple. Once again, I turn away to lower my head. I had expected their relationship to be much more hostile but more than anything, it seems as though his father is trying to get his attention, in the worst possible way.

CHAPTER FORTY-NINE

Grady

He demands we go to IHOP.

I immediately wonder at the impact on his liver but of course, no appreciation or ear will be given to me if I voice the concern so I keep my opinions to myself and just drive them to it.

I want to wait in the car so they both get what they want but when Blair turns around to see my intention, she hurries back.

“What are you doing? C’mon,” she says.

I shake my head. “Just get what you both want. I’ll wait here.”

She frowns at me. “I’m beginning to see what the problem is between you two. He’s trying to get your attention and you’re just proud enough to keep ignoring him.”

“What?” My face wrinkles. “What are you talking about?”

With a sigh, she pulls on the latch of the door. “Grady, get out of the car!”

Her gaze is fixed on mine.

At the rare defiance in her expression, I decide to concede.

We head towards the blue roofed building together and just before she goes in, I stop her briefly to ask. "How are you able to communicate with him?"

"It's easy," she says with a smile as she pulls the door open for me to get through. "He's not my dad, and I don't have an ego. Oh, and there's one more thing that we have in common."

My eyebrows arch in wait for her statement.

"We both have an innate desire to mock you, because no one else dares to."

My automatic response to her is amusement, but then when I realize that my father is probably watching us, I school my expression and return to being stoic.

"Wow," she says to me.

I ignore her. Soon, we are seated in a booth with Blair by my side and my father opposite her.

He really does look quite disheveled and battered and at the sunlight coming in through the window by his side, I can see just how sunken and exhausted he is. His gaze is the same one I've stared into for the past decade... almost blank and lifeless but I can't help but notice that today, with his attention solely on Blair, he looks just a little bit... awake.

"What kind of pancakes do you like?" he asks her.

"Hmm..." she peruses through the menu.

I think I already know what she is going to say.

"The taco pancake-paco."

For the first time in perhaps a decade, I watch a smile appear on his face. "We seem to have similar tastes."

I set my gaze on hers and I'm sure she can feel it burning through her skin. Although I don't say a word, it's quite interesting to watch the dynamics between them both. The waitress comes to take our orders with the both of them ordering the same taco pancakes, while I order what I know she will actually like which is the sweet blueberry pancake.

The pancakes are delivered soon enough and we all begin our meal quietly.

About halfway through however, my father suddenly speaks, "What's your name?"

"I'm Blair Tatum, sir," she replies.

At the mention of the name, something shadowy seems to pass across his graze. "Tatum?" he asks.

She nods as she chews on her pancake. "Yes, sir."

He lowers his head and continues with his food as though the name itself holds the key to every problem he has ever encountered.

I don't dwell too much on it, as I'm much more enthralled with seeing my father not act hostile for the first time in as long as I can remember.

Is it because he is exhausted? Or is it just because of Blair?

I turn to her, wondering what the connection is between them that has made him quite mellow or is it just because she's a woman?

"I used to know a Tatum," my father says, and then drains his bottle of water. "Simon Tatum. Great guy... but died young."

The conversation is becoming gloomy, and since it's beginning to drift towards his dark and unpleasant memories from his military service, I suspect that the somewhat peaceful camaraderie we have established is soon about to be extinguished.

"Simon? That was my father's name!"

Both my father and I turn to Blair at the sudden announcement.

"How can your father's name be Simon Tatum?" My father half growls at her.

She is a bit taken aback.

I put my fork down, completely unwilling to tolerate any hostility whatsoever from him to her.

Both of their gazes are drawn to the clink of my fork on the plate, and then I feel her hand on my thigh.

Her smile is bright and welcoming to him. "Life can have the strangest coincidences, sir."

He stares at her long and hard, and then cocks his head. "Was your father by any chance a soldier?"

I'm taken aback, and then I stare at her

Blair's eyes are nearly popping out of the sockets. "Yes, he was... how do you- You served with him?"

For the first time in my entire life, an emotion creeps into my father's eyes that I have never seen before. I've seen him angry, excited, and expressionless but what I have never seen in his eyes is pain.

He watches her tenderly, as though she is his own child, and then his eyes redden and fill with tears. Before those tears can drop however, he rises to his feet and walks out of the restaurant.

I'm thrown even more into a daze.

Blair turns to me, completely confused.

I also can't understand what is happening. Neither of us has much of an appetite to continue with our meals, so we both rise to our feet, pay the bill and exit the pancake shop. When I arrive at my parked vehicle and see that my father is not by it, I'm further worried.

I look around for him to no avail, so we get into the car. I have a suspicion so I drive slowly and pretty soon we find him walking in a daze down the street.

"Mr. Abbott," Blair calls out through the window.

I come to a stop on the side of the road.

She jumps out to get him. She goes close to him without any caution and touches his arm softly.

He looks up at her, listening quietly to her gentle coaxing to get into the car with us. He doesn't respond and just continues to stare at her, almost as though he has gone deaf and can't understand a single word.

I release the latch of my seatbelt and push the door open to get out.

Just then, it seems she has succeeded in getting him to come with her. Her hand is holding onto his arm and gently pulling him towards the passenger's door and he is complying.

He gets in, and we continue on our way.

The car is incredibly quiet as we drive back to his trailer in Aurora, but about halfway into the commute he speaks. "Your father," he says. "He passed away in 2010 right?"

A quick glance at her shows that she is looking at him through the rearview mirror.

"Yes, sir," she replies, clearly disconcerted.

"July tenth, two weeks before your sister's birthday."

She turns around fully then to face him, her face showing amazement. "How do you know all this? You knew my father?"

My father's sigh is heavy enough to collapse the roof of the vehicle. "I did," is his response. "I was the QRF Lieutenant Commander for his SEAL team."

CHAPTER FIFTY

Blair

There is very little currently going through my head. But a lot is happening in my heart. I feel confused, anxious and incredibly sad, all at the same time.

I try my hardest but it's difficult not to steal glances at the quiet broken man in the back seat.

He isn't looking at me anymore, not being bold, defiant, or even grumpy. He's just mellow, as though his soul has been sucked out of him.

Grady has also remained watchful and quiet throughout this entire meeting and at first, my suspicion was that it was because he had a strained relationship with his father, but now I'm not sure if things are this simple.

"Where do you live?" he asks in a quiet voice. "Let's get you home."

I lift my gaze to the rear view mirror once again. "Not at all," I reply waving my hands. "You're the one we came to get, sir. We'll get you home."

He watches me long and hard, so I ask what I want to while his eyes are on me. "I'd also really love to hear some stories about my father. We never really heard stories about his time in the military, so to know that you worked with him is quite amazing."

His gaze falters from mine as his hands intertwine on his lap. "Your father," he says, "was a great man. But I failed him. I failed all of them. My ego took down fourteen great men and irreversibly, wounded their families. And I'm alive to bear the torment of that grief forever."

Something grabs my heart at his words, and squeezes so hard that it becomes difficult to breathe. I turn to Grady, my gaze filled with questions that haven't even yet been formed in my brain.

He is attentive and briefly returns the glance before his attention goes back on the road, however his expression is unreadable.

"What happened?" I ask.

His father doesn't respond immediately, so I wait.

His countenance is dejected; his head hanging low and his shoulders drooping.

I can't even believe that this is the same man I met just barely an hour earlier, hollering and cursing at everything and everyone.

"I was their commander," he begins.

I hang onto every word.

"Seal team five. They were on a special reconnaissance mission across a mountain range in Afghanistan at the time, to gather information about a Taliban leader that had been killing military men and refugees. These were the most dangerous types of missions because they could only go in small numbers so there were just four of them." He inhales a deep, shaky breath and then his gaze turns to stare out of the window. He doesn't speak for a few minutes, as though he is preoccupied with reliving every single second of the ordeal. "Simon- your dad, Eaton, Jack and Steve. Their team was experienced, with the highest rate of reconnaissance success we had seen in over half a century. They understood and trusted each other, so when they went out in the field, they were in perfect synch. But then Jack messed up. I don't even remember what he did." He laughs.

The tone in his laugh is so bitter that it sends a chill through my body.

"That's what's the most funny about this because I don't even remember just exactly what he did but it pissed me off enough to replace him, the main sniper on the team with a twenty year old officer with barely any experience. I wanted to humiliate Jack and because of that, your father and fourteen others lost their lives."

I'm trembling and don't even realize it until I feel a hand cover mine. My hazy, tear filled eyes lift to meet Grady watching me again with that unreadable expression on his face.

I pull my hands away from his, uncomfortable and unhappy.

It is only then I realize that we have arrived. I look around me and see we are on an expansive plot, lined with trailers. Our vehicle is parked in front of one in particular with overgrown shrubs, and a pile of junk out in front. An abandoned, rotting car seat, rusted implements, and a broken trampoline.

The entire car is silent, and then his father speaks, "I'm sorry," he says. "That because of what I did, you had to grow up without your father. And even though I don't deserve it, seeing you work with Grady makes me breathe just a bit easier."

Before I can say a word in response, he pulls the latch on the door open and gets out of the car.

CHAPTER FIFTY-ONE

Grady

The moment the door is pulled open, Allen's face is filled with shock. "What are you doing here? On a Monday!"

"Well, you're not at work," I respond as I walk into his house, almost having to push him aside since he has forgotten to invite me in.

He shuts the door behind him and turns around to face me.

I'm a bit surprised by how different he looks from his usually suited appearance at the office. His hair is disheveled and caked with something white which I suspect is an incident from feeding time with his toddler. All he has on is a pair of shorts and a grey T-shirt. He's barefoot, unshaven and his eyes seem bloodshot. He however looks relaxed and happy

For a moment, I envy him.

Suddenly, there's a shriek resounding through the house and it startles him. With a groan, he turns to hurry towards the kitchen with a flap of his hand at me to come with him. "My master calls," he says.

With a smile, I stroll behind him.

By the time I arrive in the kitchen, I see that he has settled down on one of the stools at the counter, and before him in a high chair is his pudgy, adorable baby, Alexa. I haven't seen her in almost a year, so I take a seat on the stool beside him to watch her. Her cheeks are soaked with tears, while her mouth and bib are stained with the pudding like meal he is feeding her.

"Here we go," he says in a playful voice, complete with sound effects and as a result, yet another spoonful is accepted into her mouth. He does this for about a minute and then places the spoon down to turn to me. "She's been running a small fever since yesterday, so she's been restless. But things are calming down now. What's up? Everything okay?"

I nod in response.

He narrows his gaze at me before turning to pick up a small bottle of water to place in his daughter's mouth. "I can't have my full attention on you but I can listen," he says

An easy silence floats across the room for a while before I speak up, "Blair didn't come to work today."

He glances at me, a bit surprised to hear this. "Why? Is everything okay?"

"I received her text this morning, and all she said was that she wasn't feeling very well. But I doubt that she'll come in tomorrow either."

He turns his full attention to me now, so I fill him in on what happened between her and my father the previous day.

For the first time ever, I watch Allen get stunned into silence. "Are you serious right now?"

I cross my arms and lean against the counter. "I'm just as shocked as you are. From the moment we left my father's place till when we arrived at her house, she didn't say a single word.

"And then this morning she calls to tell you that she's not coming in."

"She didn't call. She sent a text."

"Well, maybe she just needs a day to process all of this. That's pretty normal isn't it?"

"Perhaps," I reply, a little forlorn knowing his response is not exactly what I want to hear, but aware that it's the only one he can give with his still limited knowledge of the depth of the relationship between Blair and me. I contemplate whether to share this with him, truly at my wits end on how to proceed with the current complications.

"There are some things though that I still don't understand from your father's story," Allen says. "How did the other fourteen men get involved in the mission? Wasn't it just the four that were sent in?"

"Blair's father was finally able to find the signal to contact the base for help. After that, a helicopter was sent after them with other soldiers on board. But as they neared the mountains, they were shot down from the sky."

"My God," Allen says quietly. He returns to feeding his daughter, but soon has another question for me, "Why does your father think that he is responsible for this? None of the men from the original team returned alive right?"

"Right, and I asked him that when I returned to his place after dropping Blair off. He said that during that last call, the report he got was that '*Laine lost his footing and tumbled down the mountain. His gun went off. We're fucked.*' He was the kid that he sent in place of Jack, so he gathered that the mistake of doing that put the others in jeopardy."

"But that is just speculation is it not? Anyone amongst the original team members could have also lost their footing or dozed off."

"Maybe, but bearing this guilt and carrying it like a cross is the only way that he can continue to live with himself, otherwise he might have long ago committed suicide."

Allen's sigh is heavy. "Did you know anything prior to this?"

"I did not. I found out at the same time Blair did, and it's finally made me realize what had been eating him up for the last decade."

"Wow," he says and rises to his feet. We are both silent as he processes all that I have just said to him. He cleans his daughter's mouth from all the smeared food, and takes off her bib. Then he heads over to the sink with the used plates and quickly rinses them off.

I have now locked eyes with his baby and it's fascinating just how huge and blue her irises are. She is indeed striking and her eyes remind me of another set of deep green eyes that I truly want to look into.

Allen comes over to lift his baby into his arms, and we head over to one of his living rooms. There, he puts her on the carpet in her play corner and she proceeds to keep herself busy with the blocks of toys around.

I'm already seated on one of the sofa's, so he comes over to join me on it. He watches me for a brief moment before speaking again, "All of this is truly shocking and I can especially understand that Blair would feel quite disconcerted. Do you want me to contact her on your behalf?"

I'm not sure what to say to this, so I just stare blankly at him.

He then pulls his phone out of his shorts.

My reaction is immediate. "No!" I jump to my feet.

Allen looks startled by the outburst. "Wha- What's wrong?"

I withdraw my outstretched hands and slip them back into my pocket. I can't exactly return to my seat, so I just hold his gaze.

"Grady, what's going on? Do you want me to contact her or not? Isn't it your concern that she might be taking things too hard and you want to find out how she's doing?"

"Yeah." I nod.

"So, what's the problem?"

"I think I should be the one to do it."

He seems confused. "Then what's stopping you? Is it because the both of you aren't close?"

I keep staring at him and then I see the moment that something clicks in his mind.

"You have a thing for her?"

My expression is of exhaustion.

"You have a thing for her!"

I return to the seat with the mind to deny this, but not a single protest comes to mind, so I just plaster a frown on my face and focus my gaze on his baby.

"Oh God! When did this happen?" His eyes are bright with excitement and wonder. "Wait? You both saw your father yesterday. What was she doing with you on a Sunday? And why were both of you with your father? Even I've never met your father. Hell, I didn't even know you had one and I've known you for almost a decade."

I don't think I have to respond to any of this as he is going to pretty much figure it all out. So I lean into the tan leather sofa with a sigh.

"Grady!"

"Fine," I groan. "We're not dating but..."

"You're just sleeping together?" His tone is disappointed.

"This started before she ever came to the office. We met at a bar the weekend before, and hooked up. And then the next Monday you bring her in as my secretary? I was fucking shocked."

Allen's mouth falls open. "What?" He then looks away to think and then his eyes widen with amazement. "So that was why... was that why you immediately rejected her? And then she..." He rises to his feet. "She was shocked too, but I thought- how did she manage to convince you then? She came in alone to talk to you right? What did you say? Why did you hire her?"

I cannot help but smile at the reminder. "She threatened to sue me."

"What? Blair?"

"Yup," I reply. "Your ball of sunshine is actually a lethal piranha."

"What the fuck did she want to sue you for?"

"Wrongful termination of employment."

"What employment? She hadn't officially gotten the job then."

"You'd verbally promised it to her after the interview. You made the offer and she accepted it."

"That couldn't have been proven."

"It didn't matter, I wanted her around anyway. Her wit was more than an excuse."

His smile is broad and full of glee. "I can't believe it. It worked out perfectly. I didn't even need to be involved. And here I thought my efforts had crashed and burned."

"Well, they might have. My father's twist has landed the biggest blow. For all I know, she might have even left town."

"She wouldn't do that," Allen says.

A part of me believes him. But then another part fully expects her to, unsure that our connection is strong enough to survive the recent revelations. "Well, I hope so."

Silence punctuates our thoughts.

Then he asks, "Should I call her, or should you?"

"I'll call her," I respond. "But not now. Later in the evening."

CHAPTER FIFTY-TWO

Blair

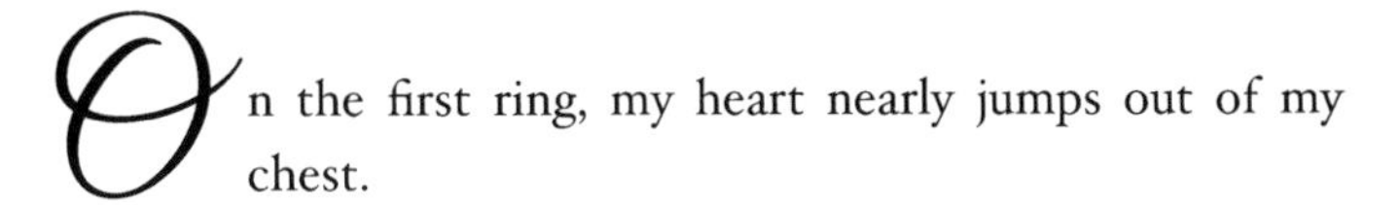

On the first ring, my heart nearly jumps out of my chest.

My phone is all the way on my bed, while I'm in the closet packing up the clothes I've accumulated over my short time here in Denver. It was originally meant to be just a weekend trip to see Layne but yet things escalated into so much more. So much more that I'm still unable to properly process very much.

I don't bother going over to the phone to check who is calling, because I fear who it is and at the same time, I'm afraid of who it is not. It disconnects and I continue with folding my clothes into my luggage.

The memories of my father come to mind- the one person that was always on my side. And it stings my eyes with tears. I have pictures of him I have always carried with me. The first half of the day was spent going through them and reliving the excruciating grief I had gone through as an eleven year old, mourning her father.

And to now find out according to Grady's father's confession, that it could have been avoided, I truly don't know the right reaction to have. All I know is that there is a heavy weight in my heart. All the held back tears from over the years, from the minutes and hours of missing him, have finally been given the permission to flow today.

The phone rings again.

I ignore it, a frown permanently etched to my face as I fold my clothes.

On the third ring, Layne comes into the room. She is surprised to see me on the floor, surrounded by my clothes and my phone being purposely ignored. "I thought you were in the bathroom or something. Why aren't you picking up?"

Without waiting for a response, she goes over to the bed to lift the phone. "Grady Abbott," she reads. "Isn't this your boss?"

My stomach does a little flip at the mere mention of his name, but I don't respond.

She comes over and realizes what I'm doing. She gazes at the pile on the floor, and the half-filled luggage. Her voice is smaller when she speaks again, "What's going on?"

"I think I'm going to take a little break. Go back to Houston for a while to see if I can put my feet on the ground over there."

"That doesn't sound like a little break to me. What happened?"

I don't respond.

"Why are you leaving Denver? Did something happen at work? With your boss?"

I pause my folding then, and gaze up at her. I haven't yet told her about Gary's revelation to our father's history in the military, and I wonder if it's necessary to tell her, but without that, I will not be able to explain why I'm seriously considering leaving. So I turn around to face her and fold my legs underneath me. "Where's Matthew?" I ask.

"He went out to grab some snacks from the store."

"Okay. Sit down or something."

She heads over to my bed and sits on the edge, her face filled with concern. "What happened?"

I then narrate to her all that Grady's father said and just as I expect, she's speechless.

Then her eyes fill with tears and she turns her face away.

I allow her the time that she needs until she's ready to speak to me.

"Wow, I can't believe it. He's your boss's father. Is this why you want to leave?"

"It's part of it," I respond.

"Why? What's the relation?"

I'm a bit taken aback by her comment. "He caused dad's death."

"You don't know that. And dad was a Navy Seal. His missions were dangerous and he could have been killed anytime."

"He also could have lived," I argue, upset at her words.

She realizes this and goes quiet. "Okay," she says. "Maybe it was your boss's father's fault, but what does that change now?"

I turn to her. "Nothing. Absolutely nothing. But is it decent that I continue to work for the son of the man whose actions killed my father?"

"You're not just working for him. You're also building a path for yourself and you've told me that his company is a golden opportunity to do that. Dad wouldn't be happy if you gave that up."

I'm perplexed. "How is this so simple to you?"

"Why isn't it to you?" She shoots back... then she stops. Her eyes bore into mine and she straightens. "Ah, I get it. You have feelings for your boss. Are you two involved now?"

I turn away from her, feeling exposed, but truthfully, I can't even trace the true source of my anger. All I know is that I'm furious at Grady, at his father, at myself, at Layne and at life in general and how fucking sucky and unfair it is.

"Blair," she calls. "Talk to me. What's the problem?"

I erupt in a scream at her, tears bursting from my eyes. "His father fucking killed Dad! How the hell am I supposed to have anything to do with him?"

She watches me ever so calmly. "His father," she says. "His father made the mistake, not him. Or wait? Is all of this connected? Him meeting and hiring you? Has he known about it from the very beginning?"

My eyes widen slightly in amazement. That hadn't even crossed my mind. "No, I don't think so. I met him at the bar, remember, and... he wasn't the one that invited me for the interview."

"Sure, but doesn't your burrito boss get his instructions from him? Maybe your boss told him to hire you."

I ponder more on the speculation. "That can't be. I got the call before we went out that weekend. Before I met him at the bar."

"What does that have to do with anything? Maybe he didn't even know your face but was just aware of the story. "

"I don't think that's it, Layne. He seemed just as shocked as I was when I came into the office for the first time."

"Alright," she says, "then let's move on. If you're involved with him and you think based on this revelation, you can't continue to do that then why don't you put an end to it and just continue on with your job?"

"Is it really that easy? He owns the company."

"Okay," she says. "Then look for another job. Or don't you like living in Denver?"

I hear the unhappiness in her tone and finally understand what she is dreading. I release a heavy sigh. "Layne, I don't mind living here, and I don't mind living in Houston either but I was beginning to love it here because of you. The problem is that I just don't know if I'll be able to move on and heal from this if I'm here. I will definitely come back. I'm not going to miss being around my niece for anything in the world which is why I'm thinking that maybe this is the best way. Leaving for a little while to get my perspective and emotions in order, and then returning to start anew."

She nods. "I understand what you mean."

"It might be a week or two or more, but I don't want to wallow and I feel as though if I remained here, then that is all that I'll do."

"You're right but... what about him? Will he care that you left?"

I feel an ache in my heart but force myself to ignore it. "He probably won't. It's not as if we were in a relationship or something." I continue with my packing.

Layne rises from the bed. She comes over to me and wraps her arms around me for a hug which I reluctantly lean into.

I hold on tightly to her locked hands and almost wish that she would never let go. The tears once again fall from my eyes and wet her arms. "It still feels like it just happened," I managed to croak out. "Like we just lost him."

"I know," she says. "I feel it too. When you love someone and lose them, you'll most likely cry forever. But don't let it overwhelm you Blair and definitely do not let it completely affect the present."

I pull away and wipe the tears off my face. "I know," I respond. "I know. I'll be fine."

With a kiss to my forehead, she turns and exits the room.

CHAPTER FIFTY-THREE

Grady

I have arrived, Sir. I'll wait till you're done with your meeting.

I'm in the conference room when her text arrives on my phone and from that moment onwards, my attention is completely removed from the room full of executives. I consider just leaving the meeting in order to settle things with her, to receive the answers I need, so I can move on with the rest of my life.

But despite my agitation, I can't get myself to rise from the chair. My heart is apprehensive as I suspect that not the very best news awaits me. For one, she didn't resume her normal time and instead, informed me she would be coming in later on to speak to me. If that is not the sign of trouble then I don't know what is.

After the meeting, I take my time speaking with the executives and only when I'm finally done, do I quietly head back up to my floor.

I recall the days of walking together with her, discussing projects and schedules as I realize just how accustomed to them I became. Now, the previously quiet commutes and ambience that once used to comfort me, no longer seems as desirable.

I get into the office and just as I expect, she's seated at her desk and waiting. She rises to her feet in greeting and I respond with a nod before heading to my office. I'm certain now that she is specifically here to torment me because somehow, she seems to have become more beautiful in the last two days. Her hair isn't falling down her back as usual but is secured in a tight ponytail to the back of her head. Then her dress, patterned with little grey and white flowers is molded to her curves, stopping just below her knee and revealing the smooth, glistening skin of her legs. Her makeup is minimal, her lips peach and plump, and her gaze piercing.

She's no longer looking at me with the timidness of an employee.

I can't help but sigh. After settling down behind my desk, I lock my hands together and face her fully.

She walks forward and places a letter on the table.

I don't need to look at it to see what it is.

Then she begins her speech, "Sir, I truly appreciate the opportunities that I have been awarded here, especially the privilege of working as your personal assistant, but I think it's time for me to move on."

I don't miss the slight tremble in her tone.

She goes on, "I will properly assign my project before I leave so the clients will be thoroughly taken care of."

"Sir?" I say. "You're handing in your resignation and you're calling me sir? As if there's nothing more between us? Or do you plan to break the news in private to me later on and then call me by my name?"

She doesn't respond and the silence between us stretches endlessly. She does however hold my gaze and I can see the redness and slight dampness in her eyes.

"I truly apologize for this. I didn't know that things would turn out this way but they have and I need the time away to sort it out."

"Then take a leave," I snap. "Why are you quitting? Is it because you got the job so easily, so it can just as easily be of no value to you?"

Her eyes widen in alarm at the statement. "Nothing has changed for you since Sunday has it? The fact that your father was responsible for my father's death... it doesn't mean much to you, does it?"

I don't have a response.

"Well, Grady, it means a lot to me and because of that I don't want anything to do with you or your father. Because your presence in my life will always remind me that it came at the cost of my father's life. You can have your own opinion about this stance and I don't care. I am entitled to be hurt and furious and to deal with this in the way that I want to." With that, she turns around, and walks away.

I watch her, but then at the last moment I jump to my feet. "What about us?" I ask.

She halts, and inclines her head to the side to glance at me. "What 'us'? You made it clear from the very beginning that there can't be an us. You said you don't do relationships. Remember? Or do you think that after this, I'm still going to subject myself to not even being worthy enough in your eyes to be committed to?" With a glare, she continues on her way and slams the door behind her.

I remain standing in that spot for a long time, refusing to take a seat until I make some sort of plan... until the turmoil currently wreaking havoc in my chest is sorted out.

When I eventually decide, I grab my phone and hurry out of the office.

I dismiss Andrew and get behind the wheel myself.

About an hour later, I arrive at my father's trailer home and meet him weeding out the overgrown shrubs in his tiny yard out front. This is a first, by this time he's usually sitting in front of his television with some liquor in hand.

I stand behind him for a while and neither of us speaks.

"I owe you an apology," he suddenly begins. "I didn't have the courage to admit it but I realize now that I didn't really want you to join the military because I believed it was the most noble of pursuits. It was because the guilt that I thought I could carry was killing me, and I was looking for a way out. To somehow ease my conscience and the only way I could think of was offering you to the military with the buried and twisted hope that perhaps something would happen to you. And you would die a hero. Then as a result, those fathers, sons and brothers that I snatched from their families would somehow be appeased, because I had offered up my own son to serve and lost him too. Instead, you went your own way and I lost my bargaining chip. And I resented you for it." His laugh is bitter.

I'm seething, with anger and frustration and a deep seated sadness for the father that I had lost a long time ago and for the woman that I'm about to lose.

"I am one hell of a man aren't I? I sacrifice the life of my unit for my ego and then I am just as eager to sacrifice the life of my own son to ease my conscience. I should have taken my life a long time ago."

"Yeah," I reply. "You should have."

He goes still, the hand holding a hoe stopping in midair.

"I just turned twenty when you were discharged and more than at any other time in life, I needed you then. To guide me and direct me and to support me. But instead, you did all you could to push me down a path that I had no business going down and when I didn't conform to that, you made me feel like shit and more or less disowned me. You left me alone, to find my way on my own and I did just that. But even afterwards, you still couldn't celebrate me, when the world did. After all the shit I went through to make something of myself, strangers patted me on my shoulder, instead of my own father. I have wished a million times that I could completely look away from your existence but I'm not as cold blooded as you are, so when you've needed help I have always made myself available."

He went utterly silent.

"But today, I want to make something clear to you; I don't want your apology and I don't suddenly want any sort of concern from you. What I want right now is for you to fix the damage that you have done. The woman you spilled your guts to, she matters to me. I don't know how much yet but I suspect that it's going to be a whole lot, so the last thing I want to do is lose her. I don't care if you have to get on your knees to beg her. I don't care if you even offer your head to appease her, but you're going to get her back. She now wants nothing to do with me and I won't allow you to once again take away someone that means the world to me. If you don't somehow fix this, then I just might kill you with my own hands and I swear it. And don't think either that I need to be a Navy Seal to know how to do that effortlessly. I'm giving you today. After today, your conscience isn't what you should be afraid of anymore. In fact, maybe you should even be relieved because it will be gone, along with you."

With that, I turn around and storm back to my car.

CHAPTER FIFTY-FOUR

Blair

"I'm going to miss you, Blair."

I smile at the saddened tone as I park my luggage by the front door. "I'll be back." I turn to her. "At least, by your seventh month. There's no way I'm letting you go through those last two months alone, especially when Matthew might not be here."

"Alright," she says. "Do you have everything?"

"Yeah, except my purse, flats and belt. They're on my bed. I'll go get them." With that, I hurry away just as the doorbell rings.

I grab the remaining things I have in the room and head back out into the living room. My soul nearly leaves my body however when I see who's standing at the door.

Grady's father removes his hat from his head.

For a second, I have to confirm if he's even the same person. The last time I met him, he had been beyond disheveled and dirty, his clothes in tatters, his white beard overgrown and unkempt, but right now the man before me looks like a completely different person. His head is completely shaved, his beard neatly trimmed, and he has on a clean pair of jeans and a black dress shirt.

"Can I come in?" he asks.

Layne looks at me with the questions in her eyes.

"You can," I reply. "Layne, this is my ex-boss's father."

"Oh," she replies. "Hello. Good morning."

"Good morning," he replies. "This is your sister?"

"Yes, she is," I respond

His smile is sad. "Your father used to talk about you both all the time. She is the one that used to call you blah, I suppose?"

Tears sting my eyes. How the hell did he know that?

Even Layne looks startled to her core. She leads him to the living room.

"Can I get you something to drink?" I ask. "Tea? Water? Juice?"

"Just water will be fine," he replies.

As I fetch it for him, my mind goes into overdrive wondering why in the hell he could possibly be here. Perhaps to offer some sort of condolence? Perhaps on behalf of Grady?

With a shuddering exhale, I take the glass over and offer it to him. Then I stand by Layne who is seated in the armchair as we both watch him take a sip.

He looks at the both of us and gives a heartfelt smile. “I’m sure that I’m not exactly welcome here,” he says “But I couldn't stop myself from coming. For one, Grady threatened my life if I didn't come over to fix the damage I have caused between the both of you.”

My heart drops into my stomach.

“He’s in love with you, you know,” he says. “I don’t know if you realize it and I don’t know if he does either, but there is a connection between you both that I have never seen him have with anyone.”

I shift my weight from one leg to the other, as I feel Layne’s gaze settle on me.

“Anyway,” he continues. “I want to formally apologize to the both of you. Everyone I have told my story to has tried to console me, that the accident was not my fault and that any of the other soldiers could have slipped or gotten into some sort of trouble but I have never agreed to accept that way out. And I don’t think I ever will. It is my cross to bear and I will continue to carry it. But I will be damned if I let this also affect Grady. I’ve hurt him and neglected him over the years and the last thing that I want is for me to do it all over again with this revelation. When the accident happened, I went to all of the soldier’s families to deliver the news of their loved ones demise. I saw them break down in tears and be torn apart by the pain, and I soaked it all in. I remember visiting your home and I met your mother. I didn’t meet either of you then but I knew of you as your father carried your pictures in his wallet. I handed them over to her then. I also have one of the both of us during one of our happier times at our base. I thought that maybe you’d like to have it. It was one of his absolutely enthralling moments of just pure joy. He was laughing as we drank together and I've kept it to myself all these years to remember him by. But I think it's time to hand it over." He reaches into his pocket and retrieves the small envelope then passes it over.

I accept it. I open the envelope and indeed, see a somewhat wrinkled picture of my father, along with a few of his military buddies. There are guns all around them, and in his hand is a bottle of beer lifted to his lips. There is also the very familiar and contagious smile across his face.

Quietly, both Layne and I study the picture with a sad smile, then we put it away, so we can pay attention to him.

"I only a-apologized to your mother back then," he says, "But today, I want to apologize to the both of you. I'm incredibly sorry from the bottom of my heart for what my ego cost your family. I do not expect you to forgive me but I do hope that you will gain some sort of solace from the fact that I am tormented by it every single second of my life. Blair," he calls to me.

I drag my gaze to him.

"Please don't abandon Grady because of me. I am the one who committed these wrongs, but he is completely innocent. I deserve your hate and rejection but he doesn't, so I hope that you will be able to look past the misfortune of him having me for a father."

I look away from him.

He rises to his feet. After a deep bow to the both of us, he replaces his hat on his head and exits our home.

After he closes the door behind him, Layne and I are quiet for a very long time.

And then she turns to me. "Are you still going to leave?"

I turn my gaze towards my packed luggage at the entrance to the house and release a heavy sigh.

"It all depends on Grady, I guess."

CHAPTER FIFTY-FIVE

Grady

"*I heard you might be in love with me.*"

I have a cigarette between my lips and at her words, it is quite easy to forget this fact. So it isn't until I'm almost choking to death at the smoke, do I remember to take it out of my mouth.

"Grady," she calls through the receiver. "Are you okay?"

I throw the butt across the counter and take deep breaths. "I'm fine," I reply. "I'm fine."

"I'm at your front desk," she says. "Can you tell them to let me in?"

My heart slams into my chest. "You're here? Right now?"

"Yeah, I-is that okay?"

Is she joking? "Of course. Sure. I'll tell them to let you in right now." I immediately place the call to the front desk, and hurry to my front door to wait for her. I pace in front of it a bit and then decide to just go to the elevator. A few minutes later, it dings its arrival and the double doors slide open.

“Hey,” she says

“Hey,” I respond.

She then looks to the elevator’s control board. “I asked for a key.”

My brows furrow at her. A day ago, she was telling me that she would be quitting her job and now, she’s back here asking for a key?

She notices my surprised gaze and slips her hands into her pocket. “Your dad came over to see me and my sister today. He apologized... for everything and told me not to leave.”

I’m taken aback at her words. “You were going to leave town?”

She nods.

My blood begins to simmer in anger. With a glare at her, I turn around and head back towards the apartment. I make sure to leave the door wide open so she isn’t locked out, and head over to the kitchen.

It smells like cigarettes and she immediately notice’s this the moment she comes in. “Have you been smoking?”

I retrieve a bottle of water from the refrigerator without responding, and just watch her as I down the water.

She however comes over without a care and sits on one of the island stools. “What are you angry about?” she asks. “That I was going to leave? I came to your office yesterday to quit.”

"But you didn't mention anything about leaving," I retort. "You were just going to disappear without a word?"

"Grady," she says. "The kind of relationship we have is the kind where I don't have to tell you the things I'm doing. No strings attached remember?"

Fuck, she's right.

"Anyway, I'm here to tell you that I'll still be leaving for a little while. Just to clear my head, away from here. But I'll be back. So I don't want you to think that I'm just completely disappearing as originally planned. But when I come back and if you're still interested in me then I'd love to give us a chance. A real chance at truly being together and not just sleeping together. This is my offer, so think about it. You can let me know your response at any time." With this, she sends a soft smile and gets up from the stool. She begins to come around the counter and when she reaches me, she places a hand on my arm and it seems to burn through the shirt that I have on.

"I used to be so intimidated by that look on your face," she says. With a lift to the tip of her toes, she presses a kiss to the side of my face. "Bye Grady, and don't be so harsh on your father. He already has a lot of demons to deal with." With that, she turns around.

Before I can stop myself, my hand reaches out to grab her. "Don't go," I say, my voice quieter than I've ever heard.

"Why she asks," and turns around.

My gaze is looking so directly into her eyes in this moment.

"Why? Because I'm fucking in love with you Blair"

"Oh Grady, you have no idea how long I've wished to hear those words. I really thought that I didn't mean enough for you to commit to me" she responds.

"I'm truly sorry Blair if I hurt you and I guess I've known it for some time but with the mess with my father and me being such a stubborn A-hole I couldn't admit to myself the truth."

" My bags were packed and I really thought that you would let me go Grady but I am so glad you haven't because I truly love you." I pull her into the tightest embrace and we just hold each other in complete silence. When we finally let go I see the tears of joy in her face and use my thumb to brush them away.

"I don't smoke," I tell her. "At least I haven't in a while. I needed it today to calm myself because... I have this assistant that drives me crazy."

She looks at me. "She sounds like a tool."

"She is, but I also don't know how the fuck I could ever function without her now and that is the strangest thing I've ever heard myself say. I think she did something to me."

She laughs softly. "I think she did."

"Grady," she breathes my name as I wrap my arms underneath her ass and lift her feet clear off the floor. In no time, her legs are wrapped around my waist, her arms around my shoulders and her lips are entangled with mine. I take her straight to my bedroom, and the moment she sinks into the soft mattress I begin to trace kisses across every inch of her skin.

I'm trembling with excitement at the impending bliss of once again being joined with her.

My lips suck hard on her beautiful breasts. It sends her hands digging into the mattress as she writhes beneath me. "Grady," she gasps when my lips begin to trace down her stomach and in no time, is at the center of her desire. My tongue, fingers and lips devour her mercilessly and by the time the orgasm hits her, she nearly pulls my hair off my scalp.

My thrust into her is just as vicious and urgent as the other times but this time around, my motion is not the usual, and almost a frantic rhythm solely directed at the chase of a release. No, this time, I go slow, driving my cock with precision in and out of her, and it sends her eyes rolling into the back of her head. I find the spot inside of her that drives her wild and inclining my hips, send my cock grating through her slick sensitive walls, hitting that spot over and over again.

The clench of her sex around my hard cock with it's slickness and scent solely of her, messes with my coherence.

"Grady," she screams into the quiet space, her voice and harsh breathing and quiet sobs bouncing off the walls.

There's a wide smile across my face and a contentment in my heart that I never believed possible. I pull her into my arms. "You are the most beautiful woman I've ever made love to. "

She kisses me, deeply and passionately.

With this heartfelt action, I know that a future with Blair will be bliss.

EPILOGUE

Blair

One Year Later

"So? How is it?"

"Allen, you need to let her swallow first," Grady says.

Amused, I chew on the huge piece of the green chili smothered burrito, garnished with swirls of shredded cheese, beans, and beef tucked into the tortilla wrap. The flavors burst in my mouth and although I know Allen is waiting, his gaze is sparkling with excitement at what my comment will be, I take my time in responding.

His wife, Meredith is amused at the both of us as she rocks her baby in her arms, and at our never ending comparisons between the Tex-Mex and the smothered chili.

Today and finally, he is getting the chance to wow me and put the argument of which is the better burrito to rest.

He should know however, that I'm not going to concede so easily. The bite is like an orgasm in my mouth, but I try all I can to keep a straight face, much to Grady's amusement.

He's a small distance away from me with Alexa in his arm, and the other grilling our carefully marinated chicken. He is the one who suggested this early evening poolside gathering with family- himself and Allen's family and of course, Layne's but they are yet to arrive.

I eventually swallow the burrito and calmly brush my hair across my shoulder.

"I know that look," Allen says. "You're about to lie."

Grady's laughter resounds from across the garden.

I can't help but yell out at him. "Stop, he's going to think I'm actually lying."

"You can't do that, it's foul play," Allen accuses. "And for fuck's sake, can you just admit that Denver's burrito beats Texas's, hands down."

"I won't," I shake my head and rise to my feet. With a smile, I start to walk away but then remember my plate.

Allen however, has already grabbed it.

I snatch it back from him before he can eat it. "That's mine, sir," I say.

He scowls at me, much to his wife's amusement.

I can't wait for us to be done with dinner, so we can all take a dip in the penthouse's pool. It's an especially beautiful evening with the space overlooking the setting sun and Denver's panoramic skyline. I give Grady a quick kiss when I get to him and quickly mutter my truth, "That is the best damn burrito I've ever had in my life."

He laughs out and readily accepts the bite that I give to him.

"What did she say Grady?" Allen calls out. "She admitted it didn't she?"

"Nope, she says it tastes terrible."

I kiss him again for the support and continue with my plate as he grills his chicken.

"Alexa, go over to your mom," he says and lets the little girl down.

I watch her go, my heart filled to bursting at her unstable steps as she returns to her parents. Then my eyes light up when I see that Layne and her husband have arrived.

Grady puts his tongs down, and then retrieves something from his pocket. "I'm thinking of telling Allen the truth," he says.

I turn from waving at my sister, as I'm shocked at the threat of betrayal. "What?"

"It all depends on how you respond to what I'm about to ask you."

I know he's playing with me, but I also know him well enough to realize he is also deadly serious at the same time and just a bit nervous. I also note the little rooftop garden has gone quiet, so I turn to see that both Allen, Meredith, along with Layne are watching us with wide smiles on their faces. "What's going on..." I pause as my gaze drops downward.

My heart is in my throat at the sight before me. "Oh, my God!" A half scream leaves my lips.

Grady is on his knee and in his hand is an opened box, revealing a sparkling diamond ring.

I can't breathe. "Grady?"

"Blair," he says. "I never expected you and I didn't even know that I needed you. But this past year with you in my life, has brought me happiness that I didn't even know was possible. Please do me the honor of marrying me? I love you from the depths of my soul, and I promise to do my very best to show this to you every single day for the rest of my life."

My eyes burn with such tears that I can barely see him. Until I blink and they come rolling down my cheeks. I nod my head, unable to speak.

The cheers erupt seemingly from everywhere.

He rises back to his feet, slips the beautiful ring onto my finger, and pulls me into his arms for the warmest, most loving hug.

"Yes," I respond, finally able to speak. "Yes. Yes. Yes I'll marry you. I love you Grady, with all my heart."

He pulls away from me, his eyes sparkling.

" You're the single greatest thing that ever happened to me Blair."

I crush my lips to his.

"To forever," Meredith calls out from the table.

"To love," Layne calls out.

"To telling the truth," Allen toasts.

Grady and I get lost in each other.

The End.

COMING SOON...

Forbidden Touch

Chapter One
Brooke

"Can you believe that we have finally done it?" I asked my best friend, Blaze. We stood in the middle of the moldy smelling living room and stared at the two-family home townhouse that now belonged to us.

"Yep, I do," Blaze said. "Were those cracks there last week?" he asked wrinkling his nose at the peeling walls.

I closed the distance between us and placed my hands on his massive shoulders. I stared at Blaze fondly then wrapped my hands around his neck and hugged him. Having a house was my dream, not his, but he had agreed to partner with me in buying the dilapidated town home.

The clincher had been that after we finish renovating it, we would each have an apartment. Mine would be on the top floor and Blaze would take the ground floor one. With our combined savings and a gift of fifty thousand worth of bonds from my late grandmother, we had done it.

Now, all that remained was to start working on it.

"Thank you Blaze," I mumbled into his shirt. He smelled so good. I didn't want to break contact but I had to. I'd been fighting my physical attraction to Blaze for years. He was my best friend and my secret crush. One that I would never act upon. I reluctantly stepped away. "I can't wait to get started," I told him, rubbing my hands together in anticipated glee.

"Me too," Blaze said.

"Let's go sit on the backyard steps and have our lunch."

We had bought takeout grilled chicken sandwiches and bottles of water to toast to our new home. I grabbed Blaze by the hand and tugged him through the kitchen to the back.

Turning the key, I pushed the door open. The backyard had been part of the reason why I had fallen in love with the town house. It was unkempt with overgrown grass and bushes but the potential was there. I could imagine Saturday afternoons spent outdoors sipping ice-cold wine and watching the day drift by. With Blaze in the downstairs apartment, it meant I would always have someone to hang out with.

This had a downside to it though. Blaze could decide to live with a girlfriend. Luckily, there was little risk of that happening. He changed girlfriends the way people changed clothes. Blaze was your textbook player, though he insisted he was a short-term one-woman man.

I'd come prepared and I had a small blanket in my handbag which I laid on the dirty steps and we sat down.

"Now, this, I can visualize the end result," Blaze said as he reached for a sandwich and bit into it.

His words excited me and made me feel less guilty about pushing him into buying a house with me.

"Yeah, a beautiful lawn with flower gardens at the edges and maybe a table and some chairs," he said.

"That right there, is why you're still my best friend," I exclaimed.

Blaze and I had met in kindergarten. We rode the same school bus and I had always found him in the very back seat when I entered the bus in the morning. He had smiled at me the first day and then looked away.

On the way home, I'd gone to sit with him and we had chatted all the way to my stop, counting all the white cars we saw. Even then, I'd been drawn to him but all we had ever been was friends. Which was a good thing, I told myself firmly.

There were times when I'd allowed myself to imagine Blaze as my boyfriend. He was hot and all my friends had had a crush on him at one time or another. But even in my fantasies, the relationship ended badly. I loved Blaze too much to jeopardize what we had.

"I'm the luckiest guy in the whole world," Blaze said.

"Why?" I asked as I watched the movements of his mouth. Blaze had to be the only guy I knew who made chewing look sexy.

"I get to have lunch with my best friend every day!" he said and smiled.

In addition to being best friends, Blaze and I worked for the same recruiting company. He was a head recruiter, in charge of five other recruiters and I was in the accounts department. We'd worked together for two years now, and the worries I'd had when he suggested that I apply for the opening, had not materialized.

I'd worried that we'd bring over any conflict we had in our personal lives to work. I had worried for nothing. For one, Blaze and I rarely fought. And two, we were in different departments and company politics did not affect us.

We ate lunch together every day in the café next to our office and met for drinks after work sometimes.

"I love you Blaze," I said and leaned on his shoulder.

"I love you right back, Hot Sauce," he said.

"I hate that stupid nickname," I protested mildly. Blaze had been calling me the name for years and I had grown into it. It had started when we were both fifteen and my body had sprouted curves overnight.

Teenage pimpled boys had suddenly developed an interest in me and guess who they went through? Blaze of course and he'd started calling me hot sauce.

I thought again about the sacrifices he had made so my dream of being a home owner would come true. "If there's anything that you ever want me to do for you, all you have to do is ask," I said in an emotion filled voice.

"Yeah?" Blaze said, a playful tone in his voice.

It hit me then how open my offer was. Definitely not the kind of offer you wanted to make as a woman loving Blaze.

Though I wasn't his type. He loved his women with nothing between the ears. "I'm not giving you a blowjob Blaze."

He feigned disappointment and then grew serious. "There is something you can do for me."

"Sure, what?" I asked.

"Go with me to Jack and Amelia's wedding."

"To Hawaii?" I shrieked, angling my body to face him.

Jack was Blaze's younger brother. He and his fiancée were getting married in a month's time, if I remembered the dates correctly. Because of how far the wedding was and the coordination involved, they had opted for a small wedding with family and their very close friends. "Why are you asking me? Why not one of your many conquests?"

I couldn't imagine anything worse than going with Blaze to a Hawaiian wedding. It would be more temptation than I could handle. More than our friendship could handle.

More than once, when we'd both had a little too much to drink, attraction had sizzled between us but we'd ignored it and our friendship had survived. Blaze was family to me and no matter how attracted I was to him; it wasn't something I would ever act upon.

But it didn't mean I would allow myself to be tempted beyond my endurance. I could just imagine being in Hawaii. White, sandy beaches and the waves lapping at the shore. A sigh escaped my lips.

"You know how women are," Blaze said.

Something sharp pierced at my chest. Blaze never considered me a woman. To him, I was one of the guys. I felt stupid to feel bad that I was one of the guys to him. It meant our friendship was safe.

"They'll misconstrue the invitation and make it out to be more than it is. Then of course, there's my family. They'll pester me with questions that I don't want to answer."

Everything he said made sense.

"Everything's paid for Brooke. The flights, the beach condo. All you have to do is show up." He turned to face me and then treated me to one of his jaw dropping, panty melting dimpled smiles.

Having Blaze as my best friend was like being treated to a toothpaste ad, intermingled with an underwear ad, every day. "I can't take a week off work," I said lamely. "I already took my vacation days."

"You have ten days remaining," Blaze said. "I checked."

I shouldn't have been surprised by that. As a head recruiter, Blaze was very thorough in his work and always did his homework. Being prepared all the time.

That excuse had been my last line of defense.

Guilt flooded me. I had refused to accompany Blaze to Hawaii when just a few minutes ago, I'd said how willing I was to do anything for him. I meant it too. But going to Hawaii would be a mistake. The end of our friendship. And knowing Blaze, if anything did happen between us, it would only ever be sex.

That was just how he rolled. He loved women and he loved sex. He hated commitment. I really, really didn't want to go.

Besides, we had just bought a house. I was itching to get started on fixing it.

“I hope this house is not what is stopping you from saying yes. It’s only a week, Brooke. Work can continue while we are away.”

He did sound convincing but I was determined. “I’ll make a deal with you,” I said, suddenly inspired by an idea. Something Blaze could not manage to do. “If you can go a month without sex, I’ll go with you.”

He laughed. “Easy. Start packing your bags, Hot Sauce.”

I was sure his confidence was fake. Blaze needed sex the way the rest of us needed oxygen to live. “Deal,” I said and we shook hands on it.

We finished our lunch, locked up the house and took an uber back to the office.

“A penny for your thoughts?” Blaze asked me in the uber. “You’re very quiet.”

I smiled at him and said nothing. I felt pretty sure my thoughts would not only shock him, they would disgust him. I kept picturing him in a speedo with his package on display. Madness.

Chapter Two
Blaze

“Home at last!” Brooke said and let herself fall on the unmade bed.

My eyes roamed over her body, taking in the swell of her incredible breasts and the curve of her hips. She wore a short black skirt and my eyes seemed glued to the view of her creamy thighs. I managed to tear my eyes away but it was too late. I'd gotten hard, so I walked to the window and pretended to look at the view. It had been three weeks since that ridiculous bet with Brook. She'd actually thought I couldn't survive a month without sex.

Brooke was my best friend but she knew very little of my private life. Sure, I'd dated many women, but none had ever held my interest for long. I'd even gone out with women for more than two months and not slept with them. Unlike what Brooke believed, I didn't jump into bed with every woman I dated. There had to be chemistry and some kind of connection. If it wasn't there, I never bothered to go for the homerun

I felt proud of the work we'd had done on the house. In three weeks, we had managed to get the first-floor apartment renovated to livable standards and today was moving day for Brooke.

If there was one smart thing I'd done in my life up to this point, was to have Brooke as my best friend. Because of her, I now owned a house. Debt free. Well, it needed a lot of work to make it habitable, but Brooke and I had decided to undertake most of the work ourselves, for the first floor apartment.

Our bank accounts were crying now, so it was time to put on our aprons and get working. But we had Hawaii to enjoy first and I couldn't wait.

"Blaze, come and take a look. There's a stain on the ceiling," Brooke said.

Thankfully, my cock had gotten the message that Brooke was my best friend, not some random girl I had picked up in a club.

She lay in the same position and she patted the empty space beside her.

I had no choice but to lie down next to her. "It's a stain all right," I said to her. We were both versed in DIY and I did small repairs in both our rented apartments. "Looks like too much moisture. At least, we know that it's not structural. We'll sort it when we get back from Hawaii."

"I suppose I should concede defeat and start packing," Brooke said in an exaggerated sigh.

I turned to my side to face her. Big mistake. Her scent surrounded me and I found myself becoming hard again. I quickly shifted to my earlier position, facing the ceiling. I loved Brooke like a sister.

At least that was what I told myself. It also wasn't strictly true because I'd woken up in a cold sweat in the last couple of years after dreaming of Brooke and me having sex. Mind blowing sex. But those were dreams and I could not control what my fucked-up mind conjured up during the night.

But I could control what my hands and my mouth did. And what they would not do was screw things up with Brook. She was the sweetest, kindest human being I know. A perfect best friend for a guy like me, more inclined to think of the now, rather that the future.

Except I had moments when I believed Brooke was my soul mate and I was a fool for not dating her.

"Do you want some help?" I asked her.

"Not with the packing but you could help me choose," Brooke said. "I bought some stuff online and I'm not too sure how appropriate they are." She rose from the bed. "If I can find them that is." Her bedroom looked a mess but that was expected on moving day.

Boxes stood everywhere but in a true Brooke fashion, they were all labelled with the rooms they were meant to be. I felt excited too, about moving downstairs. I looked forward to living close to Brooke. It wasn't enough that I saw her at work, it would be nice to see her at home too.

But this was only because she was my best friend. The only woman—no, person who understood me and whom I understood. We were soulmates, Brooke and I.

"Found it!" Brooke said and held up a brown bag. "I'll go and change in the next room. Promise you'll give me your honest opinion. I don't want to look like a fool in front of anyone."

"You would never look like a fool," I told her.

She smiled.

Dammit, my heart skipped a beat. Brooke was all sweetness and sugar and every time she dumped a guy, I usually went out to celebrate. She was smart and beautiful but she always picked losers for boyfriends. I wanted her to be happy but I didn't want her to fall in love with some guy. I'd tried to be mature about it and think to the future. Brooke getting married. Brooke having a family with some guy. I hated the idea. She was my best friend and I wanted us to remain exactly as we were...Unattached.

Wishful thinking.

She was beautiful and sooner or later, some guy would snatch her up. My heart pounded as I mulled over it. I didn't want to lose Brooke to someone, yet I was frightened of rocking the boat. I'd always had a thing for Brooke. What normal functioning hot-blooded male wouldn't? Built like a pin up model with curves for days and incredible looking breasts. A body that made me want to do dirty things to her.

I had a problem and had known it for some time. I wanted Brooke. I always had. If it had been just sex, I would have continued as I always had, wanting her from a distance but respecting our friendship.

The problem as I saw it now, had been when I had started fantasizing about other things with her other than sex. Maybe buying a house together had made my fantasies go into overdrive. Whatever the reason, I'd started to see Brook in my future. Living with me. Sharing my bed. And it did not frighten me at all.

I had a decision to make.

"Ready?" Brooke asked from the door.

I sat up and swung my legs to the side of the bed. "I'm ready."

Brooke sashayed in wearing a pale blue dress that knocked the wind out of me. It clung to her curves but the plunging neckline was what had gotten my mouth to water. I couldn't take my eyes from the swell of her breasts and her deep cleavage. I imagined how it would feel to run my tongue over her soft skin. Would she moan or cry out or would she stifle her pleasure? I imagined Brooke's hot body writhing under mine as I pressed my cock between her legs.

"Get your mind out of the gutter Blaze," Brooke snapped.

A denial sprung to my lips but I swallowed it back. "You look beautiful Brooke."

"You don't think it's too sexy for the wedding?" she asked, looking down at herself.

I cleared my throat. Was it me or had the room suddenly become stifling hot? "No, it's perfect."

She grinned. "Thanks Blaze. I'll try on one more. I think I might have gone overboard with this one." She giggled. "This trip is bringing out my wild side. I want to be wild for a week. Does that make sense?"

I nodded, unable to speak. If Brooke wanted to be wild, I'd definitely be there to witness it. Then a thought crossed my mind. Just what kind of wildness was she talking about? Did it involve guys, because if it did...?

A few minutes, Brooke's footsteps sounded and I looked up expectantly towards the door.

When she emerged, I lost all my powers of speech. The only movement came from the lower half of me. My cock – acknowledging never having witnessed such sexiness – pulsed to life.

She wore what was technically a bikini but in reality, was a scrap of cloth barely covering anything. I saw skin everywhere I looked. She had thick mouthwatering hips and I couldn't help but stare at the swell of her pussy and imagine licking it, tasting it, inhaling it.

I must have groaned out aloud, because Brooke asked me in a concerned voice if I was okay.

I cleared my voice. "I'm good. You look amazing." I sounded how I felt. Lust filled. Out of my mind desperate to touch, to see if her skin felt as soft as it looked. To plant kisses on her belly. To cup her pussy in my big hand and claim it as mine with my cock.

She entered the room and walked the length as if she were on a catwalk.

I kept ogling her but I didn't care. The scrap of cloth disappeared somewhere in her ass crack, leaving her ass bare. All the blood left my body and dropped to my cock.

I had never wanted a woman as much as I wanted my best friend in this very moment. I needed a cold shower desperately. Anything to take my mind off her hot body and my crazy fantasies of claiming her. Making her mine. My decision was made.

I had a new mission for Hawaii.

Want to read more?

:-)

Pre-order here:

Forbidden Touch

ABOUT THE AUTHOR

Thank you so much for reading!
If you have enjoyed the book and would like to leave a precious review for me, please kindly do so here:
Craving The CEO

Please click on the link below to receive info about my latest releases and giveaways.
NEVER MISS A THING

Or
come and say hello here:

ALSO BY IONA ROSE

Nanny Wanted

CEO's Secret Baby

New Boss, Old Enemy

Made in United States
Orlando, FL
29 May 2022